ALSO BY LARA VAPNYAR

There Are Jews in My House

Memoirs of a Muse

Memoirs of a Muse

Lara Vapnyar

PANTHEON BOOKS · NEW YORK

Copyright © 2006 by Lara Vapnyar
All rights reserved. Published in the United States by Pantheon Books,
a division of Random House, Inc., New York, and in Canada
by Random House of Canada Limited, Toronto.

Pantheon Books and colophon are registered
trademarks of Random House, Inc.

A portion of this work previously appeared in
slightly different form in *The New Yorker.*

Library of Congress Cataloging-in-Publication Data
Vapnyar, Lara, [date]
Memoirs of a muse / Lara Vapnyar.
p.   cm.
ISBN 0-375-42296-X
1. Russian American women—Fiction.   2. Fiction—Authorship—Fiction.
3. Women immigrants—Fiction.   4. New York (N.Y.)—Fiction.
5. Inspiration—Fiction.   6. Novelists—Fiction.   I. Title.
PS3622.A68M46 2006
813'.6—dc22   2005048883

www.pantheonbooks.com

Printed in the United States of America
First Edition
2   4   6   8   9   7   5   3   1

Memoirs of a Muse

Chapter One

A Parisian hotel room. A man sits at a round table across from a woman. There is a tea tray between them: two glasses in silver holders, with a transparent liquid changing from muddy brown to dark red depending on the light. A saucer with pale lemon wedges, a crystal sugar bowl, a plate of French pastry, two silver spoons lost on the shiny surface of the tray.

The woman is young, with a broad, well-defined face framed with heavy waves of auburn hair. Her lips are squeezed tight. Her small eyes are intense, alert. She is watching the man. The man is in his forties, short, heavy, with a scant beard and a lumpy bald patch, visible to the woman because his head is hung low. He has sinewy hands and the prominent forehead of a great Russian writer.

He is, in fact, a great Russian writer. He is Fedor Dostoevsky. And the woman is Apollinaria Suslova, his lover. Or his former lover, because she has just informed him that she has fallen in love with somebody else.

He is kneading his face with his hands. His large thumbs are stretching the skin on his cheeks, his index fingers are pressing into his temples. Beads of sweat form between the rare hairs on his crown and crawl down, lingering in every wrinkle on his forehead. Some of

3

them dissolve in his skin, others make it as far as his brows, only to be crushed by his fast, cruel fingers. Two blue veins throb on his forehead. He is suffering. She can't take her eyes away.

"Polya," he suddenly whispers. He raises his wet, shaking face to meet her eyes. "Have you given yourself to him? Have you given yourself completely?"

His voice is thin, hysterical. She recoils. Even now, now! That is all he could ever think about.

"I won't answer that," she says.

"Oh!" he groans. His head drops back and his fingers resume their frenzy.

She stretches her legs under the table. She'd never imagined that inner turmoil could take such a physical form. She can smell the heavy odor of his sweat, she could reach with her hand and feel his veins throb under her fingers, she could taste his tears. She could take him into her arms and let her body shake with those powerful convulsions of his.

She doesn't budge.

"Cruel, coldhearted, unkind," people called her.

Dostoevsky was one of them. "She desperately wanted and tortured herself to become somewhat kind," he wrote about one of his heroines, one of many inspired by Polina.

So was it true? Was she cruel? Does a muse have to be cruel? Does a muse have to be able to induce a certain amount of pain? I want to know that.

I want to know why I failed.

"Here, I see the brilliant, wondrous future spread out for both of you," the old governess said to little Polya and her younger sister, Nadya, pointing to the coffee cups with her clean, chubby hand. She had seated the girls around the big, empty table and placed a coffee cup in front of each of them. Polya climbed onto the seat of her chair and peered into her cup. The dim candlelight made their plump, round-faced governess look like a mysterious sibyl.

"You see that? See that?" the governess said, pointing at the barely visible holes and furrows in the grounds in Nadya's cup. "Our Nadya will be a heroine, a conqueror. She will fight for a great cause, she will reach unreachable heights."

Nadya nodded—she saw the furrows.

"Now, let's look at yours, Polya." Polya licked her parched lips. "I see Polya as a great beauty and as a great conqueror too, but she will conquer men's hearts and inspire them. She will be a muse."

Later Polya sobbed in her bed, pounding on the mattress with her little fists. She saw a muse as a lapdog with a devoted expression in her wet, bulging eyes. She wanted to be a heroine. She didn't want to be somebody's lapdog!

That scene about the governess I made up. I'm not sure that the sisters even had a governess. But I know that Apollinaria's younger sister, Nadezhda, achieved great success: as the first Russian medicine woman, as an accomplished writer, as a political activist, as a wife. While Apollinaria . . . Apollinaria failed at just about everything she attempted. She failed as a scholar. She failed as a teacher. She failed as a writer. She failed as a wife. What else? Oh, yes, she failed as a lover; she failed as a lover several times.

Apollinaria Suslova didn't succeed at anything, except immortality. But what good has immortality ever done anyone?

As a child, I used to think that Dostoevsky's muse was his second wife, Anna Grigorievna. I knew her story before I knew anything else about Dostoevsky, before I'd read any of his books.

When I was three, my father left to marry a tall, square-shouldered woman named Marina; shortly after that, he died. To my mother and me it was a kind of double betrayal. Around that time, photographs of the major Russian writers began to line the wall in my mother's room, replacing pictures of my father.

I never liked Tolstoy's portrait—he looked like a mean Santa Claus, the one who won't bring you anything good, the one who would leave a knitted scarf or a pair of socks under the tree. The existence of a mean Santa Claus was one of my early beliefs. There were two Santas, two brothers. The good one left glossy boxes with dolls, dolls' furniture, or dolls' dishes for me. The mean one left nothing but clothes—a huge waste. My mother would've bought me clothes anyway.

I didn't like Chekhov's portrait either. There was something suspicious about his grin and his pince-nez. What if he knew something that I didn't want him or anybody else to know? What if he even knew about my aunt's favorite vase, which I accidentally broke, disposing of the shards and then pretending not to know anything about it? I definitely didn't like Chekhov!

Pushkin . . . well, Pushkin was okay. He seemed to be a nice guy, but he didn't look serious enough for a writer.

Dostoevsky was the one whom I loved. He had strong hands and a large forehead, so large that it seemed to burst through his skin. He had serious eyes, and he looked straight at me, without hiding, without the fake playful expression of other adults. "Dostoevsky had different eyes," my mother said when she spotted me staring at him. "One brown and one black."

"Different eyes!" I repeated, awestruck, and asked if he had a wife. "He is dead" was the answer. "But he did have a wife, when he was alive. Her name was Anna Grigorievna."

I liked her name. "Was she nice?"

"Oh, yes, she was very nice. She took very good care of him."

"I could do that too!" I said.

I imagined Dostoevsky sharing a dinner table with my dolls. I knew how to prepare kasha for dolls and serve them tea. I would've spread a napkin on his lap and fed him my kasha, then I would've put him to bed, tucked his blanket around him and taken his temperature with my toy thermometer, just in case.

Dostoevsky stayed for me a dead writer with different eyes and a nice wife up until I turned ten and my grandmother got sick. Then I learned some more details about his life.

"Dostoevsky's name was Fedor Mikhailovich, and so was your grandfather's! Dostoevsky was crazy, but your grandfather even more so!" My grandmother told me this as I stood cutting her hair. I had no experience cutting hair, except for chopping up the coarse ringlets of my dolls' curls.

My grandmother's hair was white with a faint tint of yellow, light and slippery in my fingers. She'd always worn it in a neat chin-length cut with a thin blue band to keep the bangs from falling over her eyes. After the first few months she spent bedridden, her hair barely reached her shoulders, like feeble thawing icicles. She complained that long hair made her neck itchy, she complained that it made her hot, she complained that she looked like Robinson Crusoe. I said that she would need a beard to really look like Robinson Crusoe. I said that she'd better stop complaining. I said, "Enough, Ba." But she kept insisting on a haircut.

"You should try it," my mother said to me. "You're good with your hands."

My hand skills had only recently been discovered. Just a few weeks before that, I'd fallen victim to severe rainy-day boredom and pulled an old (probably left from my kindergarten days) box of white clay out of the closet. I sculpted a fat, curly sheep, hardened it in the oven, painted it off-white, sheep color, and presented it a week later to my uncle for his birthday.

"Oh, we have hands, don't we?" my aunt Maya commented. Up until that moment it was thought that my mother and I were equally bad at all hands-involving activities: sewing, knitting, cooking, making sheep out of clay. I stood in front of Maya, staring at my hands as if they'd been slowly coming out of nonbeing. I had hands!

Having hands saddled me with new duties. I was to be the one to cut my grandmother's hair.

I moved a chair to the edge of the bed, sat my grandmother up, and slowly dragged her from the bed and onto the chair's seat, holding her under the arms. She looked weightless, but felt awfully heavy. After those months in bed she seemed to have lost all the substance that used to fill the space between her bones and her skin. I imagined she was completely empty in there, her bones rattling inside of the withered sack of her self, like my wooden building blocks in their canvas bag. I wrapped a sheet around her neck, untied her blue band and combed her hair, trying to avoid touching her scalp. Her skin, though warm, had a corpselike softness about it. I felt that if I pressed my finger hard enough, it would break her skin and fall into some deathly depths that reached further than the inside of my grandmother's body.

I took the scissors—large stainless-steel shears, usually used for cutting fabric and trimming fish tails—and snapped with them a couple of times, then put them down and combed her hair some more. Her eyes, wet and alert, took in the scissors, the comb, my hands, and seemed to creep into my face.

"Sit still, Ba," I said, turning away from her stare. I called her a short and intimidating "Ba" instead of a long "Babushka." I loved to bully her. "Sit straight, Ba, you don't want to spill your soup." "Here is your potty. You better do it now, because I have lots of homework and I'm not going to run in here every second." She never complained. She moved the way I told her to. She tried to eat as fast as possible and to go to the bathroom as neatly as she could. She praised the food I served. She sang to me. She told me stories. She met me with an eager smile. She tried to humor me.

Tough but efficient, I thought myself a perfect nurse.

"You wouldn't believe what this girl of ten can do. I've been training my nurses for years and they are not half as accurate or reliable," my uncle said, introducing me to his doctor friends, who shook their heads in disbelief and smiled at me. I knew I was special! I'd always known! No other girl of my age could take blood pressure, run an ECG machine, or administer injections. Not even my uncle's daughter, Dena. Dena, who was nine years older than me, a very good student, perfect in every way, and preparing to go to the U.S. There was no saying what I would be able to do when I got older!

It was only years later, when the doubts started gnawing at me, that I thought very few girls of ten were ever assigned to giving injections or running echocardiogram machines, and if they were, they might have done no worse than me.

And still later, a sickening suspicion suddenly crept in: my grandmother was so smiley and acquiescent not because I was a perfect nurse, but because she was afraid of me.

Before her stroke my grandmother had lived in her own apartment "a half of Moscow away from us," as my mother had said. We visited her once a month. To get to her part of Moscow we had to switch from a bus to a subway and then to another bus. The trip back and forth took us more than two hours. I thought that the hour spent at my grandmother's place wasn't worth it. She always served us cake that I hated—a stale, crumbly sponge smeared with sour cream and bitter wild strawberry jam, and she kept asking if I'd at last learned how to make my bed and spread my bread with butter. My grandmother's apartment didn't have any toys, or any fun or beautiful objects—only books, which lay everywhere with neat paper bookmarks stuck between the pages, and a few photographs: of my dead grandfather, my uncle, my mother, and myself at the age of two. I would rather she had a more recent photo. She talked about her health, the problems she encountered while paying her electricity bills or applying for her special war widow pension, the sidewalks covered with thin ice in the mornings. My grandmother often attempted to talk about my father, but seemed unsure if she should weep over his tragic, untimely death or condemn his behavior when he was alive, so she switched to my uncle's wife, Maya, who was not dead and thus not protected from criticism.

My grandmother had a stroke on her seventieth birthday. We came to her door smartly dressed, with a cake, a bottle of Soviet champagne, a knitted shawl, which my mother had bought because she couldn't knit, and the birthday card, which I had decorated with stickers because I couldn't draw. My uncle was to join us later. We rang the doorbell, then we knocked, then my mother pulled the keys from her purse and told me to stay on the staircase. In a few seconds, I heard her scream. She ran out of the apartment, grabbed me by the sleeve, and dragged me to the next-door apartment. A short, chubby woman opened the door and took me in after my mother whispered something into her ear. Inside, a fat man in a white tank shirt was eating his dinner in front of the blaring TV. "Are you hungry, my little chick?" the woman asked me. I shook my head and went back to the front door, where I flattened my face against the cold wood of the door's surface and watched through the peephole what was happening on the staircase. Nothing happened for a long time. Then I saw my uncle and people in white gowns running up the stairs. My mother was crying and shaking when she opened the door for them.

In a few moments I saw my grandmother strapped to the stretcher. My mother ran down the stairs after the stretcher, trying to throw the knitted shawl over my grandmother's legs. That means she is alive, I thought, wiping the tears away from my eyes so I would be able to see. There is no need to cover the legs of a dead person.

"She'll be home soon. It was just a mild stroke," my mother told me later. "She'll just have to live with us now. She really is fine."

The chilling preparations for my grandmother's arrival made me doubt my mother's words. A big bed was installed in the living room. A waterproof sheet was carefully tucked over the new mattress and covered with a regular sheet. Then my uncle came with a special chair he had made in his garage. You could remove the chair's seat, place a potty under, and there, you had a toilet. He raved about his creation. "Eh? What do you say? After she's done, you can put the seat back and use it as a table for her meals."

"A table?" my mother gasped. "A table! On the same chair, where she . . ."

"So what? The seat is removable, right? Anyway, I talked to Mother and she didn't mind."

I wondered what had happened to my squeamish grandmother. If she didn't mind taking her meals on the toilet, she couldn't possibly be fine.

She looked fine, though. She looked the same, I decided when I came home from school on the day of her discharge from the hospital and saw her in the new bed. She was pale, and she'd lost some weight, and she wore a nightgown instead of her usual dress, but she smiled and talked and made sense when she did. "The food in the hospital wasn't as bad as I'd expected. Yesterday they even served cream puffs, and I wanted to save one for Tanechka, but they didn't allow me," she said. My uncle spent some time teaching my mother how to remove the chair seat and how to move my grandmother onto it without having to lift her. My mother practiced a couple of times. My grandmother didn't protest. Then we all had tea in the living room so my grandmother wouldn't feel left out. She had some tea too, leaning over the new chair.

"I want to see my little girl," my grandmother requested the following morning. I walked up to her, but she shook her head. "Who is that?"

"This is Tanya," my mother said. "Our little girl."

My grandmother laughed. "You two think you can deceive me like that? Our Tanya is no more than two or three and she doesn't look like this one at all. You think I won't know the difference? You think I went funny in the head?"

It was stupid of me, but I ran out and locked myself in my room and said that I wouldn't come out. "She has crazy eyes!" I yelled through the door. "Wet and crazy!"

"A stroke has everything to do with food," my uncle explained to me on the phone. "The brain is usually fed on blood. After a stroke the brain isn't fed properly, and that causes all kinds of disturbances. That's why your grandmother might fall when she walks, and that's why she has memory lapses, and that's why, well . . . you see, that's why she sometimes doesn't have a clear mind."

Her brain wasn't fed properly. I understood that my uncle was talking about the quantity of blood, that the brain didn't get enough. But I imagined that my grandmother's brain was getting junk food, and thus producing junk.

"As improbable as it sounds," my uncle added, "the state of her mind won't stay the same. It can change from better to worse and back. Hopefully it will change back. Just remember that she is not crazy, it's just a question of brain food."

I decided I wasn't afraid of her anymore.

The schedule of caring for my grandmother was established. My mother was to switch to an afternoon shift at work, and would be at my grandmother's side in the mornings and late nights. My hours were from two to eight p.m., after I came home from school and before my mother came from work. And my uncle promised to visit whenever he had the time, a statement met with a sarcastic grin from my mother's side.

"I'm home, Ba!" I yelled when I opened the door with my key upon returning from school. I dropped my schoolbag on the floor and marched into the room, ready to check on the patient, who was to be in my power for the next six hours. Her mental state was the first thing I checked on. My uncle was right; it wavered back and forth. At times she didn't recognize anybody. She pushed me away and said that her granddaughter was a little girl and asked what we had done to that little girl. She took my mother for her late sister, Zeena. She read her books upside down. She called for Hitler and Shakespeare. "Hitler, Hitler, help me die," she sang in her tiny voice. Why Hitler? we wondered. Was she thinking about the Jews and, having suddenly regained her Jewish conscience, wanting to share their fate? No. She said that she wanted him to poison her the way he had poisoned himself and Eva Braun.

Then she would sing for Shakespeare. I asked if she needed Shakespeare to kill her off the way he had killed off all his tragic characters. But I was wrong again. She needed Shakespeare, she said, to record her story. Why Shakespeare, of all writers? She didn't give an answer to that. After her quest for Shakespeare, she usually sneaked out of the bed and wandered off with a pillow under her arm, swaying on her thin and dry spaghetti–like legs. I felt that it was really her poor underfed mind that left her body and went wandering with a pillow under its arm.

Then her mind would return to her. She would lull herself to sleep singing of Hitler and Shakespeare and wake up with a clear mind. She would look around her in disbelief, slowly taking in the room, the bed, the nightstand with its colorful disarray of medicine bottles, the chair with its removable seat. She would peer into our faces and say that she was sorry, so sorry to be a burden. She would grab my mother's or my hand when we approached the bed and beg us to say goodbye to her now, because she was afraid that one day her mind would go and wouldn't return. My mother would hold her hand and say goodbye to her, even though she'd already said it the day before, and the week before. But I refused to do that—I'd run into my room and slam the door.

Fortunately her sane days weren't frequent. For the most part her mind drifted in a weird, transitional state that I called "medium-crazy." Her mind was almost clear: She didn't confuse our names, she didn't attempt to wander off or eat soup with a fork. She be-haved like a proper invalid: subdued and grateful with me, weepy and whimsical with my mother. Still, something betrayed the sick-ness of her mind to those who knew her well. It was her passion for storytelling, the unhealthy vigor that didn't let her rest, that made her talk abruptly, confessionally, that made her greedy for an audi-ence. My late grandfather, a man we avoided in family conversa-tion, was the main hero of her stories. He, and another Fedor Mikhailovich: Dostoevsky. Both men emerged as bright and sinister characters, as fairy-tale villains, endowed with juicy real-life details.

"Do you know how it came about that I married your grand-father? He forced me!"

Forced her? Nobody'd ever talked to me about that! I was all ears.

"A fat chance he would've married me, if not for the Revolution. I came from a good family. And he was . . . He was . . . He didn't have a spare pair of pants to cover his . . . his male belongings!"

I couldn't believe nobody was there to stop my listening to this.

I hadn't known much about my grandfather. He died shortly after I was born, and whenever somebody was around to talk about him in my presence, my mother sent the person a warning look, and he or she hurriedly changed the subject. My grandfather was a Communist and a war hero—that much I knew because I had often heard my mother plead to social workers, "My father was a member of the Communist Party for thirty years, he defended Stalingrad, he has two medals of honor—you can't just cut his wife's pension." He was a handsome man; he looked like a thirties movie star in photographs, with a big lock of hair on his forehead, brilliant eyes, and a powerful jaw. At various times in his life he worked as a full-time reporter, a freelance photographer, a wine taster, an assistant to a judge, a vegetable store manager, and an amateur theater critic. (The last in the list was based on the acid letters he liked to send to newspapers whenever he disliked a play.) When I asked why he switched jobs, I was met with that wary look on my mother's face. I knew that he loved me very much. "Your grandfather was so happy when you were born that he promised to stop drinking and actually didn't drink for eight months," my uncle managed to tell me once, before my mother silenced him with her stare.

My grandfather was also a revolutionary. "A first-class revolutionary! A Communist, a proletarian, a top student in a political awareness school! I met him at just the right time," my grandmother said. "You see, my father used to own a tiny grocery store before the Revolution. And he was labeled a capitalist and an enemy of the people. We needed clean documents, we needed proof of residence . . . Your grandfather promised to help. I married him fictitiously. Fictitiously! But you know what he did? After a couple of days he just climbed into my bed and said that fictitious marriages were against the Soviet law, and he, as a Communist, couldn't possibly break the law!"

"So, what happened next, Grandma?"

"What happened next? What could happen next? He went on proving the truth of our marriage every night, sometimes twice a night. Sometimes three times!"

I didn't mind my grandmother's "medium-crazy" state at all! The only thing that bothered me was her eyes. I did what I could to avoid looking at her. Her eyes chased me. They were ready to seize me whenever I slipped and looked up at her. Then her face bloomed into a smile—half sly, half delirious.

Such was her state on the day I cut her hair. "Dostoevsky, note it—also Fedor Mikhailovich, just like your grandpa—was a terrible, terrible man," she said as I reached for the scissors.

"Now sit still, Ba," I ordered as her body tilted to the side of the bed.

"How he tortured his poor wife! His muse! She was his muse, you know. Without her he wouldn't have written shit."

"I know her name. Anna Grigorievna," I said.

"Anna Grigorievna. That's right. Oh, how he tortured her!"

"Damn! I told you to sit still!" I said as her body tilted to the other side. It wouldn't be such a big deal if she fell onto the bed, I thought, but I knew only too well how those waiflike limbs turned into dumbbells as soon as you had to pick her up. A cream-colored knitted shawl, which my grandmother liked to wrap around her legs, not so much for warmth as for its softness, drew my attention.

"I am going to tie you up, Ba. If you want to have a haircut, I'll have to tie you up." She didn't resist while I circled around her with the shawl, weaving it between the chair back's rails and under her breasts, then tied it in a big knot between her shoulder blades. She sat as still as she could, nodding eagerly, following my hands with restless, glistening eyes.

"Better? Isn't it?" I asked my prisoner and took the scissors off the nightstand.

The first snap was a signal for her to continue the story.

"Fedor Mikhailovich would take all the money and gamble it away, and then he would come back for more—but there wasn't any—and pawn all of the good things only to gamble the money away. He gambled away her ring, her earrings, her shawl, and once even her shoes and her dress, so she couldn't even go shopping."

"What was the point in going shopping if he'd already gambled away all the money?"

"Well, maybe she hoped to ask a nice salesman for credit, or just wanted to window-shop. . . . And when he came back, instead of apologizing he yelled at her for not fixing his supper on time!"

"Did she yell back at him?"

"Never! She apologized for not fixing supper. You see, *she* was a very good wife."

"All right, now shut your eyes."

I let her long bangs fall down on her forehead and snapped the scissors there, careful not to scratch the skin. It was easier to look at her when her eyes were closed. She looked relaxed, smoother, more alive, almost normal, until one sly, glistening eye opened under my snapping hand.

"Geniuses are a crazy lot. They're crazy like hell! You never know how to please them. You think that you do. You keep track of the things that please them. But they are fickle, they change their likings on a whim. You serve them tea with sugar and cream—their favorite, and you had just gone out specially to buy that cream—and they yell that they wanted coffee with lemon. You want to throw that tea into their red, ugly mugs and then break the cup against their head, but you don't do it. You apologize. And then when they come home drunk and in soiled pants—yes, they do that, they soil their pants—you don't throw them out! You take them in, you undress them, you scrape the shit off them, and put them to bed. And after that you go to your communal bathroom to wash their pants. And it's not an easy thing, I tell you, to wash shitty pants in a communal bathroom, with all the neighbors watching and yelling at you because of the stench! But you do it for them all the same."

"Do it for *whom,* Ba? *Who* soils their pants?"

Both eyes open at me like nimble animals lurking between the locks of hair, waiting to burn me with their sparks.

"That's them, who do it! Them! Geniuses!"

So, okay, the geniuses are bad, I thought as I cut the rest of my grandmother's hair. She closed her eyes, hung her head down, and sat silently without moving—very convenient for chopping the hair on her crown. She must have been out of breath after her tirade.

So, Dostoevsky, a writer with different eyes, was a bad man. Geniuses are bad, and you have to wash their shit off, and that is probably it. That is what it takes to be a muse. There is not much else to it.

No, I wasn't a wise child. I didn't think about that until years later. Many years later.

When I cut my grandmother's hair, I was too preoccupied with making the layers even. Something had gone wrong in the middle of the process. It could be that my ten-year-old overconfidence let me down at some point. By the end of the session, my grandmother's hairdo consisted of rows of hair of various lengths encircling her head in various directions. I tried to even the hair's length but wound up cutting too close to the skin. When my grandmother raised her head and opened her eyes, there was nothing but yellow-white down fluttering on her bare scalp. With her neck thinned by the illness, and her beaky nose, she looked like a baby chick. A sick baby chick. An old and sick baby chick, if that was possible. An old and sick baby chick tied to a chair with a shawl. A large, hard lump rose in my throat, hurting me, making me want to hide, to escape. As if sensing my distress, my grandmother moved her neck from side to side and shook her head.

"Nice and cool," she commented.

The tears gushed out of my eyes, while my whole body shook with laughter. "You're cute like that, Ba," I said. "You're funny."

Chapter Two

$\mathcal{I}$ wasn't home when my grandmother died. I had gone to my friend Lida's house in the country for two weeks, and the date of my return coincided with the date of the funeral. I didn't even have to cut short my vacation. Convenient timing, Lida's mother commented when my mother called.

My mother told me the news on the phone. Your grandmother died. It didn't sound shocking. I knew that it would happen. I had gotten used to the thought. I didn't think it would change anything.

During the five years of her illness, my grandmother's condition was slowly slipping. And the two last years she'd spent in a state not much different from a coma. The sane, medium-crazy, and crazy days were long gone. There were no more stories, no more frightening, wet eyes, no more wandering with a pillow. Even the chair became useless after a while. The potty had been replaced with a bedpan, the cup with a baby bottle, the pills with a syringe. My chores had become so mechanical that I barely noticed them. On coming home from school, I had to change a sheet, give my grandmother a drink, then give her the bedpan and apply ointment to her bedsores. I always wondered why the skin on her back was so soft.

Everything else crumpled like used wrapping paper, but the skin on her back stayed perfectly smooth and tender, just like my own, even more delicate than my own. And it seemed that the skin on her back was the only part of her that reacted to the outside world. It usually became irritated and broke into annoying, wet sores, but at least it was something. The rest of her didn't react at all. She didn't try to communicate. Her eyes were open, but she never looked at me. I wasn't sure if she recognized me. I didn't feel that there was another living person in the house when I sat in my room doing my homework or reading a book. I felt that I was left alone or with a strange big doll that required changing and feeding and sometimes made tiny, quiet whimpers that didn't mean anything.

My reaction upon hearing my mother's announcement was, "Oh, so it did happen after all."

Just as I had expected, I didn't find any drastic changes when I came home from my vacation. The apartment had always seemed a little different at the end of a summer: the ceiling seemed lower or higher than I'd remembered, the rooms emptier or more cluttered, the bed softer, the armchair firmer. I couldn't tell whether the differences were real or imaginary. Now, when I saw on my return that my grandmother's bed was empty and her table/toilet chair was covered with a piece of cloth, I had to struggle to remember if they had really looked different before I left. I caught myself being disturbed by the fact that death wasn't anything extravagant. She had just disappeared. She used to be there, and then she wasn't there anymore. Not that she was anywhere else. She wasn't even buried in the ground. She'd been cremated, turned into nothing.

My uncle sat by the phone with his plump notebook, calling everybody he knew, saying a formal, "My mother *has ended.*" Ended. As if she were a book or a movie.

On the day of the funeral reception our kitchen filled with strange women wearing our stained aprons over their dark dresses and heavy jewelry. Were they my mother's friends? My uncle's colleagues? They sat on low stools (I didn't know that we had so many kitchen stools), peeling potatoes and chopping vegetables for salads, sneaking to the bathroom. Then the doorbell started ringing. The guests came: men in dark suits, more women in dark dresses and heavy jewelry. They rustled their wet, smelly bouquets, hugged my mother, slapped my uncle on the back, tried to pat me on the head, confirming my fears that at fifteen I still looked like a young child.

The heavy, slow eating followed. The relentless destroying of food. The mounds of salad in salad bowls, melted down like snowdrifts. The thin slices of meat, first pierced with a fork and then slashed by a knife, were torn apart by somebody's teeth. The bottles were drained and sent from the center of the table to their graveyard under my uncle's chair, where they were knocked over and spun about the floor with a sad hollow sound.

The people at the table weren't sad, though. The more bottles accumulated under my uncle's chair, the more cheerful they became. The apologetic, uncertain whispering—"Could you, please, pass me that fish? I'm sorry . . . No, no, that's enough, thank you. Don't worry"—was replaced by bright comments like "Whoever made this salad is a genius!" or "Don't you have horseradish? It goes very well with horseradish. Ah, what the hell, I'll try it with mustard!" The timid smiles were replaced with bursts of laughter, and the appropriate toasts with inappropriate toasts. One of the last celebrated the coming of spring, even though it was late summer, and the very last invited us to drink to the health of the wonderful Berta Arkadievna, my late grandmother. After that toast they started to leave. Slowly. Crawling off the table and into the hall, squeezing themselves into their shoes and raincoats, and through the door to crawl to the sidewalk and into a taxicab. My aunt was the last to leave. Her gait, unlike that of the others, was firm. She marched into the hall, snatched her jacket off the hook, and left without even putting it on. My uncle didn't follow her. He couldn't. He sat on the floor with his head on the chair seat with his eyes closed. He had been sleeping for some time. My mother and I dragged him to bed, to my grandmother's bed, but we couldn't lift him up. We put a pillow under his head and let him sleep on the floor, which was littered with soiled paper napkins, dabs of food, wine puddles, and empty bottles. "We'll clean up tomorrow," my mother said, leading me away from the room where the piles of dirty dishes and trash seemed to be the only things left of my grandmother's existence.

I woke up in the middle of the night and lay cuddled in my blanket, listening carefully and afraid to hear what I thought I had heard. It wasn't a dream. It wasn't a nightmare. It was very real. My grandmother was there, on her bed, in her usual place, behind the thin wall dividing our rooms. She moaned, she coughed, she cried for help.

"She's back!" I yelled, shaking my mother up. "She's here! She wants us!" My mother's face was red and crossed with pillow creases, one of her eyes still closed, the other only half open.

"Tanya, calm down. She's dead. She can't come back." The words that came off her chapped lips seemed stranded and coated with bad breath. Then she heard something too. "Shit," she groaned and sat up in bed.

It was my uncle, moaning and retching and crying for help. "You see," my mother said, wiping the floor while my uncle, now sitting on the bed, sipped carbonated water. "There are no ghosts. Only human beings. Very real, very alive human beings. If you can call that human, of course."

"It's my mother's funeral," my uncle whispered by way of explanation.

"Exactly!" my mother said, slapping the wet cloth against the linoleum.

I didn't fall asleep right after that. My mother's lips flashed in my head. Letting out those coarse, definite words. "She's dead. She can't come back."

Once you're dead—that's it. You won't come back. There won't be anything at all left. It happened to my grandmother. It happens to everybody. It will happen to me.

"I'm going to die!" I sobbed, shaking in my bed.

"You are not going to die," my mother chanted, rocking on the edge of my bed in half sleep. "You are not going to die," stretching. "You are not going to die," rubbing her eyes. "You are not going to die," yawning. She stroked my head and her hand brushed against my ear in the dark, making a rustle, which drowned out her words. "Your grandmother was old and sick. You're still young and healthy."

But I'm going to die then, I thought. I cried thinking of "then" until I fell asleep.

"What is death? Death is nothing," my uncle said the following morning, pouring spoons of instant coffee into his cup. He looked rumpled, but brisk. My mother, with her puffed-up eyes and red nose, looked much worse, even though she hadn't drunk. "We are atheists, so there is no afterlife for us. Thus, death is nothing."

My mother must have asked him to talk to me. I wished she hadn't.

I stared into my plate filled with reception leftovers, too embarrassed to eat or talk. But if I had been able to talk I would've argued that any kind of afterlife was better than nothing at all.

"You don't want to wind up in hell, do you?" my uncle asked, reading my thoughts. "And you don't want to be reincarnated and turn into somebody really sick or into a dog or a cow?"

"Enough! I spent two hours in line to buy this coffee," my mother said, taking the coffee jar away from my uncle. "The best way to deal with death is to ignore it. If you don't think about death, it's not there, it's not looming on the horizon, you know. And it works. I know it's hard for you to believe right now, but it works. You simply don't think about it."

"And here you are wrong," my uncle said, taking a piece of cheese from the plate and buttering it on both sides. "The whole point is not to forget about it. You know about Adam and Eve? How God punished them and made them mortal? He didn't know it, but in fact he didn't punish them. Just the opposite—he gave them the gift of life! Because, you see, you can't appreciate something unless you know that it's going to end."

"We are atheists," I said mechanically. "There wasn't any Adam and Eve."

"Kid, we are all Adams and Eves. We know that we are going to die."

I winced at his words.

"We know that, so we must live while we can. You see that?" He threw the piece of cheese into his mouth and reached for another. "We must live to the utmost degree."

"Right," my mother snorted. "As if you could live like that with your wife. To the utmost degree! Are you even allowed to eat cheese without bread at home? Or put two spoons of coffee into your cup? Are you?"

"I live to the utmost degree when and where I can" was the answer.

·   ·   ·

25

I spent the next few days alone in the apartment. My mother was working, even more than usual, as if she wanted to make up for all her absences during the five years of my grandmother's illness. School wouldn't start for a few more weeks, and I had no desire to savor the last days of summer in the park like I usually did. I smirked ironically when I thought that, only a year ago, I couldn't stand sitting at home during the last days of summer. I would stick my head out the window and inhale the sour smell of hot August leaves in the neglected park downstairs, thinking that in just a week or two, the weather would turn bad and I wouldn't be able to run out without putting on my old, ugly ankle boots, a raincoat, and a scarf. I cursed my mother for staying late at work and my grandmother—for what? For not dying sooner? I didn't want to think about that.

Now, when I had at last achieved the freedom to do whatever I wanted, I didn't know what to want. I aimlessly dragged my feet around the apartment, trying out the various pieces of furniture to find which was best suited for pondering death. I stood leaning against a wardrobe, I lay facedown on my bed, I sat perched on the kitchen stool, I sat cross-legged between the bookcase and my mother's desk.

The thought that I could simply ignore death, "forget about it," as my mother had said, puzzled me. Forget about it? How? Death was like a fresh wound: every movement, every smallest touch reminded me of it. Death was everywhere: lurking in the velvet bedspread on my grandmother's bed, waiting for me on the sunlit street, entering the room through the blinking TV screen. Death was in the smiling face of a TV anchor, who spoke of current events as if he were inviting his audience to a picnic. You're going to die, I thought, looking into the sparkly teethed TV anchor's mouth. Yes, you are. You can smile all you want, you will die anyway. And this fussy baby on the playground, whom I saw through the window, was going to die too. And his mother, who was scolding him for dropping a piece of carrot into the sandbox, would die. And the stray dog, who tinkled on that unfortunate piece of carrot, would die his animal death. I couldn't look at anybody without pronouncing a death verdict for him.

No, I couldn't possibly ignore death. Could I fight it by living my life to the utmost degree? If only I knew how.

Eating cheese buttered on both sides somehow didn't seem fulfilling enough, especially considering that I didn't like cheese or butter. What other options did I have? To become somebody really accomplished, a luminary? That sounded nice, even ticklish, but a luminary in the field of what? Where could I display any extraordinary abilities? What if there weren't any? "She is a gifted girl," people said about me, sending chills down my bones, because I knew that if I had been really gifted they wouldn't have called me "a gifted girl." They would have said "a gifted artist" or "a gifted musician." This hadn't bothered me when I was younger. Big deal! I used to think when I'd hear my aunt or my mother's friends boasting of one or another child who had won a prestigious chess competition or was advancing as a promising violinist. They were talented, yes, but talented in a field overcrowded with other talents. Would they get to the very top? Most probably not. I used to think of my lack of obvious conventional talents as a guarantee that I had something bigger hidden in me, much bigger than the simple ability to make musical instruments produce passable tunes, or to move chess figures to the right places at the right time. But now I was fifteen, and that long-anticipated extraordinary talent still hadn't emerged. My many gifts rattled about like cheap jewelry in a sequined bag—there wasn't a single gemstone. Now what kind of fulfilling life could the likes of me lead?

The life of the freedom fighter . . . If you believed Soviet movies about the revolution, the civil war, or antifascist resistance, that kind of life was exciting enough and didn't require any special talents, except for a willingness to bear various hardships. I would be hiding in my co-conspirators' apartments, lurking in the shadows of fences, staring at store windows to see if somebody was following me, consuming ham sandwiches on the run. Unfortunately, I didn't buy the romanticism of Soviet movies anymore. Present-time freedom fighters, as I'd heard, were caught very quickly and sent to labor camps or mental institutions, where it was unlikely that the food ration included ham sandwiches.

Traveling around the world . . . That could be worthwhile. But the plane tickets were so damn expensive. Plus, if you believed my uncle, it was a pain to obtain a visa, even to enter close and friendly Bulgaria, in spite of the common saying that "chicken wasn't a bird, and Bulgaria wasn't abroad."

Sex . . . Sex had hovered in the back of my mind for quite some time. Could sex make your life worthwhile? If it was a great passion? Something extraordinary? In other words something other than my next-door neighbor's affair, the developments of which I had often watched through the peephole in our door.

The neighbors' girl was just two years older than me, but was already leading a very different life. Independent. Unsheltered. Tough. She worked as an apprentice in the supermarket. She bought clothes and makeup with the money she earned. "Get lost, you moron!" she yelled at her father exactly the same way her mother did. "Shut up, you bitch!" she yelled at her mother when they argued. Argued like equals. Not in the whiny vs. accusing manner in which I argued with my mother. She looked different from me too. She looked thirty, as my mother commented. I looked twelve, as some of my classmates said. Probably even less than twelve. "Tanya has preschool boobs," the girls whispered behind my back.

For about a year, every Wednesday and Friday, around ten or eleven at night, the neighbors' girl had come home with a boy. My mother was working late shifts then, and my grandmother was usually asleep at that hour, so I had all the time in the world to spend by the peephole. As soon as I heard the bang of the elevator opening on our floor, I hurried into the hall to press my face to the cold wood of the door. There she was—sailing out of the elevator with her eyes half closed, her winter coat half open, the boy's body pressed to her behind. They moved to the staircase and leaned against the railing. I never saw the boy's face, only his hands, his large red hands fumbling across her chest, struggling with the layers of fabric (fur, wool, cotton, satin), attacking her buttons, burying his fingers deeper and deeper. I saw her flushed face and her opened lips, which she licked from time to time. I heard their panting and their coarse voices. His chanting, "Where are they? Where are they? Here they are! Here they are . . . ," and her moaning, "Shut up, you moron," in a tone so different from the one she used with her father and mother.

I went back to my bed, dove under the blanket, and lowered my pajama pants to my knees. I didn't fantasize about the neighbors' girl and her boyfriend. On the contrary, as soon as I got to the bed, I found the image of them repulsive. I fantasized about the dead old writers whose works we studied in class and whose serious faces permeated the greasy pages of our schoolbooks. Gogol, Chekhov, Turgenev, Dostoevsky. Graying hair, prominent foreheads, knowing eyes. At times the face of a writer in my fantasy would suddenly turn into the face of one or another of my uncle's friends, but if that happened I banished him from my fantasy immediately: It was too weird, too shameful to imagine how I would react when I saw that man and he gave me a certain look, as he always did. It was safer to stick with the dead.

A dead old writer would materialize in my room in his shabby—

for some reason I always imagined them shabby—nineteenth-century clothes and sit down on the edge of my bed with an expression so serious and so kind that it made me want to cry. He would gently sit me up, supporting my back with his hand, and press my hand to his chest. He would stroke my hair and stroke my back and then unbutton my pajama top, slowly, button by button, whispering gentle words. I was completely naked with a fully clothed dead old writer in my bed (I didn't find naked dead old writers appealing), waiting for something wonderful to happen. I didn't know exactly what. At thirteen, I still had a very vague idea of the sexual act. I knew that it would involve that little throbbing burrow in my body that I probed with my hand so often, but I didn't know how.

Then the dead old writer left my bed and my room, went back to the safe confinement of my textbooks. I was left all alone. With my pajama pants down. With my finger puckered. Ashamed, lonely. While the neighbors' girl was with a real, live boy. Or was she? Didn't I hear the bang of the closing elevator? And then the creak of the door of her apartment. He must have left. She was now in her room. All alone just like me. With her panties rolled to her knees and her own puckered finger.

This kind of sex certainly wasn't enough to make life worthwhile, I thought while wandering around the apartment in the days after my grandmother's death. Yet, there was a certain promise in it, a glimpse of something bigger (much bigger) lurking about in the shadow of puckered fingers and unbuttoned blouses. It was that promise that made the thoughts of death fade and gradually leave me alone.

Polina liked to be one of the first to enter the auditorium. She liked to listen to how the sound of her steps brightened the silent room.

She liked to squeeze between the narrow wooden benches, clearly not designed for women in full skirts, and she liked the excitement of the fact that she was a woman in a full skirt, yet attending classes in the university. She liked to watch how professors entered the room, making the steady rumble of students' voices instantly fade. She liked how professors cleared their throats before they began a lecture. She would lean in then, prepared to be initiated into the wonderful, busy, vibrating world of thought. There were times, though, when she wondered if the idea of initiating was actually more exciting than the classes themselves. She never felt the same thrill when reading assigned books or deciphering her notes. And during the lectures too she would sometimes catch herself fidgeting, daydreaming, forgetting to listen.

Polina walked up the steps to the third row and moved sideways, closer to the center. Soon other students started filling the room, and Polina listened to how the separate sounds of coughing, giggling, chatting, gradually expanded into a steady din. The auditorium was more crowded than ever. The elbows and thighs squashed against other elbows and thighs. The air grew heavy with sweat and the odor of damp clothes. Then the murmur rippled throughout the audience: "He's coming, he's coming." Polina tucked red wisps of hair behind her ears and took a deep breath.

Dostoevsky walked up on the platform in hurried, unsteady steps. He kept his head bowed to the right side, as if ducking some invisible enemy, and he avoided looking at the audience, except to throw one or two wary glances above students' heads. When the room erupted in applause, he smiled, but again without looking at the audience. He kept rubbing his twitching right eye. The first couple of sentences came out a little slurred, and Polina leaned in to hear him better. Slowly his voice was gaining strength, and the words that he read seemed to bounce off the pages of the book, empowered by the double dose of emotion (the first given them during the process of creation and the second breathed into them by his reading), and explode in the students' minds. Polina had read *The Notes from the House of the Dead,* and she loved and admired the book, but she hadn't been moved like this before, not by any book. He, a short, unimpressive man, was so powerful that he made the whole auditorium full of students groan in a unison of emotion. Polina had tried writing, but she had been familiar with the frustration of the process rather than the joy. There were thousands and thousands of words in the Russian language. How many would she need for her story? Which ones would she choose? Why give one word preference over another? And wouldn't the chosen word betray her by looking wrong in her writing, sounding wrong, having the wrong meaning? The right choice eluded her, making what was so perfect and beautiful in her mind helpless and ugly on paper. But here was Fedor Dostoevsky, the true writer. The true master of the world of thought, where she wanted so much to belong. More powerful than any of her professors. Yet, a man so vulnerable that his eyes actually clouded with tears when he read the passages about suffering.

In the end, as he stood, waiting through the ovation, he took a long, lingering look at the audience. His and Polina's eyes met, if only for a second. Or at least Polina thought that their eyes met.

It took her forever to squeeze past lazy, immobile, infuriating students out into the aisle, and then she had to run down the three steps to the floor, and walk very fast, pushing through a crowd of people following him, until she caught up with him in the hallway. "Fedor Mikhailovich," she shouted into his back. And when he turned, for lack of better words, she said, "My name is Apollinaria Suslova." His eyes were different, Polina noticed, one black and one light, glistening, of an indefinable color.

The furnished room smelled of people who had used it not a very long time ago. Candle wax, cognac, and sweat. Dostoevsky drew the blinds together in one swift movement and then darted back to the door to lock it properly. "That little man downstairs gave us a look," he muttered, fumbling with the key.

Polina took a few steps toward the window, listening to the sad rustle her skirt made against the shabby carpet. She tried to evoke the thrill of the previous months, the thrill she felt when they'd first met. He, Dostoevsky, the author of *The House of the Dead,* was interested in her, wanted to see her, wanted to talk to her, had told her that he loved her. Instead, she thought that the threadbare patches on the carpet looked just like the bald patch on his head. Polina bit her lip. She considered herself a free spirit and she'd always known that once she found a man worthy of her love, there wouldn't be any petty reservations for her. She tried to disregard his appearance the way she disregarded the fact that he was married. But now she found that she couldn't entirely forget about his marriage either. He had been separated from his wife for a long time. Where, then, did his anxiety come from? His fear of discovery? His petty worries that people "gave them looks"?

He was still busy with the key. Polina walked to the toilet table and tucked wisps of hair behind her ears. She looked calm enough. Her lips were a little dry, but other than that nothing betrayed her unease.

A week ago, in a dimly lit back room at his brother's apartment, Dostoevsky had asked Polina if she would be his. He was kneading her hand in his, his right eye twitching with anxiety. Polina whispered, "Yes." Her voice sounded coarse, and too quiet—she was afraid that he hadn't heard, so she cleared her throat and said "yes" again, that time louder. He let go of her hand and stared at her for some time, intently, questioningly, as if afraid that he might have misunderstood, but then he grabbed her by the shoulders and started covering her in kisses, shy and grateful at first, then more and more forceful, arousing sensations that she hadn't yet experienced, that made her blush and hide her face on his chest. It was just a beginning, she thought, a beginning of something wonderful, something grandiose.

Polina turned now to look at him. The door was at last safely locked, and he stood leaning against it, facing her. His shoulders were stooped, his chest thrust forward as if he were about to pounce. His mouth twitched. His different eyes peered at her: his healthy eye took her whole body in, scanning her neck, her shoulders, and her legs, while his black, unmoving eye pierced her through. Polina took a step back, then another, until she grasped the cold brass railing of the bed.

In a second her back bounced against the mattress. He was on top of her. His chest was pressing hard onto her breasts, his teeth crushing her mouth, his hands hurting her, pushing her down. Trying to get away from his kiss, she hit her head against the bed railing.

"I'm sorry, *dushen'ka.*" Softer notes came through the hoarseness of his voice. Softer touches. He is taking her shoes off. A thud of a shoe against the floor. Another thud. He is touching her feet. He is gently squeezing her toes. He is stroking the underside of her feet with his thumbs. His thumbs are hard and warm. Polina moans, but then he lets go of her feet, and a new sound startles her. The long sound of the ripping cloth.

Is that my dress? she thought. He's tearing my dress. Those are my buttons. One button. Another button. That's my bodice. The push, the yank, the chill on the ever-widening triangle of her exposed skin. His hands didn't feel warm anymore.

"Poterpi, dushen'ka. Poterpi," he whispered softly, interrupting the cacophony of his panting and moans. *"Poterpi, dushen'ka."*

Poterpet! The silent Polina revolted. All the great love she hoped to find came down to "yield and endure"?

But she shut her eyes and did just that, yielded and endured. It was easier in the blindness. She felt herself being pushed, pulled, touched, but it didn't bother her as much, because she couldn't see. It could very well have been somebody else's body in this whirlpool of big and small pains, mixed with the occasional bubble of pleasure swimming to the surface here and there. She didn't mind the pain as much as she minded those flimsy pathetic bubbles. Feeling the pleasure was confusing, humiliating. It made her an accomplice to the act.

He finished quietly—there wasn't any explosion or burst, as she'd expected. She heard his deep sigh, after which he stopped moving and rolled off her. Polina limped away to wash off then. She poured some water from a jug into a bowl, dipped a washcloth in, and raised her crumpled skirts. The sight of her stained thighs made her gag. She didn't mind the blood; she was prepared for the blood. But this! The blood that trickled down her thighs was mixed with thick, cloudy slime smelling of rotten eggs. She squeezed the washcloth over her thighs and then rubbed very hard, as if she wanted to scrape her skin off along with the slime.

He had his pants on and the shirt with unfastened cuff links, but his shoes were still resting by the bed. His flat, yellow feet trampled the woven rug in heavy confident strokes. He looked calm and cheerful, if a little tired. There was none of the crazy desperation in his eyes, none of the strained force in his body, none of the coarseness left in his voice.

"Polya, *dushen'ka,* do you think Turgenev will agree to my offer? The offer was pretty good, but you know Turgenev . . ." Polina stopped in disbelief. Turgenev? He wants to talk about his magazine now? Now? She had dreamed of having literary conversations with him, so that was probably it. They were having one right now.

"You can't be too pushy with Turgenev, Fedor Mikhailovich. I'm quite certain that he will agree, if you give him some time," Polina said, determined not to let him see her disappointment or her distress.

"*Umnitsa! Dushen'ka!* That's just what I thought. Isn't it a thrill to be with a smart woman!" He smothered her in a bear hug, devoid of passion but full of gratefulness. Polina smiled and reached to stroke his face. Maybe it would become easier with time. It must.

"Polya, *dushen'ka,* you'd better go now. We can't exit this place together. You go first, and I'll follow you in ten minutes or so."

Polina walked down the corridor, then down the creaky stairs. Out on the gray Petersburg street. Trying to keep her back straight and take large, even steps. Trying not to limp. Trying not to wince in pain when she had to raise her leg to step over a pile of horseshit on the pavement. Trying not to meet people's eyes, and when she did meet them not to wonder whether there were traces of the bloody slime on her dress. Trying to walk with dignity.

Chapter Three

A week after high school graduation about twenty of us squeezed into the crowded car of a suburban train. We were dressed in khaki pants and rubber boots with our backpacks made enormous by folded tents, tin kettles, and volleyballs. We laughed and shrieked as we elbowed away the timid crowd of suburban commuters. "Always take your backpack off and carry it in front of you when you board a train," my uncle had taught me. "It's part of an unwritten code." But here, I felt, the code was different; it required being loud and pushy, and ignoring the other passengers. I pushed and shrieked and followed my classmates between the wooden benches to the back of the car.

Someone had offered to organize a class camping trip the weekend after our prom. The history teacher was to supervise and protect us from various camping-trip dangers. And for me this particular teacher belonged to a category of dangers rather than supervisors. Or at least I hoped so.

"You know, I'm not sure if I want to go on this trip," my best friend, Lida, whispered, as we settled in a quiet corner between the last bench and the exit door of the train. I knew exactly what she meant. She was afraid that we would be ignored, just as we always were.

On the way to the train station some girls were relieved of their loads by the boys, but not us. The lucky ones walked proudly next to the boys, now bent under a double burden. They whistled and smiled, and straightened their backs, and made fun of the boys, and did everything to show how pleasant and easy it was to walk without a backpack. We whistled, hummed, and straightened our backs too, to show that our backpacks weren't heavy at all and that the only reason why we hadn't been relieved by the boys was that we simply didn't need their help.

At the prom too, the boys had ignored us. Not that we expected much from the prom. We told each other that we didn't. What good could possibly happen in a room decorated with stupid balloons and stupid paper garlands? Could one of the boys whom we knew since first grade suddenly shed whatever had always constituted him and turn into a romantic object? Or, rather, see one of us as a romantic object, which would probably be enough to make him desirable? And could we then have a romantic moment while sliding on the freshly waxed linoleum of the gym to the sounds of the old tape recorder in a brightly lit room smelling of cheap deodorant and cheaper lip gloss?

It turned out we were right. Nothing happened. Girls took up the space in front and tried to dance sexily: they closed their eyes, lifted their arms above their heads, swayed their hips, threw their heads back and tossed their hair. Boys either danced wildly, jumping very high and stomping their feet in the back of the gym, or they stood by the walls under the basketball hoops, chuckling and making fun of the girls. There were only two or three couples on the dance floor, and those were old, almost legitimate couples, the ones who had been going together for years.

Lida and I spent the entire prom by the refreshments table, drinking glass after glass of lemonade that we poured from half-liter glass bottles.

"I just don't get it," Lida had confessed once. I didn't get it either. I mean I got it about Lida—she had short legs, a thick neck, and a very serious, at times even scornful expression. It was natural that she was ignored. I didn't get it about me.

Why? Why? the question popped up in my mind more and more frequently.

My grandmother's death had robbed me of my favorite excuse for not having a boyfriend: I was too busy caring for my sick grandmother. Now that she was dead, the only reason I had to stay home nights was that nobody wanted to take me out. Could it be that I was unattractive? I would study my reflection in the mirror while brushing my teeth and wonder about that. I knew that I could be remarkably pretty, but at certain hours and in certain lighting. In the mornings, in the harsh light of our bathroom or under the fluorescent lamp in the school lobby, I was almost never pretty. By the end of the school day, I was decidedly ugly—unless we had ski practice or running practice, which gave great color to my cheeks, which in their turn gave great color to my eyes, brows, and hair. Then I became almost pretty. When I got home after school I was ugly for the most part. Especially in the bathroom mirror, which made my nose look too long. But at night, when dressed in my yellow pajamas and with my hair braided, and while looking in the wall mirror illuminated by the soft cone of light coming from my desk lamp, I wasn't just pretty, I was fantastically beautiful, charming, magical. If only the boys could see me then!

And even if I was pretty at certain times, did it mean that I was sexy? What if being sexy was an entirely different thing? What if it was more than a combination of the right sizes and shapes of legs, hips, and breasts? What if it was a secret formula I didn't have?

Or maybe I did have it?

I thought of the way my uncle's friends looked at me sometimes. Their stares were so intense that they seemed to leave stains, like quick strokes of a paintbrush all over my body. They found me attractive. I couldn't be mistaken about that. Or could I?

And there was the history teacher, Vladimir Ivanovich, or Vovik, as most girls affectionately called him. He had been transferred to our school from across town at the beginning of that year and, although he wasn't particularly handsome (he was bowlegged) or smart (he confused historical figures), he immediately caused a school-wide wave of crushes. "He likes schoolgirls," they gossiped about him. "He may even have had an affair with one. That may even have been a reason for his changing schools."

"Nonsense!" Lida usually said. "They fired him because he is dumb. He confuses names, and he doesn't know the difference between *esoteric* and *exoteric*." I didn't argue (especially since I didn't know the difference between *esoteric* and *exoteric* myself), but I didn't forget about the schoolgirl gossip either.

I was pretty sure I didn't have a crush on Vovik, though. I thought that if you had a crush on somebody, you were supposed to idealize that person. I couldn't possibly have a crush on somebody whom I found stupid, arrogant, vain, and, most important, bowlegged. Or could I? Because if having a crush consisted of unceasing wondering whether that person had a crush on me, blushing, and feeling my heartbeat race whenever that person approached me, then I certainly had a crush on Vovik.

Starting in January, Vovik began calling me up in the beginning of each class. He would scan the class journal first, but he would invariably call on me.

"Tatiana Doomer," he would say and peer at me, although my name was Tatiana Rumer and it was clearly typed in the class journal. But I was the only Tatiana in class, and he was staring right at me.

"Tatiana Doomer," he would repeat. I would look at him calmly for some time, refusing to acknowledge the wrong name, then drop my eyes and stare at the blurred edge of my desk.

"Tanya, it's you. He's calling you," eager teacher's suck-ups whispered.

"Tanya, it's not worth it," Lida hissed from two desks behind me.

"It's you!" My seatmate prodded me with his ink-covered fist.

"Tatiana Doomer."

I squeezed my lips and made rapid swallowing movements—it helped to fight back the tears, but it also made me short of breath. I felt a lump in my throat, big, round, and unmoving. I knew that the lump would stay there, getting bigger and bigger, more and more painful, unless I either started to cry or answered to that wrong, humiliating name. I knew that I would give in sooner or later and I wished that I had done it sooner—it would have been less embarrassing—but I also knew that the next time it happened I would behave just the same.

"Yes?" I said at last, my voice thin and strained because of the lump.

"To the blackboard!"

I walked up, hearing the class's disappointed murmur—the best part of the show was over.

"Here, Tatiana," Vovik said. He handed me a long—very long—and very heavy teacher's stick best suited for a game of pool.

"Show me Stalingrad."

I turned to a map that with all of its brilliant colors looked like a giant candy wrapper through the screen of my hovering tears. I couldn't see a thing.

"Stalingrad, Tatiana, the site of the famous battle?"

I ran the stick around the map, hoping that Stalingrad would magically pop up somewhere, greeting me with a rumble of explosions, gunfire, and soldiers' yells.

"Good, Tatiana, good," Vovik said. "At least you are in the right hemisphere."

I stood with my back to the class and thought of my skinny ankles and protruding shoulder blades and the shiny patch on my old skirt. I thought that if I had been one of those other, popular girls, the boys wouldn't have chuckled, as they did now, but instead would have admired me. If I had been attractive, I could have stood there until the bell rang, just running my stick over the map and enjoying the attention. I would have won the game then.

But I wasn't such a girl and I wanted the ordeal to end as soon as possible. I pointed at something conveniently close to the tip of my stick.

"Stalingrad," I said.

"Are you sure?"

"Yes, I am sure!" If I had to lose, I would at least do it with dignity.

"Go back to your place then," he said, scribbling something in his journal. It could be a D, but could just as well be an A.

"Do you hate him?" Lida asked me.

"Oh, yes," I answered without thinking, but I wasn't sure if I did.

Vovik didn't stare at me as intently as my uncle's friends usually did, but I had a similar feeling when I stood by the blackboard with my back to him. Swift, tiny paintbrush strokes circled my legs, my back, my neck. Especially my neck. I imagined him staring at the narrow strip of my skin between my ponytail and the white collar of my school uniform. I imagined him getting out of his teacher's desk, walking up very close to me, moving my hair away, and brushing his lips against my neck. I imagined him sitting at his desk as I searched for Stalingrad and wanting to do just that. I had been teased before. I had been tortured before. I had been pushed, I had been called bad names and I had been humiliated. But those insults were made by people who either were indifferent to me or plainly didn't like me. There was something different about humiliation combined with those stares, those brushstrokes. Very different and very pleasant.

At the prom, Vovik walked up to me at the very end of the night, tapped me on the shoulder, took the glass of lemonade out of my hand, and led me to the dance floor.

I was much shorter than he: My head barely reached to his chest. I had to raise my head at a funny angle and crane my neck to see his face. I kept looking down at my dancing feet, wondering when I would stumble. My feet seemed to glide and fly chaotically. I couldn't follow their movements. Vovik's hand on my back felt like an iron left on a piece of thin cloth for too long. The sensation was so strong that I half expected to hear the hissing and find an iron-shaped brown imprint on my blouse after the dance was over.

"Never look down when you dance," he said. "When you dance and when you ski. Otherwise you'll fall. Look up, face the danger!"

I thought about his words when packing for the camping trip, and so I had put a colorful box of "morning-after" pills (stolen a few days before from my uncle's gynecologist friend) in the pocket of my jeans.

Our camp was set up in a round clearing framed on all sides by tall pine trees. Inside the tree circle, we set up our tents—also in a circle—and inside that smaller circle, big logs were placed in a ring around a crackling fire. I, along with Lida and several other girls, was put in charge of food. We sat on the logs in the smallest circle by the fire. Each of us had a small pile of potatoes. We each took a potato from the pile, rinsed it in a pail of icy cold water, stripped the skin off with a sharp penknife, rinsed it again, then tossed the puny white thing into the big pot, and the peel right into the fire. Once we had finished with potatoes, we would have to empty paper packs of soup into another pot, open cans, brew the tea. And then after everybody had eaten, we would surely have to do the dishes, using icy cold water from the river and sand instead of dishwashing soap. We were "good" girls. And that was what good girls always did on camping trips.

Not all girls were good. Some didn't come near our "kitchen" circle, except when they wanted to eat. Some lurked between tents, crawled in and out, whispered things to one another, changed their lipstick, their shirts, and sometimes their pants, laughed, and from time to time crossed the boundaries of the outer circle of our camp and disappeared in the pine trees with one or another of the boys. They came back from the woods smelling of cigarettes, and with dark musty leaves and brown pine needles stuck to their backs. They then scraped the dirt off in a leisurely, boasting way.

In my heart I was one of them. It was just a mistake that I had to sit with the good girls and pluck sprouts out of potatoes and scrape carrots. It was a mistake that I had to listen to them gossiping about the "bad" girls, and scrunch my face in disgust when they told how one of them asked a boy to pull her pants down because she wanted to pee. It was a mistake that I had to nod and say with them, "What a slut!"

I was not a good girl! I thought, fingering the box of contraception pills in my pocket. I needed a prince who would save me from being a potato-peeling Cinderella and turn me into a Princess/Bad Girl by offering me a cigarette and dragging me into the woods.

Since the beginning of the trip, Vovik hadn't given me much

hope that the magical transformation would happen soon. He had been setting up tents at first, then he carried the logs to the campfire site with the boys, then he chopped firewood, then he helped to start a fire . . . and now he was sleeping. I could see his feet in old gym shoes sticking out of the tent and the thin walls of the tent trembling slightly when he snored. He was snoring when it was almost dinnertime, and we would have to eat around the campfire, and after dinner we would sing songs and then crawl into our tents, which each of us shared with three other people! We wouldn't have any time left for what I'd planned!

"My mom wants me to be a doctor," Alyosha Durov said after dinner. We laughed, sleepily, halfheartedly.

"Come on, you are not a doctor!"

"I know, but my mom wants me to become one."

I don't remember how the campfire conversation landed on the subject of our future professions. It was completely dark by then, and the only part of the camp we could see was the small circle lit by the cone-shaped campfire flames. The soup and potatoes were all eaten and the pots wiped clean with pieces of bread. The dishes lay in a big pile by a pine tree, waiting for the good girls' hands to scrub them in the morning. The songs were all sung, and the people who played guitar rested, warming their hands against aluminum mugs full of steaming tea.

"Alyoshka, you are not a doctor," Vovik said. "You are . . . What are you? You are . . . a biologist! That's it. You're a biologist. It's close to medicine, but you don't have to deal with people."

I don't think Vovik took his words seriously. He certainly didn't expect that they would be taken as a revelation. But suddenly everybody stared at him as if he were an oracle. The campfire stupor was shaken off in a matter of seconds. Everybody had become eager and alert. "What about me? What about me?" we asked Vovik, vying with one another, some of us aloud, others in a whisper, still others silently, like me.

Was it the night, the weird shadows creeping up on our faces, the crackling of the burning logs, that went to our heads? That special campfire smell of strong tea, smoldering logs, burnt pine needles, and the soil soaking up chicken soup from somebody's toppled bowl? Or was it the crazy imbalance in temperature, because when you sit by the fire, your back and feet are freezing while your knees and your face are blazing hot?

What about me? What about me? I kept repeating silently, half listening to the destinies of the others while trying to slow my racing heart. Why wasn't he telling my fortune? What was he waiting for? Was it because he didn't see anything good for me? What if he said, "And you, Tatiana, are good for nothing. What? Does that surprise you? Didn't you know?" And I would have to agree with him, because I knew that. I'd known for a long time . . . I wasn't very smart the way Lida, for example, was smart. Hell! I couldn't even find Stalingrad! I wasn't sexy. If I were sexy, Vovik wouldn't have slept through half the day when he could've been with me. And worse than that—I was a "good" girl. I was a good girl who tried to fool herself by bringing contraception pills on a camping trip, but whose fate really was to peel potatoes and scrub pots.

"Hey, Tatiana," Vovik suddenly said, prodding me with his fist somewhere above my denim-clad knee. "Hey, are you asleep?" Somebody laughed. I couldn't breathe. I felt the same lump in my throat that I had felt when he called me "Tatiana Doomer." If he makes fun of me now, I thought, I will run away, I will run right into the woods where the boys took the chosen girls. I will run and run until I get lost, and then I'll fall on the ground littered with used condoms and cigarette butts and die right there.

He put an arm around me. I couldn't feel it because of all the layers of my camping gear, but I saw his fingers (scratches, black fingernails) on my shoulder, and more important, I saw mortal envy in the eyes of other girls.

"Want to hear yours, Tatiana?"

I nodded.

"You should be the companion to a great man," he said. "You should be near him, you should support him, entertain him, make him happy and"—a squeeze on my shoulder that I barely felt—"you should inspire him for his great man's deeds."

My soul (or whatever it was that we atheists had) soared far, far up, racing the campfire flames and then dispersing around the woods along with campfire sparks. That was it! I knew it! I'd always known. I was good for something after all, for something special, for something much better than what was in store for my classmates, for Lida. "You're smart, Lida, you're going to be a lawyer." A lawyer? How boring! I was going to be the muse to a great man!

My mother's face flashed in my mind for a second. She wouldn't have liked it: "He said 'entertain,' didn't he? Are you happy to have entertaining a man as your destiny?" she would've asked.

But you don't understand, Mom, I thought. She wouldn't understand. For as long as I could remember I was fed the stories of my mother's hard-achieved but wonderful success. She was a scrawny, sickly girl from a very poor family, with a worn-out mother and an ailing father, yet she always yearned for a bigger life. She finished college while working full time, she wrote her dissertation while working *and* changing my diapers. And now look what she'd become—a famous professor, a celebrated author of textbooks. As a child, I loved her life story, I thought of it as a variation on a Cinderella tale, where hard work substituted for the magic, and a brilliant career for the prince. I always felt a thrill when she took me to work with her. She would walk up to the lectern at the front of a huge room bursting with her students, all of them staring at her with awe and armed with ballpoint pens and notebooks to put her precious words down on paper. And she was so confident, so powerful, so big, glowing with the sense of her own authority, accepting the attention with a patronizing smile. But as I grew up, I became more and more aware of her other persona, concealed from the public, but naked in front of my eyes. That other woman was small and miserable. Plagued with constant colds. With either a woolen scarf wrapped around her throat or a piece of cotton wool sticking out of her ear. Sobbing into her pillow at night. Giving dirty looks to couples. Wincing whenever Maya described her marital bliss: "I told your brother, 'Stop it, people will see!' But no, he can't help it, he has to touch me all the time." And then waiting and waiting and waiting for a call from her boring, unattractive, married male colleague, who might or might not be interested in her. That was the role model she wanted me to follow? That?

A muse, on the other hand, doesn't simply entertain. She inspires, she influences the great man's work. In some very subtle and magical way—it's elusive, it's indescribable. He, the great man, would be sitting frozen in front of a blank sheet of paper, empty canvas, silent piano, and I would walk in. Five feet five, flat-chested, and skinny, but with a great fire in my eyes, or a strange remarkable gait or carriage, or speaking in an especially melodic or powerful voice, and he—the writer, artist, or composer—would snap his fingers and say, "Yes!" and hit his piano, slab of marble, or creaky typewriter, and create with great fire in his eyes an enormous, magnificent work. And then generations and generations of people would admire that work and see the fire that would still burn behind it centuries later. And it would be I who had lit that fire!

I could live with being unpopular. I could live with being ignored by the majority. For there would be one man, the most desirable man, who would pick me out of the crowd. He would pick me because I was able to inspire!

I felt Lida's grip on my elbow. "Gosh, it's so cold." The fire had been put out. Everybody was moving toward their tents, carrying the smell of smoke and bits of campfire warmth with them. "Such a jerk!" Lida said. "He meant himself, didn't he? He is that great man. He has a crush on you and he is disgusting!"

It was the first time Lida had acknowledged Vovik's interest in me. A day before I would've been elated. Now I felt a harsh wave of night cold washing over me. He meant himself? Only himself? But what great deeds could *he* possibly need me to inspire in him?

"Tatiana." I heard Vovik's whisper. "Tatiana, come here."

He stood leaning against a tree, barely visible except for the light of a cigarette dangling below his mouth. I walked in his direction until his outstretched hand grazed my stomach. He planted his other hand on my back and pressed me to him. Somehow it didn't feel as exciting as when we had danced. A light dropped out of his mouth and hit the ground with a quick hiss. I felt his wet, meaty tongue in my mouth. Tasting of tobacco, chicken soup, and ashes. After a while he took it out and made a wet path down my neck, so my chilled skin broke out in goose bumps. And then he let me go and whispered, "Come out here when the other girls in your tent fall asleep."

I thought about the cold, as I lay in my tent waiting for the girls to drop off. Nights in the woods were very cold. I started to shiver imagining how cold I would be when he lifted up my sweater or pulled down my pants. It would be so cold, but I had to do it, didn't I? I needed to do it. The box with the pills in my right pocket pressed into my hipbone, making me really uncomfortable. I turned onto my other side, facing the sleeping Lida. Lida was big, warm, and comfy. She snored softly, letting out cozy puffs of well-heated breath. I moved closer to her and shut my eyes.

I woke up when it was already full morning. I woke up because Lida pulled on my toe and told me that they were folding our tent. I seemed to be the only one who'd had a good sleep. Others had creased faces and half-open eyes. They moved as if in a stupor, collapsing the tents, dragging their rumpled backpacks back and forth, mixing trash into the cooled coals with their boot-clad toes. Vovik sat on a log with his back to the former campfire and picked hardened pieces of meat from a can of stew. His face was even more creased and rumpled than the faces of the others. He had smudges of ketchup around his mouth and pine needles stuck in his hair. I hadn't noticed before that his ears moved when he ate.

I considered throwing my box of pills in the coals and burying it with my foot as a symbolic gesture, but then I thought better of it. Now that I had proof that I was wanted, I knew I would need them soon. Hopefully, very soon.

Once at home I rushed to make a raid on my grandmother's things. Shortly after her death my mother had put all her belongings into three boxes: clothes in a big one, documents in a small one, and everything that was neither clothes nor documents in a medium-size box. I found what I needed in the third box, which was buried under faded postcards, broken pairs of reading glasses, and bottles of unused and expired medicine. A small, shabby book. Anna Grigorievna's diary.

I brushed the dust off the cover, carried the book to my mother's room (I liked to read there when my mother was at work), and slumped on the couch. I was going to read about the writer with different eyes and what it was like to be his muse, a muse, just like I would be one day. To my surprise, the excitement vanished as soon as I read the first couple of pages. There was something wrong, very wrong, either with me or with the book, and I couldn't understand what.

Here she was, Anna Grigorievna Snitkina, a young stenographer fresh from school. A lucky chance brought to her an assignment to work for Fedor Dostoevsky. He needed a stenographer because he was in a hurry to finish a novel (some complicated contractual obligations—I skipped the boring parts). They arranged that he would dictate and she would write in shorthand, and then later transcribe what she had written. They worked like that for about a month, got attached to each other, he proposed, she accepted.

When she came to his flat for the first time, she brought her neat stenographer's notebook and a supply of sharpened pencils of the very best quality. She described in minute detail how she went to buy those pencils, how she chose them in a stationery store. Wanted to impress him with her pencils! She didn't describe how much time she spent tending to her hair though, choosing a ribbon, trying to make herself look pretty! Liar! Liar! I smacked the book against the couch with the force of my sixteen-year-old hatred, but I couldn't put it down. I read on, turning to my imagination for the details that Anna Grigorievna had omitted.

She sat bending over her work, she didn't lift her eyes, but she felt his presence. He was pacing back and forth, back and forth. The folds of his coat brushed against her back from time to time, his heavy feet made the floorboards creak. He sighed. He groaned. He murmured some unintelligible sounds. He looked at her. At first without realizing that he was looking at her, but gradually becoming more and more aware of her presence. He stared at her delicate girlish neck bent over the manuscript. He took in the shape of her back, the color of her hair, the quick, firm movements of her hand, all of that while speaking out the brilliant sentences of his novel.

I hated Anna Grigorievna. I hated her guts. I choked with rage when she described how Dostoevsky called her affectionate names, bought her fruit and sweets, and declared his love on his knees (that usually happened after he had gambled yet another sum of money away—but I was too flustered to notice that at the time). I was full of the sweetest joy when I read how he yelled at her or ignored her. She portrayed Dostoevsky's stepson and the widow of his brother as her archenemies, so I immediately sided with them. I gloated over their victories in some little fight over poor Fedor Mikhailovich's time or money, and fumed if Anna Grigorievna won.

I wasn't comforted by the fact that she was your most average girl, not particularly pretty, not particularly smart, unremarkable in every way, practical, even petty. As ordinary as Anna Grigorievna was, she had the man of my dreams, and she was his muse. She was the one who inspired Dostoevsky to write what was called in my Russian textbook "the pearls of world literature." She was even more than a muse. Dostoevsky dictated to her, said the words aloud. But it was she who actually wrote *The Gambler.* It was her hand that touched the paper, it was the movements of her fingers that transformed short-lived sounds into the eternal letters. It was her eyes that first saw the words he uttered. It was her work that enabled others to see them.

I found it hard to breathe. Yes, in my case "the other woman," along with "the man," had been dead for almost a hundred years, but that didn't make my jealousy less real, or less painful. I couldn't bear reading this book anymore. Anna Grigorievna's diary went far under my mother's couch, where years before I had hidden my uncle's scary *Atlas of Dermatology.* The torturous book was gone, but the image of Anna Grigorievna sneakily winning Dostoevsky wouldn't let me alone. I had to read *The Gambler,* the novel that *she* had written. I found it among Dostoevsky's titles on the upper bookshelf, a thin book under a faded blue cover. I started reading right there, while standing on a chair, my feet sinking into the plush upholstery. After a few pages I stepped down, dragged my feet across the room to the couch, and cautiously lowered my butt onto the seat, all without taking my eyes away from the book.

I was soaking up every word, getting drunker as I progressed. There was something about the book that made me feel very good, almost euphoric, but I couldn't at first guess what it was. It was bigger, more important, more exciting than the characters or the plot, something that existed beyond the book's pages. In the middle of chapter six it hit me. Another woman! There was another woman, a real woman who gave life to the character of Polina and to the novel itself. She was not Anna Grigorievna. Dostoevsky had had a relationship with this other woman before he met his zealous stenographer. And it was this other woman whom Dostoevsky loved.

The magnitude of the passion in the novel was so great that I, totally unfamiliar with anything even remotely close to being in love, was able to recognize it.

What there is so attractive about her I cannot think. Yet there IS something attractive about her—something passing fair, it would seem. Others besides myself she has driven to distraction. She is tall and straight, and very slim. Her body looks as though it could be tied into a knot, or bent double, like a cord. The imprint of her foot is long and narrow. It is a maddening imprint—yes, simply a maddening one! And her hair has a reddish tint about it, and her eyes are like cat's eyes—though able also to glance with proud, disdainful mien.

"A maddening imprint" of her foot . . . That expression moved me so much that I dropped the book and fell facedown onto the couch, laughing happily, as if I'd just discovered that somebody was so passionate about me.

I didn't resemble that woman at all. I wasn't tall, I wasn't a red-head, I didn't have cat eyes, I didn't have long feet, I wasn't proud or cruel or disdainful—there wasn't one single separate trait that I could recognize as my own. But Polina was utterly different from the hated Anna Grigorievna, and that enabled me to identify with her, identify not with a particular trait of her personality but with her image as a whole. I allowed Dostoevsky to be in love with her. I blessed their love.

After two days of constant rereading, *The Gambler* went back to my mother's bookcase. One by one I took out and read Dostoevsky's other novels—*The Brothers Karamazov, A Raw Youth, The Possessed,* and *The Idiot*—all of them written while he was married to Anna Grigorievna, all of them including that other woman (whom I took to calling "Polina") as a character. In *The Idiot* she even appeared twice—as the snobbish upper-class beauty Aglaya, and as the half-mad kept woman Nastasya Filippovna. He could dress her in different clothes, but he couldn't fool me. All of them were Polina, with her maddening attractiveness, with her sick pride, with her openness to suffering and inclination to torture, with her crazy idealism.

But where was Anna Grigorievna in those books? I couldn't find a single character resembling her. Not one devoted, calm, domesticated woman. Not one practical woman. (Just think of Nastasya Filippovna throwing thousands of rubles into the flames! Anna Grigorievna wouldn't have let a single kopeck go to waste.) Anna Grigorievna didn't write shorthand for him after *The Gambler,* but she was right there all the time while he was writing *The Brothers Karamazov, A Raw Youth, The Possessed,* and *The Idiot,* in the same flat with him, behind the thin walls of his study. His wife. Moving about in her rustling Victorian skirt, giving household orders, taking care of the kids, listening to the sounds coming from his study. Ready to rush to him, whenever he called, "Anya!" Ready to ask him what he wanted, bring him his tea in a silver glass holder, offer to throw a plaid blanket over his shoulders, kiss him on his bald crown, and quietly exit the room afterward.

Dostoevsky sat at his desk sipping the tea served by Anna Grigorievna, while his quills tore the paper and spilled ink over the frenzied world of his novels, where there was no place for her. That world was dominated by Polina, who wouldn't serve him tea, offer him a plaid blanket, or kiss him on the bald crown, but who instead had the power to ignite him with the imprint of her foot, torture him, drive him mad, who had the power to make him want to grab the quill and write about her.

When I am a muse, I will be Polina, I decided. Never, never will I become Anna Grigorievna.

Chapter Four

Some time after I moved to the United States, I grew to dislike coffee. I can't say that I developed a deep distaste for it; it simply didn't please me anymore. I stopped falling asleep with the thought of tomorrow's morning cup of coffee. I stopped feeling a thrill upon breaking cappuccino froth with grains of sugar. I stopped sneakily adding cream to my espresso to make it last longer.

My enthusiasm was lost.

I still drink coffee though. One cup when I wake up, because the morning is not real morning without the sharp, optimistic scent and the percolator's grumbling. And then I drink another cup later in the day, usually after work, usually on a deck, leisurely, because it allows me to rustle with the newspaper and drift off with whatever thought or dream I might have. Sometimes I leaf through the diary I began while I was first living with Mark and then abandoned. I don't write in my diary anymore. I never read it either. I just leaf through it, without pausing to decipher the words—I know all my entries by heart.

This diary looked good when I first bought it, just the right size: small enough to fit into my pocket, but not too small to make writing uncomfortable. Ivory colored, smooth, matte paper. Soft leather cover with a flap and two soft brown laces to tie it closed. Very writerly, very romantic.

It looks even better now that it is worn, now that one of the laces has broken off, the flap on the cover is curled up, and some of the pages are greasy or coffee-stained. It looks perfect next to a coffee cup and a spoon, especially when there are a few grains of sugar on the cover.

It looks authentic and true.

I can't say that about the diary's contents though.

At the beginning every date is filled. The sentences compete with one another for space, words spilling over onto the borders. Lines burst with tiny, crisp letters and distinctive punctuation marks. The pages seem blue from ink; there is very little white space. They feel uneven when you touch them, from all the deep imprints, all the pockmarks made with a pen. They feel thin. Countless corrections and additions are squeezed in the narrow spaces between the lines. The number of corrections betrays the lying. You don't make corrections in your diary. If you do, it means you haven't been truthful either when you wrote your entry or when you corrected it.

The farther you leaf through it, the paler the diary becomes. You encounter pages with clear borders at first. Then unfinished pages, followed by unfilled pages, and toward the end by a vastness of thick, white, empty space with only occasional notes, slanting light lines made with a lazy, reluctant pen.

I close my diary when the coffee becomes cold and my dislike of it grows. There is something sad, pathetic even about cold coffee. It tastes like something unused, unfinished, unloved.

Back in Russia I used to be crazy for coffee. For the three kinds of coffee that I knew. There was "coffee beverage"—a ground mix sold in plain paper bags that didn't smell or taste like coffee, and in fact it wasn't even made of coffee beans. I didn't enjoy drinking it, but it was the first kind of coffee that I learned how to brew, and I loved guarding it from boiling over.

There was also instant coffee in brown cans, a rare treat, and a measure of a person's power. "He can get instant coffee," my mother would say about somebody, and I would become filled with awe and think of that person as if he were a fairy-tale wizard with a beard and a magic wand. My mother's wand wasn't all that powerful, so we could get only a couple of cans each year. My mother gave it to me only before big exams, and I loved drinking it while still in my pajamas, my feet dangling under the kitchen table.

But my favorite kind of coffee was Turkish, served in a little coffee shop on the Old Arbat Street. The coffee there was muddy and had an earthy smell that felt foreign but at the same time very real. It reminded me that somewhere there was other, foreign, bigger life, just waiting for me.

"Is there Turkish coffee in New York?" I asked my uncle on the phone. He and Maya emigrated to the United States soon after my grandmother's death, and he was now considered an expert on foreign life.

"Turkish coffee? To your heart's content!" he said. "Turkish coffee, Swedish coffee, Arabic coffee! There is so much Italian coffee that they don't even remember that it came from Italy. Cappuccino, espresso, iced coffee . . ." At that point Maya on the other end of earth remembered about the cost of the long-distance call and my uncle had to stop, but I was sure that if he hadn't the list of coffees would've gone on and on.

"Coffee!" was my first thought on seeing the letter from the United States Immigration Service. I will get to drink a lot of coffee! I will get to try all the different kinds, I thought, tearing the envelope right there, by the mailbox in the damp lobby of our building.

Later I became ashamed of the pettiness of my reaction. My

uncle had sent a request for my immigration documents about two years before that. As the time for the answer from United States Immigration drew close, I'd started running down to check our mailbox several times a day, silently praying to find The Envelope there before I stuck my little key into the mailbox lock. Surely I had been hoping for something more than coffee all that time.

"I will get to travel, I will get to fly on a plane," glided through my mind as I lay in my bed that night unable to sleep. "I will buy clothes I saw on the much-handled pages of foreign magazines at my friends' . . . What else? Oh, yes, I will own a videoplayer and see as many foreign videos as I want. Movies too. Foreign movies. I won't have to stand in a two-hour line to see an American movie . . ."

Too petty again. "It's important, Tanya. For your future," my mother kept telling me. She was staying. She had decided that she would be lost there, at her age (she was forty-nine at the time), without her job, without hope of ever fully mastering the language. So it was just me. My future. "Your life will be so much better in this country," my uncle kept telling me on the phone. "Better?" What did it mean? How better? "Better" was too vague, too light, and by definition too elusive. If something were better, another thing could be still better yet, so how could you strive to achieve something that was by definition surpassable? No, I refused to be excited by "better." And then, suddenly, a quick thought stirred me up. The change . . . That's what I get out of coming to the United States. The change. My whole life would be different. The word "different" had something magical about it. Now, I could see it. A genie would come out of the modest INS envelope and take everything that surrounded me now and exchange it for something else, something unknown. I had no idea what my new life would be, but I knew one thing for sure, it wouldn't be the same. It would be different! Different—no matter better or worse—could never be boring.

So far that was just what my life here had been. Boring. I couldn't yet call myself a failure, but I certainly wasn't going in the direction of success.

I didn't feel any joy when they handed me my diploma at the graduation ceremony at my Moscow college. A modest two sheets of paper stapled together under a hard blue cover (if I had been a better student it would have been a red cover), a list of subjects, most of which I hadn't enjoyed, a list of grades showing that the professors hadn't enjoyed having me either, a modest line allowing me to practice a profession that I didn't feel any desire to practice.

My subject was history. Five years before, when applying to college, I had chosen it without much consideration, simply because I had always felt irresistibly drawn to matters of the past. Soon, however, I found out that the particular matters of the past that interested me weren't considered important.

I wanted to know exactly what it was like to be a nineteenth-century Russian, eighteenth-century Frenchman, or a citizen of the Roman Empire. How people lived, what they talked about, what they ate, wore, rode, where they dumped garbage, how often they took a bath, what men used for shaving, and what women used as birth control.

No piece of information could be too petty or too repellent to me. I didn't shun the exploration of canalization plans or personal hygiene habits. It was the knowledge of those minor details that made the past breathe behind all the dusty books and artifacts, that made people who'd been dead for hundreds of years spring to life. It allowed me to take a little bite out of their experiences.

Sometimes it seemed that I knew exactly what it was like to wear a "whale teeth corsage" or a skirt with hoops. I felt the stiff bandage hugging my rib cage, I felt its sharp edge cutting into the tender skin under my breasts, I felt beads of sweat gathering in my artificially enhanced cleavage. It must have been fun to have a man undo all those fastenings on a Victorian dress. Slowly, one by one. It must have felt ticklish to kiss a man with a beard, especially one with a long, fluffy beard, the kind favored by most nineteenth-century Russian writers. It must have felt very funny to have a beard like that run down your bare neck and chest. It must have sent a tangy chill down your body, making your nipples stiff, but your skin tender and a little sore.

I spent days in the Lenin Library, the Historical Library, the Central Archive, and the Theater Library, attending to the questions that popped into my mind. I read stuffy mammoths of history books. I leafed through the fine yellow pages of old magazines. I peered into the ancient gravures, trying to determine whether the dresses drawn in them were made of velvet or wool. I scanned the menus of 1890s restaurants. I studied rosters of scarves and gloves sold in Kuznetsky Most shops in 1900s Moscow. I put long hours into my work and wrote painstakingly researched but unfocused essays, which were rarely appreciated by my teachers. Apparently, the questions that interested me didn't interest anybody else in my department. And what was worse, the questions that interested them didn't interest me.

I couldn't care less who had discovered Siberia or conquered Caucasus. I yawned through the lectures on economic and political systems. I escaped to a bathroom when a trembling-with-awe museum guide showed us a glass box containing Lenin's high school report card. I walked off to pick flowers when they brought us to the site of the great Borodino battle and described the position of the Russian soldiers and Napoleon's. Later, when we had to draw a map of the battle, all I remembered were daisies and cornflowers swaying on their thin stems in a sea of tall grass. That didn't help my grades, along with the fact that I could never remember which Russian tsar came after which, or whether a certain country was an enemy or an ally of Russia in some minor centuries-old war. Wars annoyed me the most. It seemed that there always was some hungry tsar or king behind each of them, ready to send hundreds, thousands, millions of people to ruin and death, simply for the sake of the power and fame it would give him. Most of the wars were as senseless as they were ugly, and yet they took up almost all the space in our history books. Foreign wars, civil wars, territorial wars, religious wars, political wars. Chapters and chapters of wars. And only a small, unimpressive appendix at the end of the textbook was devoted to the important scientific discoveries, cultural changes, or artistic achievements of a certain period. Physicists, artists, and writers would be all bunched up in a single sentence, while Napoleon enjoyed detailed coverage of all his major battles, many of them with charts and plans. If an alien were to look at our history books, he would be sure that humans were busy killing one another ninety-nine percent of the time. I thought sometimes that maybe if historians didn't find wars so fascinating, there would be less incentive for the tsars and kings to start them.

On my final exam, a professor asked me which tsar ruled during the Russo-Turkish War of 1877–78, and I couldn't recall his name. Was it Pavel? Or Nikolai? Nikolai II or I? "Shame on you," his assistant hissed through her teeth. I could describe in detail what people wore at that time, and what they ate, and what toys their children played with, but they hadn't asked me that.

"Makeup? History of makeup in nineteenth-century Russia? You should be ashamed," my thesis adviser said after studying my proposal. "Look at the things happening all around you. The Soviet empire is about to collapse. Look out the window! We live in a period of the greatest change. It's a dream of any historian. And you!

You, writing your thesis about creams and pomades that went ran-
cid more than a hundred years ago!"

By the time of my graduation, I knew that I didn't have much
chance to get a nice job in a museum or a research center. I couldn't
hope to be left unemployed either. There were plenty of schools on
the outskirts of Moscow, waiting for people just like me (not too
bright, not too promising) to teach teenagers about boring wars and
the boring bad tsars behind them. When they called my name at the
graduation ceremony, I had an urge to hide. I felt that after traveling
a long, hard road, I hadn't arrived at my destination but instead had
been handed a ticket for another journey, longer and harder than the
first, and possibly endless.

My romantic situation wasn't too hopeful either. For one thing
it wasn't romantic.

After that night by the campfire, boys eventually started asking
me out. From time to time a serious pimple-faced boy from my college would suggest our studying together. Or a not-so-serious boy
would sit down next to me on the subway and offer to walk me
home. A boy who wasn't serious at all would chase after me on the
street and try to get me to come with him to his grandmother's,
father's, friend's empty apartment or to take a walk in a park. I didn't
have a great flow of offers, rather a trickle, which I wouldn't have
minded if the boys had been more interesting. I had accepted not
being popular, but I had accepted it on a certain condition. Where
was that amazing, extraordinary man who was supposed to pick me
out of the crowd? I felt cheated out of my part of the bargain.

At first I refused my suitors mercilessly and resolutely. I refused
them with indignation. After a while, though, my refusals became
less resolute. Then I started making steps to accept. "I need it for
experience," I explained to my college girlfriends, who raised their

eyebrows on seeing me with somebody with whom they "would've never gone out." That is if you believed them, of course.

"I just want to know different people. Listening to a new boy is like reading a new book," I explained to my serious friend Lida, who didn't buy it and didn't approve. But I wasn't seeing her frequently anyway, preferring to be with the girls who were less smart and less interesting than Lida, but with whom I had more in common. "More" being sex.

I need to keep the motor running, I explained to myself when I woke up awash with disgust sometimes. I need to keep the motor running, so that by the time I meet my real man, I am not all rusty and creaky . . .

But I didn't want to make any one of the boys a steady boyfriend. I thought that if I settled on one of them, I would betray my dream, and then my real man would never turn up. So I met them in lecture halls, on subways, and at bus stops, went out on dates with them a couple of times, and then broke up with them just in time, before the relationship could be considered steady.

Having heard that a woman always remembers her first man, I resisted having sex with my momentary boyfriends—I didn't want to remember any of them. My resistance didn't prove to be very strong though. Slowly, hesitantly I "granted them little favors" (an expression I'd heard from my mother) or, rather, stole those favors for myself. I didn't really care what those boys felt for me—maybe only a little—because I found their desire flattering and exciting. The "favors" invariably progressed further with each new boy. The difference in degree of physical intimacy was often so little that I can't even now say who kissed me first. Was it the one who had brushed his lips shyly against my cheek? Or was it the one who had pressed his mouth to mine? Or maybe the one who had succeeded in parting my lips? Or the one who had sucked on my tongue so hard that I punched him in the chest, afraid that he would swallow it?

My relationships with boys progressed in intimacy, and simultaneously in geographic proximity to my bed. I would say "goodbye" to one boy at the bus stop, but allow another to see me to the steps of my building. The next boy would be kissing me by the radiator in the lobby of my building, pressing himself to me harder and harder, trying if not to feel, then at least to picture the contours of the female body beneath my puffy down coat. His successor would actually come up the stairs and unbutton my coat, while I would lean against the railing in exactly the same spot where the neighbors' girl used to melt in the hands of her boyfriend. And so they progressed into my apartment, but not into my bedroom; inside my bra, but not inside my panties; into my bedroom, but not into my bed; inside my panties, but not inside me . . . It all happened so gradually that I couldn't tell who was "my first man" in the conventional sense. At the time, I was glad that I couldn't tell. That meant that all the experiences that I'd had didn't count. I had yet to meet my *real* first man. With whom everything would be different. Sex, among other things.

I wasn't shocked but I was unpleasantly surprised when the mystery of the sexual act was cleared up for me at last. Or rather the absence of mystery was cleared up. I discovered that the sexual act was simple, accessible, perfectly devoid of any romantic meaning, and, what was most disgusting, very common. Everybody did it, and most people did it in exactly the same way.

I would look at my teachers, at the salesmen in a supermarket, at the fellow commuters on the subway, and think: He is doing it. She is doing it too. This ugly mustached pregnant woman must have done it at least once. Just like in the days following my grandmother's death, a new world was suddenly opened to me in a flash, showing me something appalling that I would've preferred had remained concealed. Married couples became the source of constant fascination for me. They are married, I kept thinking, looking at them; that means they are doing it. My mother's friend and her husband—so gloomy, so serious, so bored and boring—get undressed at night (does she wear that same ugly, off-white tricot that I saw when she tried on my mother's skirt?), climb into the same bed, and abandon themselves to sex. This woman in the breadline, who says that she's been married for thirty years—only imagine how many times she has done it! All those couples who look barely compatible enough to share a meal have to do something that requires at least a minimal amount of passion, and have to do it not just once but all the time. How on earth do they manage it?

Meanwhile, everybody around me was getting married.

Dena sent us photographs from her American wedding. She looked beautiful, if a little tense in her white dress, and I liked the groom very much. "A find, a real find," Maya told my mother on the phone. "Smart, hardworking, polite, from a very nice Kiev family." He was sexy too, in a shy, bespectacled kind of way. I felt a mild pang of envy when I studied the photo of their wedding kiss. I felt a stronger pang when I spotted tears in my uncle's eyes in another photo.

Every fall, a few more of my classmates came to school endowed with shiny wedding rings, hard round bellies, and a whole new set of problems that seemed to have emerged overnight. Only yesterday they'd giggled, describing the sensation of a boy's hand under their shirts, and now it was more like: "I set out to make some meatballs yesterday, but the butter had this funny smell, so I sent him to the store, but he said . . ." "And then the bitch told me, 'You might have taken my son, but never will you get my apartment!' " Even their bodies seemed to change their functions dramatically. "My nipples are all cracked." "I have a pain in my lower back like you won't believe." "I sit there for hours and nothing happens." "Did you try beets?" "I tried everything!" "It was a seventeen-hour labor, and then they had to cut me up anyway, and the wound got infected, so I still have pus coming out . . ." Then after cracked nipples, constipation, and pus, the children came, the ones who were supposed to be great fun and the reward for all the suffering, but I never heard them described as such. In the words of their young mothers, children were portrayed as sickly, annoying little beings whose sole purpose was to get on their parents' nerves and never let them go anywhere. By the time I graduated, the neighbors' girl had a six-year-old, her face perpetually covered with crusty snot. "Shut up, you little shit!" the girl now yelled.

There was no place for beets, crusted snot, or yelling in my fantasies of marriage. In fact, there wasn't a single concrete image in them. I imagined a shadowy loft apartment, which I would share with the still blurry-faced man of my dreams. The apartment would have creaky stairs, and the pale light would come through the window in a conical ray, illuminating the books and papers strewn all over the place. We would do some work, or he would do some work—some thrilling, intellectual work—and when we or he took a break, we would talk or laugh or simply be comfortably quiet. We would be very much alike, and at the same time sufficiently different, so we would never bore each other. There would be a natural, instant intimacy that you didn't have to build. A perfect harmony in everything from our choice of books to our choice of food. I never imagined what it would be like to make love to him, I just wanted it to be something different, to have the complexity, the mystery, the magic that my real sexual experience lacked.

The scary thing was that by the end of my college years, my perfect fantasies had started to fade. As much as my married friends complained about their lives, they actually didn't seem to mind.

More than that, they thought of marriage as an achievement. They all had smug expressions as though they'd earned the right to have all those maladies. There must be something good about it, I thought, something that they didn't disclose. Could it be the pleasure of having all those constant little pains that proved that you were a woman, and were alive?

This is life, I thought, when one or another of my friends gave me her warm, heavy, sleepy baby to hold. The baby fussed in my arms, the baby pulled on my hair, the baby smelled of sour milk and freshly pressed overalls. The baby was real the way my marriage fantasies and aspirations to become a muse were not. What if the life I dreamt of simply didn't exist? One day, I was afraid, I would give in and swap my dreams for a shiny ring and a fat sleepy baby.

And then I was granted an escape. Here it was, squeezed tight in my hand, in the shape of a white envelope from U.S. Immigration.

Polina arrived in Paris in the first days of June. The train pulled in at the station around six a.m., and even after she had found a coach, directed the coachman what of her luggage was supposed to go on top of what, told him the hotel's address in passable French, and took her seat, it was still very early. There were few people on the streets; the buildings, the pavements, even the pigeons were bright, cheerful, and very clean (or at least they looked so to Polina). The sounds that horses' hoofs made resonated happily against the freshly washed cobblestones. Polina, who had loosened the ribbons of her travel hat, looked, listened, and laughed. Was she alone in that coach or with a travel companion? If she did have a companion, I'd want her to be a grumpy middle-aged woman who had a habit of falling asleep as soon as she was seated in the coach. She would sleep swaying along with the ride, her prickly double chin knocking against her chest, and wake up from time to time with a jolt, looking around with a wary expression. "What?" she asked Polina. "Why are you laughing? Was I snoring?" But Polina laughed simply because she was in Paris.

In Paris, alone. In Paris, free.

She had planned to make this trip with Dostoevsky. "We shall go to Paris!" he'd said to her many times in various hotel rooms, while raising the hem of her skirt and removing her shoes. She didn't believe him because he rarely kept his promises, especially those made in shoe-removing circumstances. But by March their plans had become more certain. Dostoevsky procured foreign passports for them, put away the needed amount of money, made arrangements for somebody to care for business for him, and even set the date for their travel. Polina began preparing for the journey. She ordered a new pair of shoes, both sturdy and elegant, quite fit for walking Paris streets. She read what there was to read about Europe. She looked through heavy books full of pictures. She fantasized about three whole months with him alone, away from his family, his friends, his publishers, all those whiny, greedy people who seemed to attack him and claw out pieces of his flesh and soul, along with his money. She and Dostoevsky would not be confined to a furnished room anymore. No more brief, coarse encounters. No more canceled appointments and short, apologetic notes. No more endless, anxious, exhausting waiting that kept her from concentrating on her studies, on her books, on her dreams. To think that she had imagined the whole new world that the affair with Dostoevsky would open for her! Instead, she found her own world had shrunk. In Paris, this would all be different. In Paris, they would take long walks together, see the sights through each other's eyes, share clever observations, laugh at the ridiculousness of foreign life. There would be cheerful mornings brightened with sunlight and the smell of coffee, quiet evenings over a cup of tea, and long, leisurely nights full of gentle touching, exactly the way she liked, not the short, filthy trysts that, having failed to satisfy her, left her aroused and ashamed for days afterward. In short, Polina fantasized that in Paris their affair would at last resemble the relationship she had had in mind when she stopped him in the university hallway.

The new shoes were ready in the first days of April. They were perfect—made from reddish-brown leather with round buttons of a lighter shade of brown. Polina would get them out of their box every night, look at them, stroke them, try them on, buckle and un-buckle them. But shortly after that, Dostoevsky announced that they weren't going. Some problem had occurred with his magazine. They would have to postpone the trip, he said. The problem was serious, and Polina was required to be supportive and understanding, but she was so tired of being supportive, and positively sick of being understanding. Postpone! And then of course something else would occur, and they would have to postpone again, and again, and again. Polina sat studying the intricate ornament of another dusty fur-nished room's carpet. She was staring at the carpet the whole time: while he paced the room around her, telling her how sorry he was and how much he wanted to go on the trip; and when he fell on his knees and continued to say how sorry he was while stroking her hands and covering them in kisses; and she was still staring at the carpet when he rose off his knees, put his right hand on his chest, and swore that he would do everything possible to make the trip as soon as possible. Polina didn't raise her eyes even then. She had wanted to make the trip very much, but now she wasn't sure if she wanted to anymore. Wasn't it naïve to think that their relation-ship could change so drastically? She was tired of being naïve. Yes, it was possible that they would have some good times in Paris, but what would happen once they got back? Wasn't it logical to suppose that their relationship would go right back to the Petersburg routine, with its furnished rooms and canceled appointments?

"Our relationship made me blush," Polina wrote in a draft of a letter to Dostoevsky—I don't know if she ever mailed it to him. "I never concealed it from you, and many times wanted to break it off before going abroad."

So why didn't she?

"Why not break it off, if it's so bad?" I always asked my whiny girlfriends, and never dared to ask myself.

But I think I know why Polina didn't. If she broke it off before Paris, their relationship would've become a finished chapter, and would forever stay in the book of her life as no more and no less than what it was, not as what it might have been. It would have to be defined as a banal affair with a married man.

When I was seven or eight, I overheard a conversation my mother had with my grandmother. "Why? Just why?" my mother kept asking through the gooey mess of tears. "If he had to die so young anyway, why couldn't he die sooner? Before he left me? Why? I wouldn't have had a husband, but I would have had something. A memory . . . a myth of good life . . . This is simply unfair!"

My grandmother didn't say anything, just kept stroking my mother's head, and I tiptoed back to the room where I had been playing. I didn't understand my mother's words and I was horrified that she wished that my father had died sooner. Yet I couldn't possibly blame her. Her congested nose made her sound like a crying child, like me, and so I sided with her, and felt sorry for her, and assumed that my father must have been really awful, and it would have been better if he had died sooner. It was only years later that the meaning of her words dawned on me: Her marriage with my father became a closed chapter once he left. And no matter how good the beginning possibly was, it ended with a failure, and it stayed as a failure in the book of my mother's life. Whereas if my father were to have died before things had gone bad, their marriage would've stayed a sad, but beautiful story, made even more beautiful by the tragic ending.

No, Polina couldn't possibly break it off with Dostoevsky before Paris. She could either wait and see if it was possible to change their relationship somehow, or find another, better, worthier man so that she could close the bothersome Dostoevsky chapter with triumph rather than failure.

At the end of May, Polina packed her suitcase, took her foreign passport from her bureau drawer, put on her new shoes, and took off for France, telling Dostoevsky that she'd wait for him there, but hoping that she wouldn't have to wait.

Chapter Five

I spent my first night in America half lying on a damp rubber mat in my uncle's bathroom. At first, while I had some strength, I sat on the edge of the bathtub between my vomiting fits, but eventually I slid to the floor and rested my head against the toilet.

My head spun, my throat hurt from constant heaving, my stomach felt empty and beaten up, my whole body was drained of life.

Several hours before, we'd had a party on the occasion of my arrival. "Just you wait," my uncle had said on the way from the airport. "I bet you'll say that you've never seen so much food on the table!"

"Your uncle spent the whole morning and half of his monthly food stamps ripping off the shelves of Russian delis," Maya said, trying to keep her greasy hands away from my back as she hugged me in the little hall of their apartment.

"I've never seen so much food," I hurried to assure them.

There was indeed plenty of food on the table—sharp, heavy, loud food. Each bite had to be announced and supported with comments.

"Try cream cheese, Tanya! It tastes like nothing you ever tried before."

"They have cream cheese in Russia."

"No, they don't."

"Yes, they have."

"No, it is called 'melted cheese' and it tastes differently."

"Tanechka, put some smoked salmon on your cream cheese. Yes, like that. No, no, put some more! Don't spare it! Thank God, we're not in Russia anymore."

Except for me, my uncle, and Maya, there were only five people at the table, although it seemed like much more. Dena sat across the table from her husband, Igor, who had grown a bald patch, a pot-belly, and a weird habit of stroking Dena's neck all the time as if she were a dog and would've bitten him if he had stopped strok-ing. There were also Igor's mother—a mealy-mouthed woman with bluish hair that could rival Malvina's—and Igor's father, a handsome man with a military crew cut and a booming voice (if I remembered it correctly, he had once been a superintendent in the Soviet Army). And there was Dena's son, Danik, a thin jumpy five-year-old with a blaring toy fire truck, which he was riding back and forth under the table.

The group at the meal soon divided into what I called "well-wishers" and "advisers." Since the party was in honor of my arrival, all the wishes and nuggets of advice were directed at me. My well-wishers praised me, praised everything about me: my hair, my figure, the choice of history as my profession. They were compassionate about my mother's staying behind, although enthusiastic about my coming, and they predicted the brightest, sweetest, easiest future for me. The advisers in their turn snorted at those prognoses, showed that the sweet bright future was unattainable, and listed ways—very hard, very thorny ways—for me to arrive at a plausible future, one that wasn't sweet or bright at all. Among the well-wishers, I counted

Igor and his parents. Maya and Dena were the advisers. Only my uncle and Danik didn't join either camp. My uncle took up the passive position of an eater. And Danik kept smashing the fire truck ladder into my knees with a loud and hostile "Vroom-vroom-bam!"

"Now, listen, Tanya," Dena said. "You can forget about history."

"Yes, forget about history," Maya added.

"Mother, don't interrupt! So, Tanya, you will learn computer programming. Though it won't be easy and it won't be quick."

"Not necessarily. She can find a two-month crash course," Igor said.

"She's smart, she'll learn in no time," Igor's mother added.

"It wasn't easy for me, and it won't be easy for her. You'll have to study a lot. While you're studying, take a part-time job. It will pay your rent. Now, after you finish your studies—it will take you at least six months . . ."

I couldn't help but smile. Dena had always been like that, as long as I could remember her, and I remembered her as a twelve-year-old with pigtails teaching me how to use a fork and a knife. I was four then, and I wasn't a quick learner. "No, not like that. Look, like this. Here, put your hand right here. Mom! She's not listening!"

No, Dena hasn't changed, I thought, mentally replacing her hip hairdo with pigtails. She's only gotten older. Much older. But it's been only ten years since I saw her. She must be no more than thirty-one? Why is her complexion so sallow, what are these two deep lines doing around her mouth, why does she have those shadows under her eyes? How come she looks so hard, and bored, and exhausted?

"This is America, my dear," she was saying to me. "You don't come here to live, you come here to work."

"Dena, tell her about clothes," Maya said.

"Oh, yeah, clothes. I hope you haven't brought many Russian

clothes with you, because tomorrow you'll have to throw them away. Nothing will betray and humiliate you more than your Russian clothes."

I plunged into eating to drown out her voice, as years before I had plunged into playing with my toys whenever Dena spoke. Apparently I succeeded, because I couldn't recall anything that she said between the smoked salmon and the two kinds of chocolate cake that were served for dessert.

I was awakened from my eating reverie by two exotic foreign words that rang off Dena's tongue. "Prenup agreement." I'd never heard them before.

"What?" I asked, plowing my piece of cake with a fork.

"Ha!" Dena reacted. "You thought he would marry you without one? Ha-ha!"

Marry me? Who? I was so stunned that I put my fork down.

"Dena, a lot of people marry without a prenup," Igor said, causing an outburst, unfairly directed at me.

"So, Tatiana, you're one of those who think that they can go jogging in Central Park, and just happen to bump into a nice millionaire who won't just fuck you a couple of times and say goodbye but will want to marry you? And without a prenup? Ha!"

"Prenuptial agreement is very important," Maya said.

It turned out that while I was working on the food the conversation had switched to the possibility of my marrying a millionaire.

"Why won't he marry her? Look at her!" Dena's mother-in-law cooed. "Just look at that sweet face! She'll find a nice boy in no time." The compliment didn't fool me, because I knew that its true purpose was to spite Dena rather than to praise me. Dena knew it too; her face hardened and she made a sharp movement to shake her husband's hand off; he was still stroking her neck. "You have to aim high, whatever you do," Dena's father-in-law boomed. "A million-aire! An American! No less!"

I felt the first wave of nausea then. I thought that maybe it wasn't such a wise idea to mix smoked salmon with stuffed chicken, choco-late cake, and ice cream. It was probably even more unwise to wash it all down with cherry-flavored Manischewitz—my uncle and Maya's wine of choice—which tasted like a lollipop dissolved in alcohol, along with the stick. Yet I drank glass after glass of Manischewitz and ate spoon after spoon of ice cream, as if hoping that this might cool me under their melting stares.

"I don't plan on getting married right away," I said at some point. "I guess the millionaires are out of danger."

"Good for you, good." Dena's mother-in-law started cooing anew. "We don't need those Americans, we'll find a nice Russian boy for you. I just happen to know a wonderful boy—"

"What are you talking about?" Maya interrupted. "I promised that I'd introduce Tanya to my neighbor's son."

"But the boy I was talking about is really special."

"And mine is less special?"

I don't know for how long they let the two unknown boys com-pete for the right to be introduced to me. I guess I lost my concen-tration again. The last image of the party that stayed in my mind was of the whole group, already fully clothed to go outside, their flushed faces sticking out of sweaty coat collars, taking turns planting wet goodbye kisses on my cheek. "Call me, okay?" Dena whispered after removing her lips. "I didn't mean to frighten you; it's just better not to have great expectations. You have to trust me on that."

It took us the better part of an hour to clear the table after the party. The food had been placed into plastic containers, bundled in foil, covered with plastic wrap, and locked in the safety of the refrigerator; the table had been folded and put away to make space for unfolding the sofabed. Yet, the spirits of the food we ate refused to leave the room. They lingered about, tormenting me with sharp, heavy smells as I lay on Maya's stiff sheets trying to sleep.

I thought of my mother at the airport. Waving at me over the little fence separating the customs area from the passengers. Gray hair, wet, flabby cheeks under her knitted beret made out of two berets placed one on top of the other for warmth. Her face quivered as the customs officer motioned for me to go.

Where had I come? What was I doing here? I thought I'd escape reality by leaving Russia, but in fact I was about to enter the trap of a worse reality, filled with humiliating jobs, separate bank accounts, prenup agreements, and the smell of smoked salmon.

I felt like I had years ago at summer camp, when I ran through the scary dark woods to a battered phone booth to call my mother: "Mom, I hate it here. Please, come and pick me up."

There was something wrong with this room. The sideboard stood in exactly the same spot by the window, and it was filled with the same dishes and figurines as in my uncle's Moscow apartment. The bookshelves were in the same spot too, in the back of the room, and on the upper shelf I saw a piece of whalebone, a sea lion's tusk, and the picture of my uncle playing with polar bear cubs, and my uncle's trophies from his many expeditions to the North. But along with these objects, the shelves now boasted letters from Social Security and Medicaid offices tacked to the side, supermarket coupons, a modest black yarmulke for the trips to a Jewish center, where they gave out free gefilte fish along with other food, and a collection of cheap souvenirs—little cups with the names of American cities embossed on them in gold letters, a Mexican hat, a two-inchhigh Eiffel Tower, and a three-inch-long London double-decker. Next to them, the whalebone and the sea lion's tusk looked as if they had been bought in airport gift shops too. Or as if somebody had robbed my uncle and put my uncle's trophies here, among his own petty belongings. Somebody who didn't have the right to own those beautiful and noble things.

I had the same feeling I had when I'd seen my uncle in the airport, or the man who claimed to be my uncle but who in fact resembled him very little. Where was his thick mop of salt-and-pepper curls? Where was his Napoleonic posture (hands folded on his chest, head slightly tilted to the right)? Where was the wide smile of a person living his life to the utmost degree? The man who waved at me with a small bouquet of wilted carnations had a lost and timid expression. He was short, slouchy, and almost completely bald. He wore a shiny, dark blue club jacket and white pants. Both were clearly hand-me-downs; the sleeves and the trouser legs were too short, and the buttons were about to burst. He looked like a caricature of an American the way they were drawn in Soviet propaganda newspapers. "I know a big shot at the Society for Former Doctors from the Former Soviet Union," he boasted at the table. "I think I have a pretty good chance of getting in."

He couldn't possibly have changed like that.

Yet he had.

"Tanechka," he'd whispered, pushing the carnations toward me. "I'm so glad to see you."

"Uncle." I hugged him, inhaling the stale smell of old age, the smell of my grandmother.

He stepped away from me then and gave me the once-over, nodding approvingly, and at the same time regretfully, at what he saw. I realized that during the six years that we hadn't seen each other, I'd changed too. Changed as dramatically as my uncle had. He'd turned into an old man while I'd turned into an adult. I was sixteen when he left, pretty much still a child, and considered as such by my family.

They used to watch my growing up with cheerful amazement. "Tanechka will soon be taller than her mom. Tanechka will soon look like a woman." They sometimes listened to my opinion seriously, but it was a halfhearted seriousness, mixed with amusement that a child would say something so adultlike. So cute, so funny, like a little girl wearing her mother's size-eight pumps, or a toddler in a full suit with a tie. And there I came, after six years, dressed like an adult, looking like an adult. My hair was combed in an adult way. Estée Lauder lipstick and condoms had replaced drugstore lip gloss and stolen contraception pills in my purse. (My uncle didn't know those details, of course, but if he had stopped and thought about it, he certainly could have guessed that I'd had some adult experiences.) The image of myself as an adult was so scary and sickening that I felt another wave of nausea coming on.

The smell of food intensified. I was pretty sure that I wasn't imagining it—the food was right here, somewhere very close to me, something smoky, and garlicky and fishy.

I decided to venture to the bathroom after all. I swung my legs down and groped for the slippers with my bare feet. Something had apparently gone very wrong with one of my slippers, because it had become soft, slimy, and sticky to the touch, or else it wasn't my slipper but a piece of smoked salmon that somebody had dropped during the feast and that lay there glistening in a puddle of yellow oil.

I reached the toilet just in time.

Later, as I lay there on the floor waiting for some strength to return to my body, my eyes fell on a magazine stuck between the tiled wall and the toilet tank. Hoping for some distraction, I pulled it out. There was a picture of Central Park on its glossy, dusty, sticky cover. CENTRAL PARK, NEW YORK, the tiny caption read. I was afraid that the effort would make me gag again, but I took the risk and leaned closer to peer into the picture.

I liked what I saw. I liked Central Park. I liked the emerald green grass and the trees, and the tall castlelike buildings framing the park. But they weren't the reason why I kept peering into the picture and smoothing the creases to see it better. The reason for that was the tiny figure of a man in the lower right corner, half lying on a large black rock with a book, or a notebook—I couldn't see. His clothes were a little shabby, his posture relaxed, his features were a little smudgy, but I could decipher a beard and thin glasses—there was something painfully familiar about him. I picked the picture up and brought it closer to my eyes. Yes, as improbable as it was, he looked just like a nineteenth-century Russian writer from the pages of my textbooks; he looked very much like the blurry-faced man of my fantasies.

"Tanya! Are you okay?" My uncle knocked at the door.

I wanted to say that I was okay, that I felt better, but I seemed to forget the certain motions that I should perform with my lips, teeth, and tongue to produce the certain sounds.

"It was the salmon!" I heard my uncle hissing at Maya behind the bathroom door. "It was the salmon! I told you that I didn't want the six ninety-nine one!"

"It wasn't the salmon! She's just jet-lagged!"

"Jet-lagged! Are you crazy? It's food poisoning."

"The food was fresh. She just ate too much. She saw all that food and couldn't stop herself. I told you not to buy so much!"

I was afraid that their description of the food we had eaten would bring my nausea back, so I scrambled to my feet, opened the door, and managed "I'm better" and a smile as I trudged past them to the couch. I had the picture from the magazine with me.

When I woke up in the morning, my nausea was all gone and I was looking forward to my first American breakfast.

"Americans are so stupid," my uncle said, raising his head at me.

He was crouching on the kitchen floor with a bunch of walnuts. "They buy these expensive kinds of cereal with nuts and dried fruit in them, when you can buy a cheap kind and simply add the nuts and the raisins."

He cracked the walnuts with a chair leg, then brought them up to the table and crushed them with his fist. "I don't want you to think that I don't own a nutcracker," he said as we sat down to eat. "I do. I just don't see a point to it." He wiped some beads of sweat from his reddened forehead and sank his spoon into the bowl.

"So let's discuss what you do," Maya said, reaching for a notebook page covered with her fine script on both sides. Free of her daughter's presence, she could at last resume her comfortable, domineering manner. She lowered her glasses from the top of her head to her nose and slowly read the list that started with buying some "real clothes" on the big shopping street near my uncle's place, and continued with a schedule of cleaning and washing dishes in their apartment, which I was supposed to do between going on job interviews. Cultural pastimes weren't overlooked either.

"New York City is the world capital of culture," my aunt announced before proceeding to instruct me on how exactly I was to put all that culture to use.

"Opera is very expensive, but here is what you do: You buy a twenty-five-dollar ticket, but you don't use your seat—you can't enjoy opera from a twenty-five-dollar seat. Instead you wait until the show is about to start, and then just look for an empty seat in the orchestra. I can guarantee you some empty seats on Tuesdays and Wednesdays.

"For the Broadway shows, you go to the discount booth, where they sell tickets half-price. As for the museums you have to follow the schedule. Met is 'pay what you wish' at all times, but MoMA and Guggenheim only Fridays six to eight. Frick collection doesn't have free hours at all, but you could get tickets for a free concert, and they would allow you in half an hour before that, so you have plenty of time to explore the whole museum. Their collection is very small; half an hour is more than enough. And you'll have ten extra minutes during the intermission."

"Thanks," I said, reaching for the list and stuffing it into a pocket of my coat, where I'd already put the magazine page.

But I had decided to be rebellious—to ignore Maya's cultural schedule and spend the morning in Central Park. My other stroke of rebelliousness was a decision to wear my Russian coat, my big, bulky, brown, herringbone-patterned coat, on which Dena had pronounced a death sentence the night before.

My first impression of the park was that everything—buildings, trees, grass, horses, and people—looked vivid and brilliant, as if lit by a special, extra-powerful lamp, like the one they use on movie sets. Once on the path, I had the tickling sensation that my every move was being recorded by invisible cameras. I straightened my back and tried to walk in small, even steps, not too fast, so the cameras wouldn't miss the gracious movements of my hips and feet. I wasn't just an extra or a secondary character. I was the heroine. Everything here—the trees, benches, squirrels, bikers, passersby pretending to ignore me and mind their own business—was in fact a part of the set, providing the backdrop for me to play the main part, the part of my life. I was the heroine about to meet the hero. That was the point of the scene. Everything that had happened before was mere buildup. My whole life was a buildup.

Now, where was the hero?

Was it the smiling biker waving at me with a gloved hand? Or the man in a black beret asking me something? What is he asking me? I don't understand. The movie is running in a foreign language! Is that him? Is he the man? He shrugs and walks off. The delayed translation tells me that he was just asking for the time. Well, it's not him, then. Must be another one.

I already felt close to the man in question, even though I didn't know anything about him, not even how he would look or sound. Would he have a fair complexion, with freckles? Or would he be dark-skinned with shoulder-length wavy hair? Would he be tall? Or short? Would he have a little belly? Or athletically wide shoulders? Would his voice be deep or high? Would he stutter? Would he have a beard?

My mother had told me many years ago that she felt this way when she was expecting me. She felt that she had a perfect stranger inside her body; she had no idea how I would look, not even whether I would have a penis or a vagina (this was before ultrasound). She knew that once that stranger was born, he/she would become the most important person in her life and she would be crazy in love with him/her. "I was so impatient to know what you would look like that I spent hours studying pictures of all my and your father's relatives, trying to come up with all the possible genetic combinations. Once or twice I even attempted to draw a picture of my dream child."

"Did it look like me?" I asked with a faint jealous feeling.

"It didn't look like anything. I've always been a terrible artist."

I didn't meet anybody that first day in Central Park, although I walked there until the sunset changed the lighting to soft amber. They are turning off their lamps, I thought, and I headed back to the subway. I wasn't sad. I knew that I would meet my hero very soon. I had to meet him. Otherwise, what was the point of the whole movie?

The following weeks were spent according to Maya's schedule. I saw a few apartments—all in my uncle's neighborhood, all worse than my uncle's, and all madly, frighteningly expensive. In fact, most price tags I happened to see during my first weeks in America were frightening. Two dollars for a loaf of bread? Ten dollars for a T-shirt? Two hundred dollars for an ugly coat? Six hundred dollars for a studio apartment with a cracked wall and cockroaches in a neighborhood where people dried their underwear on clotheslines? How much was it in rubles? Could it be that much? I realized that as an adult I'd have to earn my living now. I'd have to depend on myself, which I'd never done before. I'd held a variety of jobs in Moscow, but those were fun jobs, little supplements to my college stipend and my mother's salary. "I got my money today!" I used to yell to my mother, standing on the doorstep with a big cake carton in my hands. "Money. How nice," my mother would exclaim. "Nice"— that was all you could say about the money I earned. "Nice" was enough for a cake, for a new skirt, for a short trip to Leningrad. It wasn't enough to live on.

Maya relieved me of some of my worries. She sent my uncle to talk to me, and while blushing, sputtering, and confusing words, he uttered a long tirade about how wise and practical his wife was, and how it was best to listen to her advice. And then he mumbled something about my staying with them and paying half of the rent. I was not to tell anybody about it, because they lived in a subsidized apartment, and subletting was "slightly illegal." But because they lived in a subsidized apartment, I would get a very nice bargain! He would've never thought of charging me money for the stay, but here in the United States, it was different, and you had to play by the rules and charge rent even if the person was your niece. (Rules? But didn't he say that the offer was illegal?) Maya hissed from behind the door, "Tell her about the rules, about 'play by the rules.' "

"I just did," he hissed back.

Maya then yelled (she worried that I might not hear her well from behind the door) that they had already arranged with a dentist friend that he would take me on to work for him part time. Then I would have enough money to cover my share of the rent and more than enough time for studying. "You can take up your history," Maya said. "Or, if you are a clever person, you could just go ahead and take a programmer's class."

A balding, wide-hipped guy from a nearby computer school assured me that he could teach programming to anybody, even to rabbits. "Give me a class of rabbits, I'll teach them!" "Rabbits could be very smart," I observed. He answered with a blank stare.

Next, I went to see the heads of history departments at several New York schools. "You must not abandon your academic career!" my mother pleaded into the phone receiver every time she called. "Even if it's hard and doesn't pay much, you have to do what you're good at. It's worth the sacrifice!"

That sounded right to me. But was I really good at academics? Was I so good that it would've made it worth the sacrifice?

The interviews with "the heads" made me doubt myself even more. Here I was, sitting across from these neat, imposing men, trying to prove in my broken English that I was an exceptional scholar. They grinned when I told them that courses titled "The History of the Communist Party" and "Marxism and Leninism" were in fact survey courses of twentieth-century history and philosophy. They cringed when I showed them my credentials, where Bs were as frequent as As, and Cs spiced up the mix from time to time. They cringed even more when I told them that I hoped to get a scholarship. They raised their brows when I said that my interests ranged from breakfasts in ancient Rome—historians always describe those wild Roman feasts, but what about a normal meal like breakfast?— to the history of Russian makeup. The only pleasant moment I had during those interviews was when I exited the room of one or another head at last and ran down the marble stairs, listening as my hard, urgent steps resonated in the heavy silence of the building.

I started going to the dentist's, where my job consisted of answering the phone, not being annoyed with the patients, and at times assisting the dentist's assistant. The latter privilege allowed me to look into the patients' mouths. The sight wasn't thrilling, but I knew from Dena's crash course in American life that it must not be thrilling under any circumstances. Yet at the end of a day spent hovering over somebody's suffering mouth; looking at the misery of rough, rotten, uncared-for Russian teeth; wiping blood and saliva off trembling chins, off the spitting bowl, off the floor; listening to the screech of the drill and the clanking of metal tools, groans, and sharp intakes of breath; smelling fillings and rot, I longed for distraction. Any kind of distraction.

The two dates arranged for me by Maya and Dena's mother-in-law were almost identical. Each boy kept looking at me appraisingly as if asking himself what I could do for him. And I was supposed to go out of my way to prove that I could do a lot. Apparently I failed, because neither of them called me again.

"You didn't work on it," Maya said. "A man won't just fall into your lap. You have to work on it. Seduce him. Play with him even if he doesn't seem to like you at first."

My uncle nodded with his mouth full.

"But that's humiliating!" I said.

"So?" was Maya's reaction.

Possibly humiliation was a requisite state for recent immigrants. "Humiliation, yes! That's what immigration is all about. You have to be sufficiently humiliated at first, to be able to get your rewards later," I imagined Dena saying.

The rewards seemed to come according to a schedule. A nice job within two to four months, a clean, well-paid, respectable one, with "Americans"—"I work with 'Americans,' there are hardly any Russians there." The first vacation in Europe within two years. Your own house in a nice but not particularly nice suburb within four. Skiing, tennis lessons, vacations in three- then four-star resorts. Within ten years, a better, bigger house in a better neighborhood, the best feature of the neighborhood being, of course, the absence of immigrants. Even though nobody explicitly stated it, and even though Americans were often criticized for having bad taste in clothes or ignorance of European culture, they were clearly believed to be the superior race. "I know this American . . ." or "One American told me," people kept saying, unaware of how proud they sounded.

Dena's family hadn't reached the Ultimate American Dream yet, but they were moving smoothly on schedule. Their house stood in a suburb full of immigrants, but Dena and Igor had been to Europe three times, and everybody in the family, including little Danik, was taking tennis lessons. Their furniture was all luxurious and new, having originally come as a mess of parts and fastenings in an Ikea box, and they entertained with fifty-piece sushi trays from a local "Price Club."

The women at Dena's gatherings were jittery and ferocious like a flock of seagulls; they sat perched on the sofas' armrests, shouting stories at one another. Men, who sank deep into the plush and leather, were mum and gloomy next to their wives. Sometimes a yawning shaggy-haired Danik would appear out of his bedroom in Disney-character pajamas, and Dena would drunkenly kiss him and shoo him back in. Everybody seemed miserable to me and at the same time bored with his misery.

I watched it all from the corner of the couch, where I sat with a sagging paper plate in my lap, sinking into the cold leather even deeper than the men, full of fear that eventually I'd get sucked into this life. The trap would close and before I knew it I would be well on my way to the American Dream station.

Chapter Six

Central Park seemed the only place where I could breathe. I still took every opportunity to come uptown, but not every stroll now produced such an intense feeling as the first one had. At times, I felt what I called "a high burning." The anticipation of happiness throbbed in my temples, tickled the tips of my toes, rolled into a sweet lump in my throat, behaved as something separate and alive inside of me. I would become acutely sensitive of men's presence—and buildings, trees, squirrels, and passing women and children would fade into the background, cease to exist for me. I knew that on the days when I glowed, men were able to grasp it. Never before had men noticed me in such a spontaneous way. They couldn't help but notice me, but they looked surprised, as if it happened against their will, and sometimes they would even talk to me, once again appearing surprised that they were. The high burning added some mysterious element to the formula of my attractiveness, the element that I had lacked before. Sometimes, when I passed one or another man who looked close to the perfect picture I had drawn in my imagination, the burning would become especially high and reluctant to subside even after the man was gone from my sight.

At other times, I experienced a low burning, which allowed me to admire the surroundings and feel moderately happy. Soon I expanded my routes from Central Park to the adjacent streets, where the green of the trees was dark, the buildings modest yet classy. Elegant people roamed the streets with an air of tired sophistication lurking somewhere in the corners of their mouths or the line of a cheekbone. They passed me by and disappeared in the dark, inviting portals of the buildings, or rode away in yellow cabs, or entered small, pretty shops and cozy cafés, where they sat down at the tables covered with crisp white tablecloths. The whole world of beauty and culture seemed to belong to them, to be effortlessly theirs, not stolen with discounted tickets or illegal opera seats.

I longed to follow their routes, to partake of their lives, but I didn't reside in those buildings, didn't have money for a ride in a cab, and was too afraid to ask for coffee, even in one of the cheaper cafés. Everything seemed within reach, but at the same time inaccessible, unless I could find some kind of a secret key that would open this life for me and make me belong there.

So far, the only places where I felt more or less comfortable were the neighborhood bookstores, where many people weren't buying, but browsing like me, and where I could dissolve into the scene. My favorite was the Bookend, a small store on the West Side. The shelves there were made from pretty carved wood, the books had an air of seriousness, and the two salespeople—an old woman with loose, graying hair and a young man with an earring—were always engrossed in an animated chat with one or another customer and didn't pay any attention to me. At first I would come to the Bookend whenever it rained, but after a while I caught myself wishing that it would rain so that I could go into the store, and I made the Bookend a permanent part of my route.

One Sunday evening, as I opened the Bookend's door, I saw a few rows of gray folding chairs and a big poster announcing a reading. A bearded, long-nosed man smiled at me from a blown-up photograph. His name was Mark Schneider. The title of his work was *After the Beginning.* Below the title was a succession of blurbs, each boasting fireworks of unfamiliar-to-me adjectives. The only thing I could understand was that the author was being compared to both Marcel Proust and Philip Roth. I had never heard of the latter, and had never read the first, but I had heard that Proust was a big deal. A professor of modern European history in my college used to say that "if anybody ever surpassed Dostoevsky in his treatment of the human psyche it was Proust." I took my hat and my scarf off and sat down on one of the first-row chairs, preparing to listen to the man compared to somebody who had surpassed Dostoevsky.

Mark Schneider didn't appear until a quarter past seven. All the chairs were taken by then, a few people stood leaning against the bookshelves, and some were sitting right on the floor. I heard quietly enthusiastic clapping around me, but the fear of being ridiculous prevented me from joining my palms and making a similar sound.

Mark Schneider wore the same jeans and a tweed jacket over a dark checkered shirt as in his picture. He looked older and somewhat broader though. His stomach pushed through his shirt. His beard and his short curly hair, black in the picture, turned out to be brown with streaks of gray.

He squinted at the audience, bowed his head, and jerked it back. "Thank you, thank you so much. I'll try to make up for keeping you here in wonderful weather like this." Polite chuckles broke out here and there as he climbed onto a tall stool and took one of the thin black-and-orange books from the pile.

He leafed through to the needed place and paused there, staring at the page. A tiny image of him from the back-cover photo was showing between his fingers. He cleared his throat, read a first sentence, and paused again, as if surprised by what he was finding there, as if seeing the words for the first time, not believing that he himself had written them. He seemed to be trying to get familiar with the book and make it acknowledge his authority.

It was just a book. It was a stack of white pages covered with black letters, one of the many copies of exactly the same book. But for Mark Schneider it was alive, unpredictable, difficult, so difficult, that even he, the book's creator, wasn't sure how to handle it.

I was in awe.

He cleared his throat again and started reading, swallowing words in the first couple of sentences, but regaining a normal tempo by the middle of the first page. He read well, not too fast and not too slow, making quick, unseeing eye contact with the audience from time to time. I leaned in, trying to decipher the rapidly moving sounds of foreign language, and during one of his pauses his eyes caught mine, as if asking what I thought of the text. There were too many unfamiliar words, and even when the words were familiar it took me too long to recall their meaning, so that by the time I did recall them, I had long forgotten the sentence they came bundled with. After a while, I stopped my attempts. I closed my eyes and listened to the graceful foreign sounds joining and supplanting one another as they swelled into complex, fully alive sentences. It was so beautiful that my eyes filled with tears.

Then the silence came, followed by the scattered clapping that seemed revoltingly loud. I opened my eyes and blinked off the tears and saw Mark Schneider staring at me. His expression was surprised and strangely intimate. It was then that I felt a high burning stronger than in any of my Central Park walks.

People were standing up and moving away, some in the direction of the exit, others forming a line to have their books signed. I wandered to the shelves and stood looking at the book spines and not seeing them. I heard his voice, I heard his laughter, I heard the bookstore owner thanking him, I heard him saying goodbye, I heard his quick steps toward the door, and finally, finally, after what seemed like hours of waiting, I heard him speak to me.

"You! You sat in the first row, right?"

His voice reverberated through my spine. I turned to him and nodded.

"You liked the reading, didn't you?"

"Yes. I did. Very much."

"Have you read the book?"

"No . . . I don't read in English . . . that much."

"Oh." He laughed. His eyes, small and sharp, the color of melted dark chocolate, squinted at me from the creased depths of his eyelids. I felt waves of heady heat emanating off the soft folds of his jacket and reaching my body, which felt strangely exposed.

"So what is your language then?"

"Russian."

In the next ten seconds he knew what city I came from, what I was doing in New York, and who my favorite Russian writer was.

"Dostoevsky? Is that right? Now answer me, and answer quick. What are the names of Alyosha Karamazov's mentor, the girl that Stavrogin raped, and Dostoevsky's wife? Quick!"

"Zosima! Matryosha! Polina!" I cried out, hoping that it was fast enough.

"Good." He chuckled. "The wife's name was Anna, but you got the first two right, so I forgive you. Dostoevsky's my favorite too."

Damn! How could I have said Polina? I thought, as Mark scribbled something on a crumpled grocery receipt he had dug out of his jeans pocket.

"Here is my number," he said. "Call me when you want to talk Dostoevsky again."

It took me two agonizing weeks to gather my courage and dial Mark Schneider's number. Just enough time to memorize all the items on the receipt along with the prices. "Cantaloupe—1—$1.99, Salad—1lb—$3.99, Altoids—$1.99, Total, Tax." What if he doesn't recognize me? I thought. (Tanya? Reading? What Tanya?) What if he doesn't want to have anything to do with me? (Tanya, reading. Okay. I'm sorry, but I'm terribly busy at the moment.) But when I called at last, the throaty, barely familiar voice on the other end of the receiver sounded warm: "Tanya? Reading? Of course I remember. Let me guess. You want to discuss Dostoevsky?"

We met on the corner of Central Park West and Seventy-second Street and walked through the park to the East Side. He asked me a few questions about my family, my studies, my plans, none about Dostoevsky. I answered, quickly, not turning to him, ashamed of the rough, awkward sounds of my English blended together with the soft rustle of my shoes in contact with the path's gravel. His shoes made a firm, confident crunch. Confidence filled Mark's every movement, whenever he was pressing on a door handle in a little Italian café, speaking with a waitress, unfurling a napkin on his lap, or taking a big, competent bite of a sandwich. The same sandwich on my plate seemed too tall and complicated for me to even try to eat it.

The tables in the café were so tiny that our knees and elbows often met, and for a while those accidental bumps and touches were the only thing that registered in my mind.

Mark was telling a long, intricate, possibly funny, story about how his Jewish grandfather came to America from Poland and either had his papers stolen, or lost them, or hid them on purpose. I was too nervous to concentrate on the story.

"He was a funny man, my grandfather, and a sad man at the

same time. The expression on your face reminds me of him. There is this Eastern European gloom that seems to hang around you like fog. Do you know what 'gloom' means? We Americans don't have that." Mark's neck was creased and thick. He was a man, an older man, a complete, adult, fully formed man, and he was very close. I could feel his warm breath reaching my face along with the sounds of his voice.

"Your cappuccino," the waitress said, placing two large mugs with wobbly caps of white foam in front of us. I had never seen cappuccino before, and Mark had never seen a person who had never seen cappuccino. We were equally fascinated as I watched the slow descent of sugar granules through the foam in my mug. The foam, so light and fragrant, with sprinkles of brown powder on top, looked irresistibly delicious. I was sure that it would taste very sweet and chocolatey when I took some with my spoon and brought it to my mouth. But the foam hardly tasted like anything at all, plus it wasn't warm, tepid at best. I was about to be disappointed, when Mark moved his chair closer so that his knees caught mine in a firm grip. "You are unique, do you know that?" he said, and a second later I felt his beard on my face, warm, damp, and smelling of coffee and cinnamon. I felt as if my whole being was slowly dissolving just like sugar in cappuccino.

I feel enormous. I am enormous, I thought all the long, leisurely subway ride back to Brooklyn. I gasped with pleasure as soon as I entered the car and my hand touched the cold railing, and then my bottom hit the slippery seat. There, behind the warm screen of the strangers' bodies, the nervousness of the date left me. I felt wonderfully alone, uninhibited and ready to savor the chaos of fresh recollections. Sometimes I would forget myself and moan out loud, and then be half afraid that people around me could guess why I had moaned, half wishing that they would guess. Poor little people,

I thought, watching other passengers. They were hurrying some-where, serious, tense; they had no idea how small and petty their lives really were. I felt so sorry for them, and so overcome with kind-ness and generosity that I wanted to make them smile. I came close to complimenting an old, sullen woman on her pretty embroidered scarf, a young mother on the loveliness of her baby. The only thing that stopped me from saying these things aloud was the fear of speaking English badly and getting an annoyed "What?" instead of a grateful smile in response.

My poor uncle, my poor aunt, I thought when I came back to their apartment and saw them circling sale items on a supermarket flyer with a felt pen. Discussing whether they wanted to buy a jar of Hellmann's mayonnaise for $1.99 or wait and see if it won't be two for $3.00 next time. Dena dropped in and offered to take me to the end-of-the-season sale at the New Jersey mall just a few miles away from her house. "I can guarantee you the greatest discount on designer clothes. Gucci, Versace—you name it." My mother seemed especially small, her voice coming from far away, blending with tiny specks of dust on the receiver. "So, Tanya, how are you? Did you find a good school yet?"

I found so much more! But how could she possibly under-stand that?

Polina's new lover's name was Salvador. He rented a tiny flat in the Latin Quarter. On August 19 and 22, Polina saw him there. On August 24, she came but didn't find him at home. "I was at Salvador's," she wrote in her diary. "I was at Salvador's yesterday," she wrote in her diary the following day. "I was at Salvador's, but didn't find him home," she wrote again and again. In the summer of 1863, while Polina lived in Paris and supposedly waited for

Dostoevsky, the whereabouts of a man named Salvador were the central theme of her diary.

I bought an old edition of Polina's diary from a street vendor after my second date with Mark. Usually, when I stepped off the train, I was reluctant to go straight to my uncle's place. I walked to Brighton Beach Avenue instead and slowly strolled past the vegetable and bakery stands, stopping occasionally to look at the books scattered on folding tables. The book vendors, either gloomy old men in warm jackets and baseball caps or chirpy old women with housedresses sticking out under their coats, tried to seduce me with glossy mysteries and romances. But I ignored them and dived straight for their secondhand books, kept under the tables in boxes with misleading signs: DELL LASER PRINTER or TROPICANA JUICE. Most often they were throwaway books. But that time, between *Let's Cook with a Smile: The Book of Jokes and Recipes* and the second volume of *How to Make Garden Furniture,* I found a thin beige hardcover entitled *The Years of Intimacy with Dostoevsky.* Author: Apollinaria Suslova. Inside, following the long introduction, was her diary. Her diary! I hadn't known she kept a diary. My whole life prior to meeting Mark was a series of predetermined and interconnected steps all leading me to this inevitable high point—becoming a writer's muse. Vovik's fortune-telling on a camping trip, the writers' portraits on the walls of our Moscow apartment, the fact that my grandfather's name was Fedor Mikhailovich, the fact that my grandmother's favorite book was Anna Grigorievna's reminiscences, and now the emergence of Polina's diary—everything, simply everything, fell into place.

I read the whole book as soon as I got to my uncle's place. I read it many times more in the following years, either to search for answers or to apply the ones I'd already found.

The diary begins on August 19, 1863, and catches Polina's affair with Salvador past its bloom. I don't know when exactly she met him. I assume she must've lived in Paris for several weeks at least before Salvador appeared in her life. The several weeks were spent waiting for Dostoevsky's arrival, reading letters from him, writing letters to him, saying in those letters how much she missed him. And I'm sure that she wasn't lying. She did miss him.

She was lonely there. Without her sister or her Petersburg friends, Polina didn't have anybody to talk to, nobody to share her impressions of Paris or her longing for Russia. He wrote back that he missed her too. He missed her terribly. But she knew that when he wrote that he missed her, conversations about Russia and Europe were the last thing on his mind.

"Do you miss me in that way?" Dostoevsky asked in every letter to Paris.

Did she? I think that she did. In fact, it was easier for her to miss him "in that way" in Paris, while she was far away from him, alone with her memories, which she adjusted to her taste. She thought of his hands, so large and strong, on her shoulders, turning her to him. She thought of the weight of his body on hers. She thought of his wonderful, different eyes. She didn't think of his tepid saliva invariably trickling between her breasts, or his voice turning into a thin falsetto in moments of passion.

Or maybe Polina didn't miss Dostoevsky but just missed being with a man, being in love? She saw so many couples on the streets of Paris. The whole city was teeming with lovers. Couples sneaked kisses in parks. Couples held hands under restaurants tables. Couples walked together, talking, exchanging glances and smiles.

The men were young, clean, with shiny hair and shiny eyes, healthy and simple. The women were happy.

"Mademoiselle Pauline, a woman of letters from St. Petersburg," a mutual acquaintance says in French, introducing Polina to

just such a man in a busy Latin Quarter café. He doesn't say anything, only bows in a noble, respectful gesture. She notices his
dark hair, which falls gracefully to his shoulders. She notices the self-
assured glow of his olive complexion, and the pale, masculine pink
of his large mouth. She also notices that she has made an impression.
His eyes are glued to her for the rest of the evening. He wants her in
a simple and sincere way, devoid of an older man's agenda to prove
himself on her account, to grasp for his fading life in her, to affirm
his virility. Salvador doesn't have to prove anything. His virility is
right there, breathing through every pore of his beautiful body.
There isn't, of course, much else to him, beyond this virility, but how
is Polina to know that? In spite of the fact that she was considered
a woman of "free behavior" by the standards of her time, at the
age of twenty-four, her experience was limited to only one lover,
Dostoevsky.

"I love you!" Salvador tells her in French, falling to his knees,
not long after they meet. He says that in a language that is foreign
for both of them, and often doesn't sound real. What Salvador
means is: "I find you attractive enough to sleep with you, and I won't
spare any passionate words or gestures to make the most of it."

Polina, unfortunately, fails to translate him correctly. In her version it is: "I'm yours forever. I can't go on living unless we reach the
perfect union of minds and bodies."

Polina stops writing that she misses Dostoevsky, and soon stops
writing to him altogether.

She is overwhelmed when Salvador undresses for the first time.
She can't believe that a male body could be so smooth, so beautiful,
so inviting. Shyly she begins to touch him, learning how to do it as
she goes, trembling with unmasked admiration. Salvador accepts her
awkward caresses with the kind, slightly condescending smile of a
man who's been basking in women's affection for as long as he can

remember. He encourages her with routine compliments that make him bored by sheer repetition, but she finds them new and exhilarating. As for the act itself, I have a hard time imagining Salvador as a particularly good lover. His conquests are so frequent and easy that he usually doesn't go out of his way to make the encounter memorable for a woman, getting his pleasure from novelty rather than skillful performance. I imagine his lovemaking as quick, energetic, and clean, which is, unfortunately, the best lovemaking Polina ever experienced and, therefore, easy to mistake for pure love.

The fact that Salvador is a foreigner plays its role too. He is even a double foreigner—a Spaniard in France, a foreigner in a foreign country. Polina doesn't understand him. He is, for her, like a book written in a foreign language and translated into another foreign language. She can't read him. The only way she can interpret him is to construct the meaning of his words and gestures based on her assumptions, which in their turn are based on what she wants to believe. Most people act like that in the beginning of their love affairs, when our lovers are still foreigners for us. We don't understand them and we interpret them the way we want them to be, while building dream castles based on illusion and hopes. Then, of course, we get to know them, the illusions crash, the hopes go.

Salvador is a foreigner in every sense of the word for Polina, and the time that it takes her to understand him is unfortunately long enough for her to build an impossibly tall castle of illusions and hopes, so tall that it would be simply fatal to let it crash.

But while Polina is enjoying the view from the top of her dream castle, the real Salvador is already slipping away from her. She isn't as good a lover as he'd expected. Her ineptness and shyness (the very things that fed Dostoevsky's fantasies and made his passion for her stronger) are just a nuisance for Salvador. Even the enticement of her beauty becomes questionable after a while. Square-faced, red-haired, Russian, she is exotic, true. And exotic is very appealing, that's true too. But exoticness is one thing that never lasts long; it either becomes familiar and boring, or if it manages to hold, it becomes annoying.

Within a couple of weeks, Salvador starts making gentle but obvious hints that it is time to split. Polina's vehement refusal to understand and accept those hints comes as a big surprise to him. Aren't those Russians crazy? Chasing you, showering you with letters full of threats and pleas, declarations of some weird, muddled feelings, all after having a few days of sex, and not particularly good sex?

He ducks Polina's visits, he avoids talking to her, he doesn't reply to her letters, and if she does manage to catch him, he answers her questions with silence, which is interpreted in her diary as "meaningful," "painful," "proud," or "mysterious."

"You didn't come, and haven't written that you're not coming. Maybe you haven't received my letter, but you could've written to me in any case. Don't you know how much I love you, that I'm crazy in love with you? I'm beginning to think that some terrible disaster has struck you, and the thought is making me crazy. I don't know how to express how much I love you, if only you knew that, you wouldn't have made me suffer so much, for I have suffered terribly during these two days, while I've been waiting for your letter."

Polina! Polina! Stop it! You don't write these things to a man. You don't turn yourself inside out. That won't help. That will only make him run away. Don't you know that?

"I want to tell you, how much I love you, even though I know that I'm incapable of expressing it in words," Polina wrote to Salvador. "It's necessary, however, that you know it."

No, Polina, no! It is necessary that he does *not* know. God, poor Polina!

Once, when I was a child, I happened to see the same puppet show twice. First my mother took me for my sixth birthday, then we went with my class. I watched the three little rabbits hopping happily about, and one of them, the main character, the mischievous Boonya, hopped to the right edge of the stage. But there in the wings, behind the green velvet curtain, a wolf was hiding! That wolf, big and bad, wearing gray tights and a huge head with jagged yellow teeth, was waiting for Boonya, and he would leap and grab Boonya and drag him behind the stage if nobody did anything. But nobody could do anything, because nobody knew what would happen, except for me. I was the only one able to save Boonya by the happy coincidence that I had already seen the show on my birthday. So I stood up in my seat and yelled, "Boonya, stop! There is a wolf. Stop, Boonya, stop!" I was sitting in the second row of the balcony, and Boonya couldn't hear me. But my teacher, Anna Nikolaevna, who sat just a few seats away, could hear me very well. She grabbed me by the sleeve, pulled me out of my seat, and dragged me to the exit, my little lacquered shoes scraping against the theater carpet. I managed to pull away and take a last peek, just as the heavy door was closing behind us. I saw that the wolf had seized the foolish Boonya, just as he had the previous time.

I felt the same frustration reading Polina's diary, the frustration of a knowing spectator who can't share his knowledge, who can't do anything to prevent the course of events.

At the very end of August, Polina gets the answer to her letters at last. A short note, written not by Salvador but by his friend, informing her that Salvador has typhus and is staying with some friends of the family.

So, Salvador is gravely ill. Polina's reaction is an immediate burst of joy. Oh, that's why he didn't come or write! It's not that he doesn't love her anymore. He is simply dying! What a relief.

Soon, however, the joy fades, making place for growing doubt. Polina starts writing letters again, to Salvador *and* to his friend. Begging, begging, begging him to tell her more about Salvador's state. Begging to be assured that he is really ill.

Her letters are left unanswered, and on September 1, Polina takes a little walk in the direction of the Latin Quarter. She isn't looking for Salvador. Wouldn't that be ridiculous to look for him in this gay place when he is lying in bed exhausted with illness, immobile, suffering? Of course it would, so Polina isn't looking for him, she's simply strolling along the streets. Nice little walk, a pleasant distraction from her thoughts. The problem is that she can't stop. She walks and walks, circling the same streets, swiping the littered sidewalks (pigeon droppings, tobacco crumbs, candy wrappers, or whatever constituted nineteenth-century French garbage) with the hem of her skirt. She stops by cafés and pretends to study the menus, at the same time peeks in, scans the patrons with her eyes, especially tall, dark-haired men who sit with their backs to her, hugging obnoxious French women. And then a waiter appears, a sleazy little spy, and asks her if she wants a table, but in fact knows perfectly well that she is just chasing a man. Everybody, every passerby, guesses that! And Polina hides her eyes and says, *"Non, merci,"* and quickly walks away with splotches of shame still burning on her cheeks. But she can't keep her head down; she has to raise her eyes, for she is afraid to miss Salvador, even though she is not looking for him, she is just taking her little walk.

Polina finally sees Salvador down the Sorbonne Street. Walking alone, a little pale, but obviously healthy. She can't help but see things in their true light now. Her happy blindness is at once broken, crushed, annihilated. Salvador doesn't love her. Never loved her. And with this illusion gone, everything else crumbles. What she took for Salvador's noble simplicity turns into emptiness. His striking honesty into an inability to come up with credible lies. His "meaningful" silences into stupidity. His immense love for her turns into simple interest in her body, and not too great an interest, making the whole affair even more banal than her relationship with Dostoevsky, making her sink even lower. She is confused, she is devastated, and she is desperate for revenge. "I so want to make him suffer," she writes pleadingly in her diary. But as much as she tries with threats and insults, she finds that she is simply unable to cause Salvador real pain. She can make him annoyed, she can make him angry, she can even make him scared, but she can't make him suffer. Whatever she did to him wouldn't result in anything even close to the agony she is feeling.

But wait, wait, wait. Where is Dostoevsky? When I read Polina's diary for the first time, I was so impatient to know how the Salvador story ended that I missed all the references to Dostoevsky. But the references are present. Here and there his name appears between the interpretations of Salvador's words and deeds. "Just now received a letter from F.M. He is so happy to see me soon. I feel sorry for him."

Around August 27, Dostoevsky finally manages to come to Paris. He is a little worried by Polina's continuing silence, but optimistic, in high spirits (made even higher by the substantial sum of money he wins at the roulette table on his way to France). He spends the night in his hotel room, and the next morning, refreshed but still a little tired from the trip, anxious yet hopeful, he rushes to see Polina. She says that he's come "too late."

"Do you love him?" Dostoevsky asks Polina afterward, over a tray with rapidly cooling tea.

"Yes," she answers.

"Are you happy?"

"No."

"Why?"

"Because he doesn't love me."

He groans and proceeds to knead his face with his hands, his shoulders shaking, the beads of sweat rolling down his forehead. Polina watches him in silence. As distraught as she is with her own pain, she can't help but notice that he is suffering. She is able to get to a man after all.

Chapter Seven

I don't know if it was Polina's diary that inspired me, but after my third or fourth date with Mark, I went to Kate's Paperie on Seventy-fourth and bought a journal. "Memoirs of a Muse," I wrote on the inside of the cover, giggling with a mix of embarrassment and excitement when I saw those words on paper. I couldn't wait to make my first entry, so I decided to do it right in the subway car, in a shaky hand, balancing the journal between my knees. But faced with an empty page, I suddenly got shy. I couldn't possibly describe our walks, or our kisses, or the constant, almost painful exhilaration that I felt, so I started with coffee.

"Today we drank espresso. They served it in thick tiny cups with a piece of lemon peel on the side. There was hardly enough coffee for a couple of sips, but the color was so dark that it stained the inside of the cup, and the taste was so strong that it stayed in my mouth for the better part of the day."

The second entry was devoted to Turkish coffee, the third to Vietnamese. My fourth entry described the "best coffee I'd ever tasted."

"Now you're going to have the best coffee you've ever tasted,"

Mark had announced that day, leading me away from the café area and onto a quiet residential street. We entered a big building with a big marble lobby and a fat sullen doorman. This looks like a museum, I wanted to say with a laugh, before I realized that it was Mark's building. He lived there, and that was why he walked those marble floors so nonchalantly, nodding at the doorman in passing, not looking at the mirrors or vases. His perfect ease made me more uncomfortable than the chill and grandness of the building.

Inside the apartment, I felt better.

"Look around, while I'm busy doing my alchemy," Mark said, hanging his coat on one of the funny hooks made to look like tree twigs. He then dove into a tiny doorless, tableless kitchen, so tiny that he could reach all the cabinets, the stove, the sink, and the fridge while staying in the same spot. He looked as if he were doing an exercise. Bend, squat, straighten, bend. Bang, bang, bang—the chipped blue doors opened and closed, producing an army of coffee gadgets and materials. I liked Mark's kitchen.

The tiny living room wasn't intimidating either, I decided, after making a mental inventory. Brick walls. A section of a picket fence serving as a screen. Old leather bags hanging on the posts of the fence. Dark, shabby desk in the corner with an electric typewriter on it. A couch covered with plaid fabric. A small TV. A painting of a man with a sad, dark blue face above the couch and a colorful landscape with purple grass and orange haystacks on the opposite wall. Sagging bookshelves filled with old, shabby books. Everything simple, worn out, and dignified without being pretentious.

"Sit down now," Mark said, having emerged in the kitchen doorway with a metal coffeepot in one hand and two brown mugs hanging off the fingers of his other hand. "You're about to taste magic."

The coffee was too hot for me; I burned my tongue with the first sip and couldn't quite enjoy the taste after that, but the aroma was joyful and heady, and I smiled in approval.

"Didn't I tell you it's the best?"

My eyes continued to scan the apartment as we drank, and for some reason Mark found this fascinating. "Do you want to know what that is?" he asked about one object or another.

"Toothbrushes? Pretty, aren't they? I've had them for years. I don't know why. I guess I just like to be greeted by something bright and colorful when I wake up and go to the bathroom.

"Black dots on the painting? I have no idea. Cows? Sheep? Painter's mistakes?

"And that, behind the closed door, is the bedroom. You'll get a chance to see it in a second."

Mark took me there after coffee, leading me by the hand and pushing the door open with his shoulder. The bedroom didn't have the cheerful, unruly look of the living room or the kitchen. Everything there was orderly, square, and pale in the dimness of drawn blinds. A dresser. A nightstand. A walk-in closet. A painting called *Provincetown's Dunes in the Rain*. A wide, low bed that somehow managed to make my desire for Mark disappear as soon as my body made contact with its hard surface. The desire had been constant since I met Mark, rocking inside me like heavy, glutinous liquid, erupting in bubbles of sharp sensation whenever he touched me or the image of his touch appeared in my memory. But here, on the bed, as Mark's hands and mouth set out on their leisurely journey along my body, my desire seeped out, and in my sudden emptiness I became exposed to terror. My stomach churned. My heart raced, my face burned, the tips of my fingers grew cold, and moisture left the places where it would have been appropriate, to break out in beads of sweat on my nose and forehead.

"Is it scary?" my college friend Jenya Turkina had asked me years ago, during a lecture on the history of the Communist Party. Her wedding was a week away, right after the nasty "Marxism and Leninism" exam.

"Well, not as scary as Marlenism," I said with the affectionate authority of someone who had already lost her virginity even if not so long ago.

"What if I fail both?"

"How can you possibly fail *that*?"

"But what if I do it all wrong?"

"What is there to *do*? You're not a boy."

Wasn't "performance anxiety" solely men's trouble? I thought then. Women were saddled with menstrual cramps, childbirth, pregnancy, and the worst evil of all—fear of pregnancy. It was only fair that they were spared some of the male problems. There was not a shade of performance anxiety in my earlier experiences with boys, probably because there wasn't any performance; I let the boys do things to me, and they seemed quite happy with the arrangement. Yet I believed that women differed in their qualities as lovers. Some had that mysterious talent for passion, others didn't. Some were Polinas, others Anna Grigorievnas. No technique described in the dog-eared sex manuals we hid in our laps during lectures on Marlenism could help you. You either had it or you didn't. I had always assumed that I did. The fact that none of my boyfriends had ever praised my lovemaking skills didn't dampen my spirits in the least, I was sure that the magic would somehow start working as soon as I met my true love. When one girl in my class brought in some American questionnaire asking the reader to appraise herself as a lover on a scale from one to ten, I wrote "ten" in firm, bold letters. The only thing that made me doubt myself was that seventeen out of twenty girls wrote "ten" too. (I made sure to check every answer.) Seventeen out of every twenty girls couldn't possibly all be Polinas. There simply wasn't enough room in the world for so many Polinas. That meant that most of the girls who answered the questionnaire only *thought* that they were Polinas but were in fact Anna Grigorievnas! What if that was the case with me?

Shrinking on Mark's hostile bed, I was especially doubtful. What if I simply wasn't good enough as a lover? Not good enough for Mark? I thought as his hand grazed my breasts, the cool fingers of his other hand slipped under the collar of my shirt and down my spine, his lips touched my neck, and his eyes studiously searched mine for a response. There was no response.

I'd had just the opposite problem during my former short-lived encounters. I was disgusted by my own desire for those boys. I didn't like them; they were so ordinary, and yet my body reacted to their touches fiercely and joyfully, as I had expected it to react only to somebody special. I hated my body. I felt betrayed by it.

Now I was with that special man at last, and my body chose to betray me again. Another touch, and Mark would see my lack of response and know that I wasn't the lover he needed.

"No!" I shrieked, sitting up in bed, and then added pleadingly, "No . . ."

He didn't insist. He let go at once, moved away from me, and sat there in silence, while the glazed expression in his eyes was slowly turning to normal.

And then in desperation, to make up for my failure, I turned to the only thing that could work, my fascination with his life, which never failed to engage him.

"Who is that?" I asked pointing with a trembling finger to a black-and-white photograph on his nightstand. I couldn't see it very well, but I said, "It's a beautiful picture."

"That one? That's my mother."

"She's beautiful."

"Beautiful . . . I don't know. I guess it's a little hard for me to judge. Spirited, yes. This picture really captures that, don't you think?"

The picture was faded and kind of fuzzy. You couldn't tell much about the woman, except that she had carefully styled hair, a long nose, and a mean expression.

"My mother had the ambitions of Emma Bovary but lacked her passion, her will, and her determination. She didn't take lovers, at least not that I know of. And she didn't make my father—a doctor too—perform risky operations, but she did strive for something bigger in her life. You know who Madame Bovary was, don't you?"

I nodded.

Mark continued talking about his mother, very fast and in a very quiet voice; I couldn't always follow the English.

But, once on the subway, while replaying Mark's voice in my mind, I was able to put those sounds together so they produced clues, and then from the clues I was able to assemble the sentences, and the meaning of Mark's words suddenly dawned on me. Then, afraid that the new fragile meaning could disappear, I rushed into my purse, took out the diary, and scribbled my entries in a shaking hand, balancing the diary between my knees. Perhaps I was simply replacing the words that I didn't understand with words that I wanted to hear, interpreting the whole picture until Mark became closer and closer to my understanding of life.

"Mark's mother's parents came from Poland. All her life she had been terribly ashamed of her family's immigrant status. She married up, very far up, but apparently not far enough, for she was never satisfied with her life," I put into my diary later that day. "Mark's

111

mother had a habit of bursting into tears when he brought home his school report. She said that his Bs in Math (or Cs in chemistry, or the 'isn't paying enough attention' comment) were killing her, yes, simply killing her. And then, at night, she would come into Mark's room and sit down by his bed and cry and ask him to forgive her, and tell him that it didn't matter to her in the least whether he had an A or a D in chemistry, math, or English, all the while sniffing and blowing her nose. Mark's father was oblivious to whatever ambitions his wife might have had, and to life in general. He was a quiet anesthesiologist who seemed to have inhaled too much of the sedatives he used. All his free time he had spent in the study of their house reading medical magazines and historical novels. Whenever his wife or son reminded him of their existence, he would promptly leave his study and spend some dutiful time with them—teach Mark how to play chess, accompany Mark's mother to a theater—and after the duty was over just as promptly return to his study."

And so it went on like this. I would come to Mark's place. We would go to the bedroom. I would pray and hope that I wouldn't fail again. But inevitably I would. And then I would ask for more stories or for other pictures from Mark's past.

"Do you have pictures of you as a kid?"

"Well, I must have somewhere . . . but I should warn you, I used to be very chubby. You wouldn't have liked me as a kid."

The pictures Mark kept not in photo albums but in the plump old leather bags, the ones that I had spotted hanging in the hall. Mark brought the bags in and emptied them right onto the rumpled bed. Yellowed black-and-whites, the pictures looked strangely intimate, even vulnerable against the soft light-blue cotton of Mark's sheets, next to our half-dressed bodies. A fat, unsmiling baby dressed in a suit with a bow tie. A chubby little boy with a paper boat in his hands. An older boy holding on to a baseball bat. A lean teenager with a book.

What had originally started as a distraction from failed sex soon turned into my biggest source of enjoyment.

"Who is that?" or "When was it?" or "Is it you?" I would ask, fishing out the ones that interested me the most. Later, on the subway, all the black-and-white faces, pale landscapes, and gray interiors turned colorful and came alive, joined to the stories Mark had told me.

For the coldest weeks of the winter, Mark's family traveled to Florida. On a train, because that was how people traveled to Florida in those days. How old did this make Mark, I wondered. Fifty? More than that?

At night, when the train passed the sites of the Civil War battles, the young Mark imagined dead Confederate soldiers rising from their mass graves. They were decomposed bearded corpses in gray uniforms covered with fresh and dried-up dirt. They limped closer and closer to the rails. Soon they would be able to knock at the window of his compartment with their hard, yellow fingers. Sweaty and shivering under the thin shield of his blanket, Mark crawled into the farthest corner of his berth, trying to squash his tiny body into the cold wood of the wall.

For the hottest weeks of the summer, Mark's family drove to the Catskills. There were no imaginary corpses on the way there, only the real ones of unfortunate raccoon and deer. Mark couldn't take his eyes off the swarms of flies buzzing over one or another animal's unmoving tail.

Every night before going to sleep Mark imagined what he would feel when dying. He imagined his limbs getting icy cold, his throat stuffed with asphyxia (he had thought "asphyxia" was a material object similar to cotton wool in texture but smelling like gas), his body powerless, his mind slowly going. "I hated to sleep alone in a room, still do," he said.

At thirteen, while watching Mrs. Kovalchik from the bungalow next door fan her fat, white thighs with the hem of her skirt, Mark experienced his first orgasm. The sensation nearly knocked him down. It was the most powerful and exciting thing that had ever happened to him. The habit of pondering death faded away. From then on, Mark was engaged in more satisfying activities before going to sleep every night.

The days, Mark devoted to reading. At first, he used books as a shield—he was a terrible athlete and very ashamed of it. "Schneider, you throw like a girl," the boys would yell. Or "So what that the sun was in your face, we had Schneider on our team; it's worse!" Mark's solution was to pretend to be a great reader and thinker; he went everywhere with a book under his arm, and kept saying that sports were beneath him. But gradually, while feigning deep interest in his reading, he started feeling it for real, and soon nothing could tear him away from a good book. He swallowed one book after another, with barely enough time to digest what he had read. His favorite were books from the Chip Hilton series, because they allowed him to identify with the characters and feel like a great athlete, while playing sports in real life only humiliated him. "It was then," Mark said, "that I discovered the enormous power of fiction." When Mark started the tenth grade, a new English teacher came to their school. Mr. Donner, a tall man, with a long wrinkly neck, a jutting Adam's apple, and brows that seemed frozen in ironic disagreement. Mr. Donner made fun of the boys, mocked the boys, humiliated the boys, and introduced them to truly great books, introduced them in such a way that if a boy managed to get the book at all, it stayed with him forever. "You'll have a long summer ahead of you," Mr. Donner said at the end of tenth grade. "Spend it wisely, read *Crime and Punishment*. Make sure you're alone in the room when you read it. Lock the door, tell your parents to go away if they want you, smack your siblings if they pester you, kick your pets, give the book your full attention, let it get to you."

Mark always listened to Mr. Donner. He let *Crime and Punishment* get to him. He read the book during the first week of the summer, and spent the remaining weeks boiling in rage and disgust toward his family and friends who had no clue what real poverty or real suffering was and had never even thought of committing murder in their sorry, pathetic lives. "Am I a louse or a man?" Raskolnikov wanted to find out. Mark needed to know that too. He pondered briefly whether he should commit murder or write a novel as great as *Crime and Punishment*. He chose the latter.

For about a week he didn't leave his room, pouring the whole of his consciousness into the story. He painted the picture of life the way he knew it. Ten pages. Called "Raskolnikov's Dream."

His father wasn't too impressed with the story, but his mother was. And she thought that like everything else the story should be seen by a specialist. Unable to wait for the beginning of a school year, she called Donner and begged him to see them at his house. One Sunday, she carefully typed Mark's story, styled her hair the fancy way, and told Mark to put on his suit and tie, even though it was August. Donner met them wearing rubber boots and pants covered with fresh garden dirt. He didn't seem particularly happy to see Mark or his mother, but he motioned for them to sit down on the porch and even served some tepid tap water in coffee mugs. Then he took the sheaf of pages into his hands. The reading seemed to go on forever. Mark peered into Donner's face, trying to guess which line he was reading, to interpret every frown or shrug. The face familiar to Mark from English lessons grew different, longer, as Donner read.

His chin was slowly drooping, the nose stretching down to catch up with the chin, the ears extending, the eyebrows rising, and a tiny razor's scratch on his cheek turning into a huge, creepy wound. Mark was scared in a way he hadn't experienced before, more scared even than he had been with the thoughts of death. He looked at his mother for reassurance, but she was staring at the ground, her carefully made-up face melting in the ruthless Donner's sun. A fly would land on a page from time to time, but Donner wouldn't pay any attention to it, and Mark didn't have the heart to wave it away. As stretched out as the reading seemed to Mark, when Donner finished at last, it seemed to happen too soon. "So, Schneider," he said after taking a swig of his water. "I could lie to you, but I'm not going to." Donner continued talking, but Mark couldn't hear him—the rest of the words were drowned out by the rustle Mark's new shoes made against Donner's grass as he ran to the gate. "You should be grateful to me, Schneider, I'm sparing you years of misery!" Mark heard when he was outside the gate, sobbing into his mother's thin, sweaty body.

Mark didn't write another fiction piece for almost twenty years, until his mother died and Donner's long face had faded from his mind. By that time he'd become a successful magazine editor, an admired author of witty and acerbic columns, a professor of English, and a man with substantial life experience. His friends, his readers, his women, and his therapist all asked why he didn't write a novel. And so he did. "To great acclaim, as they say," Mark added, laughing.

Photographs of women would sometimes surface in the pile. All of them appeared to be about the same age—close to mine, but their clothes and hairstyles showed that the pictures were taken throughout the decades. Some had forlorn and mysterious expressions on their faces, others were frozen while smiling. All of them were beautiful, very beautiful, and not just beautiful in a simple, physical way (although that too), but glowing with inner poise, sophistication, complexity. All of them had entered Mark's life at one time or another. All of them had been looked at by Mark, touched by Mark, kissed by Mark, had had him inside them. Probably on the very bed where I was sitting with him now.

"This one used to drive me especially crazy," Mark noted once when I fished out a picture of a thin-faced brunette in a seventies-style miniskirt.

"She is more beautiful than I am," I said, putting the brunette away.

"Well, yes, she is," he agreed, sending a sharp injection of pain through me but relieving me of it the next instant. "Yet, you've got something that none of them had. I can't quite describe what it is, but I can feel it. I used to chase after beauty when I was younger, but with the years your values change."

Yes, yes. I was a woman whose value only a brilliant, perceptive, mature man could understand. I was indescribable. I was unique. Plus, I had that mysterious Eastern European gloom. I would get to stay in Mark's bed, while the other women went back into the stuffy darkness of the old leather bag. I'd defeated them all.

How I hated the screechy voice of the subway operator announcing the Brighton Beach stop! So rude, so inconsiderate, it would make me get off the warmed seat, exit the perfect universe of my diary, and head toward the world of smelly vegetable stores, loud cars, and undignified chores. But even there the image of Mark never really left me, hovering within reach as I mopped the floors in the dentist's office, shopped for discounted rotting tomatoes in Brighton Beach, or squeezed some Palmolive over my uncle's dishes. I closed my eyes and saw Mark's pale lips, and his nose slightly slanting to the right, and the matted hair on his arms, the fine ornament of freckles and birthmarks on his chest. I would see present-time Mark as he sat cross-legged on the bed, dressed in gray boxers and an unbuttoned blue shirt, with a paunchy stomach and graying hair on his chest, and suddenly, through his adult face, the anxious eyes of the chubby little boy from the black-and-white pictures would appear, or the nose of the same boy in color, the boy of Mark's stories. At those moments, I felt as if my whole body had been hollowed out and filled with a warm, salty tenderness for all three instances of Mark.

Often, at my uncle's place, I would reach into my Russian suitcase and pull out a big, dark blue folder with my photographs, the one that my mother gave me on my last day in Moscow. Me at eight months, smiling a bottomless, toothless smile, looking the happiest I would ever be. Me at the age of three, skinny, curly-haired, and bitterly crying. My grandmother peeling potatoes with a resigned expression, a long wisp of white hair fallen over her face. My young, happy mother hugging the jagged edge of my father's side; he has been cut off from the picture. My father and mother leaning over my crib, staring in disbelief at the screaming bundle that was me at the time. Another of my father, wearing a suit and smiling tensely into the camera. My father squatting at the beach, wearing a khaki jacket, his back to the waves, his face out of focus. My father surrounded by a group of men in khaki jackets on board a small ship, most of them sporting knitted hats and short, scruffy beards. I vaguely remembered those pictures as the ones that had hung on the wall of my mother's room before the dead old writers took their place. In the group picture, my father stood next to another bearded man, whose face was strangely familiar. "Oh, yeah, yeah, that's me," my uncle said. "We used to sign up for a North Pole expedition every summer. Didn't you know that?" No, I didn't. I hardly knew anything at all. My mother never talked about my father, and I, for some reason, had never been compelled to ask her.

"I signed up as a doctor, and your father as a mechanic. He used to work in seaport docks before college, so he knew everything about ships. Waves, wind, ice, northern lights. Two months away from everything, jobs, wives . . . yeah, those were the times."

So my father liked to live to the utmost degree too, where and when he could.

"We all grew beards on the ship. Your father had a funny one. Red, when the rest of his hair was black."

My uncle wanted to tell me more, but I became wary about talking about my father. Mark was the single most important thing in my life, and I was afraid that bringing up my father, and even thinking about him, would cast a shadow on my present happiness. But at the same time I longed to show the pictures to Mark, the ones of my father and the others too. I wanted to give them to him without saying a word, to lay them out on his bed and watch his reaction as he looked at them.

Every time I was about to leave for Mark's place, I picked a few pictures from my folder and put them in my purse, but for some reason I could never find a good moment to take them out once I got there. They just traveled with me from Brooklyn and back, hidden in the dark of my purse, never shared with Mark, never exposed, except on the subway, where I took them out and tried to look at them with Mark's eyes.

I imagined Mark taking the pictures from me one by one, gently, with great care and respect, flicking the specks of dust off the worn images, smiling as he took those little bits of me in. "I just love your grandmother," he would say. "She looks resigned, but there is a hidden force to her . . ." Or "Oh, I like you as a baby." Or "This is your father, isn't it? You still miss him, don't you?" And I would nod, and smile, and melt, and tell him things that I wanted so much to tell. In my mind, while swaying in the dusty subway car, I told him my whole life. And in my mind, Mark listened to me patiently and with eager attention, marveling just as I did at the hidden similarities in our drastically different lives, understanding me better than I'd ever understood myself.

I'd never known such intimacy with anyone as I had on the subway with the Mark of my imagination.

However, after a while I stopped enjoying my subway rides back to Brooklyn. The anxiety crept into my precious recollections of the date. We still hadn't had sex, and it clearly couldn't go on like that for much longer. "It is beautiful," Mark said to me once, after yet another failed attempt. "That clever little game of yours. I never know when you're going to say 'no.' " He thought it was a game. I didn't try to dissuade him, overjoyed that there was something he found beautiful, unpredictable, or clever about me. It made me a little sad, though, that he knew me so little, though more relieved than sad. But the whole point of the game as Mark imagined it was that sooner or later I'd say "yes." If I didn't say "yes" Mark would eventually grow tired, annoyed, disappointed. He wouldn't want to see me anymore. And the longer my resistance held, the closer that moment would draw.

One night I became so overcome with anxiety that I did the unthinkable and called up Dena. For some reason she seemed very happy, even excited, to talk. "Don't you see that Mommy's on the phone! Can't you watch your child for a second?" she kept yelling.

I mumbled that I had an important job interview coming up and asked if she knew some remedy for anxiety.

Dena laughed.

"A job interview! Come on, stop it. Tell me, tell me about the guy. What do you mean you don't know what to tell? Who is he? An American? A writer? A real writer? Do they have him at Barnes and Noble? They do! Where on earth did you meet him?"

Dena grilled me with questions for a long time, but at the end promised to help.

When we met the next day, she rolled two white tablets onto my palm. "I'm taking these for my nerves, but they'll take care of your problem just as well. Here are two, just in case. But don't take more than one, if you want to enjoy it."

Enjoy it? I'd never thought of that. All I wanted was not to fail.

One tablet proved to be enough. I kept going in and out of a strange slumber. Dreaming but not exactly dreaming. Taking in what was happening, but feeling strangely excluded from the act. My legs were bound in something heavy, I couldn't move them at all. Not that I minded. I didn't mind at all. I was swaying. Very gently. I liked it. Mark's face moved rhythmically above my face, coarse hairs of his beard tickling my neck. I touched his hair with my hand and slid it down his slippery back as far as the length of my arm allowed me. I wasn't dreaming. There was a live, warm panting, Mark on top of me! Breathing rapidly and making the sharp little sounds that could only mean that he was enjoying it and I wasn't failing. I was overcome with joy. I freed my legs from under his body and wrapped them around his back very tight, feeling enormous gratitude for what was happening at last.

"Wait! Wait a little bit," he said from somewhere far above me, but it was too late.

"You overwhelmed me," he said later. "I kept waiting for your famous 'no' up to the last moment."

I overwhelmed him! I overwhelmed him!

I had a smile on my face, so wide and persistent that it made my jawbone hurt.

I marked November 14 in my diary as the official beginning of my career as a muse. It made perfect sense to me then. I decided that the great and mysterious work of a muse must start with that little shudder of a genius's body, a minor explosion, the quiet spurt of his sperm inside her. Technically, this wonder sperm didn't even enter my body, it poured into a tiny rubber bag that was swiftly withdrawn from me, along with the genius himself. But that was how a muse's influence on the work of her lover started. With this little act, otherwise so simple and trivial, if not for the genius of one of the parties involved.

Polina and Dostoevsky left Paris together.

They talked a lot during that crazy week. She told him all about her affair with Salvador. He said that he understood her. He said that he didn't blame her. He said that it had only dawned on him now, how painful, how unbearable their Petersburg relationship must have been for her. He said that he was sorry. He said he was unworthy of her. He said he was privileged to know a person as noble and pure as she. He said that there was nothing in his life he valued more than their friendship. He said that he would be her tender and devoted friend from now on. He proposed that they continue their journey to Italy as they had planned a long time ago, promising to remain like a brother to her.

"He understands me," Polina wrote in her diary.

They boarded a train in the first days of September, after a week of unceasing showers. The rain had stopped pouring by the time they got to the station, but everything—the benches, the handrails, the pavement—was wet and slimy, and the humidity seemed to hang in the air. Polina slipped on a wet boulder as they were getting off the coach and Dostoevsky hurried to place his hand at her waist to support her. Did she notice how his hand lingered there, pressing against the stiff fabric of her travel dress? Was she alarmed? Flattered? Indifferent? Whatever her reaction was, Polina didn't show it. She pulled up the damp and dirty hem of her dress and hurried toward the station, her scuffed shoes picking their way between the puddles. She looked down, wishing that the pavement, the puddles, the boots, would register in her mind as the last impression of the hated city, erasing the streets, the buildings, and all Parisians from her memory. Dostoevsky hobbled along, trying to keep pace with her, trying to slow her down, trying to tell her that there was still plenty of time before the train, trying to reason with her.

There were three other passengers in their compartment. I once saw a copy of a Victorian engraving in one of my history books, entitled *First-Class Railway Passengers*. I imagine that the people sitting next to Polina and Dostoevsky in their compartment looked exactly like those in the engraving. A fussy lady covered in frills, a fat older man buried behind a newspaper, a mustached younger man with his hands folded on his chest, throwing quick assessing looks at the frilled lady. They were all drawn in a caricatured style, and I imagine that they looked just like that to Polina and Dostoevsky: hideous caricatures rather than real people. She had to bear their presence and the knowledge that they were witnesses to her pain.

But by the time the train had passed the outskirts of Paris, the mustached man and the frilled lady had dozed off, the streets of the hated city were no longer in sight, and Polina had gradually calmed down. She wiped the rest of the bitter moisture from her eyes and even managed a smile. Dostoevsky smiled back kindly, happily, hungry to see her smile.

I picture half of their compartment in shade, the other half brightly lit by the morning sun. I'd prefer Dostoevsky to sit in shade. I hate to think of all the blemishes Polina would otherwise see on his face, which is far from attractive: angular, gaunt, pallid, showing the emotional exhaustion of their week in Paris, his brown eye twitching in the sharp light, his black eye frozen. Let him stay in the shade, let the dimness of his corner smooth out his features so that his face doesn't remind Polina of the face she used to see so appallingly close to hers. With his expression softened by the dark, his voice sounds different to her, his words full of quiet significance. They talk in Russian, which feels strangely intimate in this tight compartment filled with foreigners. Do they talk about life now? Do they learn how to be friends? Close, attentive, kind?

Baden-Baden is pulling near. The dark opening of the train station rushes to receive their train. Soon Polina and Dostoevsky will get up and move out of their compartment and into the train's narrow corridor.

I know how the story ends. Even if I didn't know, the end would have been easy to guess. Something must have gone wrong during their European journey, otherwise why would Dostoevsky end up marrying Anna Grigorievna three years later?

But for now, as they are getting ready to leave the train, I don't want to think about the end. I want the hope to live.

Chapter Eight

On January 14, I moved in with Mark. My diary says that much. "Jan. 14. Moving in."

A few days before that, as I was on my knees searching for my panty hose in a pile of Mark's clothes on the floor, Mark asked me to sit down next to him on the bed. He was comfortably stretched out on the sheets, naked, his left arm folded on the pillow under his head, his right hand idly pulling the hair on his chest. I was fully clothed except, of course, for the missing panty hose.

"You see," he said, having moved his feet to give me space, "your presence is so light that I barely notice it. But your absence makes me itchy, as if I've forgotten something important but can't think what."

"As if you couldn't remember if you turned off the gas?"

He laughed. "Exactly!"

He turned to the side to reach into his nightstand. "Here. I got a second set of keys for you."

All the way back to Brooklyn, I had the odd sensation that I had forgotten to wear my panty hose and they were still lying there on the Upper West Side, in the dark, dusty spot under Mark's couch, and my legs were still bare. I kept rubbing my knees one against the another to feel the reassuring rustle of nylon.

Was Mark's offer flattering? It was so strange and unexpected. I hadn't even spent a full night at his place yet. "The Americans guard their beds and apartments as if they were medieval fortresses. God forbid they let a woman spend the night, let alone move in with them!" Dena said to me once, when I had come to her birthday party. There was a little break between the hors d'oeuvres and the second course—the stubborn leg of lamb that just wouldn't reach the needed temperature in the oven, even though Dena's husband, Igor, had carefully followed the cookbook's instructions. Dena grabbed my hand and led me to their unfinished extra bedroom. And there, while we sat on a bare mattress facing a half-painted wall, she asked how things were with my guy. I was reluctant to answer, and luckily she was reluctant to listen; she just talked and talked about Americans, until Igor appeared in the doorway with oven mitts on his hands and said, "The leg is ready."

Mark had offered that I move in just like that. That meant our relationship was romantic, spontaneous. He said I was the kind of woman he could live with. That was good, wasn't it? I was the kind of woman a writer, a great man, could live with! But wasn't his offer a little insulting? Hadn't he compared me to a burner he'd forgotten to switch off? Well, he hadn't. It was I who'd brought up the burner. He didn't mean anything bad. But hadn't he gotten the keys made before he'd even spoken to me? Why was he so sure I'd say yes? But then why wouldn't he be sure? I didn't go to great pains to conceal my feelings from him.

By the time I reached the Brighton Beach stop, I'd decided that I should be happy with Mark's offer.

And so, a few days later, I slipped cautiously onto the cold sheets next to Mark's smooth and clean body, preparing to sleep in bed with a man for the very first time. Facing a whole new set of problems.

Was I supposed to hug him? To cuddle? How was I going to fall asleep while touching somebody else? Wouldn't I be too uncomfortable? I once caught a sight of my uncle and Maya sleeping together. Maya lay on her back with the serene expression of a corpse, and my uncle lay on his stomach, with his face buried into the pillow and his meaty arm resting across Maya's chest. How could she be comfortable, how could she sleep under that heavy load? While I was pondering appropriate bed behavior, Mark yawned, turned away from me onto his left side, and mumbled, "Sleep tight." He fell asleep in a second and soon proved himself to be a perfect sleeping partner—immobile, quiet, and undemanding about space.

The bed, on the other hand, wasn't as accommodating.

The pillow was too soft and too plump for me. After a quick fistfight, I flattened out a small part in the corner—enough to fit my right ear and right cheek there. It was fine for a while, but then my right ear grew sore and hot.

The blanket was even worse than the pillow. Too warm, too stuffy, and too heavy, it enveloped my body like a casket, making me hot and itchy. I tried to pull it down a little, but Mark grumbled in his sleep and pulled it back.

What do I do in the morning? I thought in sweaty panic. What do I say to Mark? How do I act? Am I supposed to cook breakfast? What if he hates it? What if he hates the way I clean? Didn't my aunt always scrunch her face when she picked up a plate just washed by me? Didn't my mother always remark that "wetting and washing floors were two different things"? I thought of the other dangers as well—vague, indefinable, invisible dangers that threatened even the best of couples with silence, boredom, with nagging dissatisfaction.

My mother and father had gotten into one of those traps. Dena was struggling in another. What mistakes had the women in Mark's photographs made? What was it exactly that made their presence in his life come to an end? These throbbing, poisonous thoughts were so scary that I preferred to worry about badly cooked dinners and poorly washed plates.

"Do you even know how to do it?" my mother had asked me on the phone when I told her about Mark and that we were going to live together.

"Know how to do what?"

"Oh, I don't know, how to live with somebody?"

We were both silent for some time.

"Tanya?"

"What?"

"Do you remember that fish soup I used to make? Your grandmother taught me right before my wedding. Your father liked it a lot. The soup is delicious and so simple; you'll have no trouble cooking it. You put just any kind of fish there, even canned fish, and onions. Potatoes too. Carrots? I can't remember. I'll look up the recipe for you. Tanya, call me, please keep calling me. And keep your job, okay? And promise you'll keep looking for a good school!"

I turned onto my other side and suddenly had a vision of the fish soup in my bowl. A clear pond where bright green parsley sprigs and red disks of carrots swam amid gray bits of fish. "Wait, Tanya, wait," my mother told me. "Let me put the egg in." White-and-yellow circles of hard-boiled eggs slid off the cutting board and into my bowl. They were beautiful. They were the secret ingredient for the fish soup. I could do that. I'd make the soup and slice an egg for Mark, and he would smile at me, admiring the gentle taste and aroma. I fell asleep basking in happy anticipation mixed with faint fear that Mark might not like my fish soup after all.

The delicious revving of the coffee grinder woke me up. The empty pillow next to me had a wonderful creased dent shaped like Mark's head, with a few twisty hairs stuck to the pillowcase. The dent smelled sweetly of Mark's shampoo, but mostly of something stuffy and warm, strange and dear at the same time. I pressed my cheek to Mark's pillow and lay like that for some time before getting out of bed.

The kitchen was full of coffee aroma, the floor littered with coffee beans, which felt cool and smooth like tiny seaside pebbles under my bare feet.

A rumpled Mark, dressed in boxers and an oversized T-shirt, was pouring coffee into two mugs.

"Sleep well?" he asked, his words barely decipherable through a series of big yawns. He then poured some cereal into two bowls, moved his stool closer to the table, and motioned for me to do the same. After the first slurping spoonful of cereal, he yawned and scratched his back with the handle of his spoon.

Until just a few months ago I hadn't known about this man's existence. He led his own complex, private life. And now I got to see how he looked when he woke up, and how he sounded slurping his milk, the way I had seen only my mother, my grandmother, my uncle and aunt before. But with them I hadn't appreciated these intimacies, I had taken them for granted. Here, sitting across from Mark, I felt an awed discomfort, as if it were all a part of some kind of initiation ceremony.

After breakfast, Mark showed me where to put my things. He freed a couple of bedroom drawers for me, a few hangers, and a shelf in the bathroom cabinet. He seemed to be strangely apprehensive that my stuff would mix with his. I could see that he wanted me there, but at the same time was worried about the inconveniences my intrusion would cause him. My overcoat was the only item of clothing that was allowed to be lost among his things. "My overcoat went to the front closet. It's hanging now between Mark's two leather jackets, above the messy pile of Mark's sneakers and loafers, and under the shelf with his hats and woolen scarves," I wrote in my diary that day.

And with that, my new life began.

The household panic that I had on the first night turned out to be for naught. Cleaning was done by an invisible woman who came every Wednesday and worked while Mark took me shopping. Breakfast Mark cooked himself—a strange but edible concoction of cereal with dried fruit and nuts, plain yogurt, soy milk, organic grape jelly, and some nasty powder from a plastic jar. Lunch was served to us in one of the little cafés where I had peeked longingly in the windows just months before. A dinner most often materialized from a pile of takeout menus. I soon learned to make simple sandwiches that Mark liked as a late-night snack and brew coffee or tea the way he preferred.

Despite my mother's wishes, I had quit the dentist's as soon as Mark suggested I move in with him; I simply couldn't fit this job within the high hopes and aspirations of my new life. And since I didn't have anything to do, I effortlessly adjusted my daily routine to Mark's schedule, which wasn't complicated at all.

On Tuesdays he took a train to Bard College to teach his "Defictionalization of the Novel" class. (I asked him to repeat the title three times before I lied that I understood what it meant.) On Thursdays, he taught an unimaginatively titled "Contemporary American Fiction" class in a prep school for boys. On Friday and Saturday nights, we usually went to stand-up literary parties or sit-down literary dinners. (At least I assumed they were literary, because I couldn't follow the conversation.)

The rest of Mark's week seemed to be devoted to the needs of his body rather than his mind.

Mark never went to any exhibitions or concerts; he rarely listened to a stereo. What was more puzzling, he didn't spend too much time reading. Except for the books he needed for his classes, an occasional magazine, or an old classic novel, he mostly read writers' biographies. He liked to highlight his favorite passages with multicolored markers. Sometimes he would write his name next to a highlighted passage, at other times some other name, or "Mother." He must have looked for things that made those writers' lives feel close to his. I imagined all writers belonging to some intimate club, where all members boasted the same foibles and peculiarities, and found Mark's highlighting sweet and endearing.

I decided that his lack of interest in other books was caused by the fact that he was a writer himself. His mind was constantly busy with producing and digesting its own images, so there wasn't place or time or energy for absorbing somebody else's. Geniuses created art, while struggling and suffering. And ordinary people simply consumed it, feeding off the genius's mind, like parasites off their host's body.

Mark wasn't writing either. "I'm between novels right now," he explained to me. "Gathering strength for the next one." It was okay, I thought. It was perfectly normal for a writer to take a break and gather strength. Only an idiot would think that a writer must write all the time, like a machine. Mark must put an enormous amount of energy into each of his works, and now he needed time to have that spent energy restored. Writing, I was learning, was a very delicate business.

While Mark's mind was taking a necessary rest, his body demanded a lot of attention. I marveled at how complex its needs were. Mark's body seemed to be a much more sophisticated piece of machinery than my own. It required monthly internist's and dentist's checkups, regular jogging, gym visits, massages, and countless showers—all of these things that I either skipped (the dentist), had never tried (the massage), or did quickly, nonchalantly, without tender care (the shower).

We spent mornings cruising the aisles of the supermarket and then the health food store, stopping here and there so Mark could take his time with the nutrition information on the labels. We shopped for organic toothpaste, organic shaving cream, and an organic bathbrush. (God only knows what it was made of.) We shopped for shoes that you couldn't feel on your feet and for socks that made your feet warm but not sweaty. We kneaded, stroked, and rumpled a great variety of fabrics to pick out the shirt that would feel just right against Mark's skin.

In those little cafés where we went to lunch, Mark always engaged in lengthy discussions with waiters. "Can I have that with extra lettuce and no mayo?" "Last time I ate here, they used some other, some different kind of avocado, and the guacamole turned out so much better." "Yes, garlic *and* onions, please. No, no, I'm quite sure, it won't be too overpowering. If you put in the right amount, of course."

He was so particular that I felt flattered that he'd chosen me.

He won't put just anything on or in his body, I thought with admiration. Unlike me, or my mother, my uncle, or even Dena and her successful friends. Dena could say, "Where did you buy those? Kmart? I would've never bought anything at Kmart." But she didn't mean it the way Mark did. She thought that buying inferior things would betray her lack of cultivation, while Mark, as I saw it, was truly unable to use inferior things.

Sometimes we shopped for things for me. But in this case, Mark tended to choose clothes that would "look good" rather than "feel comfortable." He was tactful and didn't want to embarrass me with questions about which designs or materials I preferred. He knew that I had no idea. He was just as tactful about the money. I developed a habit of sneaking away as soon as we reached the cash register and Mark produced his credit card to pay for the things he'd chosen for me. I feigned an interest in one or another item, running my hand over a collection of scarves or lifting and turning over a hat, while desperately trying to ignore, and thus negate, the moment of the transaction. Mark didn't seem to notice this. Soon after I moved in, he said, "Whenever you need money for something, just ask me." I never did. My heart would start beating and my tongue would go numb at the mere thought of asking Mark for money. Nor could I use his credit card, except to pay for groceries or other things he asked me to buy. The credit card was a little spy hiding in a wallet and recording every purchase to present Mark with a revealing statement. And Mark was very scrupulous about bills. "Wait, wait, wait," he often said when reading a restaurant bill. "We didn't order two appetizers? Did we?" A wave of intense shame would wash over me every time I imagined Mark scrutinizing the credit card bill. "Wait, wait, wait," he could say. "What did you buy for $39.99? A sweater? But didn't we buy you a sweater last month? You needed another one? Why?" When I needed to buy something for myself, such as medicine or underwear, I took the money from the fast-melting savings from my dentist's job. Mark must have noticed that I didn't take any money, but he never asked how I managed without it. I accepted this with gratitude, as a sign of his tact. Not that the lack of money bothered me that much; I didn't like to go shopping without Mark anyway, or even to walk the streets alone.

Now that I was a resident of the neighborhood that I knew so well from my frequent visits to Mark, it looked different to me, strange, and for some reason less welcoming. There were people who owned it, who seemed to have the right to be there, and to regard that right with elegant nonchalance. And there were people like me who struggled to fit in, and didn't fit in, precisely because they had to struggle. Often I would catch my reflection in a store window or the polished wall of the elevator of Mark's building and be amazed at how different I looked from other residents. It wasn't even my coat that betrayed me as a Russian, as a recent immigrant, but rather the strained expression in my eyes, the mouth not accustomed to smiling, the lack of ease, the lack of happiness, the lack of contentment. I would try to evoke pride at being different, at being "authentic," as Mark liked to say, but the pride wouldn't come. I was embarrassed to be a Russian, and ashamed of being embarrassed.

The only place where I had some sort of interaction with the other residents of Mark's building was the elevator, or the curved path leading to the elevator from the lobby. Most treated me as if I were invisible; they turned to the door as soon as they entered the elevator, and rode in silence, their shoulders a little tense, looking impatient to break from the transitional state of riding between the floors and engage in whatever activities they were heading toward. I watched their backs, feet, and purses from the far-right corner, slumped against the wall, hoping that somebody would talk to me or pay me just a little bit of attention, and at the same time afraid of that attention and wishing to remain invisible.

There were only two people in the whole of Mark's building who seemed to notice me. One was a strange, sickly looking woman in her fifties who lived on the eighth floor. She was always wearing men's pants, knitted hats pulled over her eyes, and a shabby, shapeless long coat that looked a little like mine. She darted for the opposite corner as soon as she entered the elevator and stood there slumped, never nodding or smiling at other people. When I first caught her looking my way, I thought she was just deep in thought, but then I realized that she was looking at me. Her stare was oddly intent and respectful, as if I were an object in a museum and she had to study me very carefully so that she wouldn't miss any details. Her big, slightly protruding eyes glistened in the dim glow of the elevator light, looking awkwardly animated in her pasty, immobile face. Her stare was weird but rather kind, and warm, and I felt strangely reassured whenever I felt it on me. Whenever I rode in the elevator, I wished that the "woman in the hat"—as I took to calling her— would be there too.

I couldn't say the same thing of the second person that noticed me in the building, Bruno, one of the doormen. Every time I had to pass through the lobby, I secretly prayed that Bruno wouldn't be there, that he would be off or sick or, better yet, dead.

Bruno wasn't his real name, wasn't in fact even close, but Mark called him that, insisting that "Bruno the doorman" sounded just right. Bruno didn't seem to mind; he responded to his new name with an approving smile and a wink, as if it were an in-joke between him and Mark. He never smiled at me though. Whenever I passed through the lobby, his broad, oily face, which pushed over the tight collar of his uniform like rising dough, assumed a strict and determined expression. Before I moved in with Mark, he would always stop me when I walked in, even though I had been there two or three times a week, even though he'd seen me with Mark countless times before. "Can I help you, miss?" he would hiss at me, accentuating the double *s*.

"Miss! Miss! Hello!" he shouted every time, when I foolishly tried to sneak to the elevator without looking at him. "What apartment, miss?" My whole body would feel slack and heavy, rocking in waves of rage and humiliation as I finally turned to him. "Penthouse B," I would say. "Penthouse B. That would be Mr. Schneider," he'd mutter, pretending to consult his book. I'd nod, feeling the treacherous tears rise up in my throat, fighting them back by biting on my lower lip and making quick swallowing movements, just as I had done years ago when Vovik called me Tatiana Doomer. Bruno would half-turn from me as if he were about to do something secret, and punch up Mark's number, slowly, digit by digit. "Your name, miss?" he'd ask me every single time.

"Tatyana."

"Tat'ya what?"

"Tatyana."

"There is a Tatti Anna for you, sir."

He'd assume a solemn expression as he waited for Mark's reply. Every time, I saw that he wished that Mark would say "no," so he could turn to me and announce that there was no need for "a Tatti Anna" upstairs. And every time, as he signaled permission for me to go up, there was a promise in his eyes that the day would come when I wouldn't get that permission. He quit stopping me after I had moved in, but the promise in his eyes stayed, and Bruno never missed the chance to convey it to me. You don't belong here, he seemed to remind me, whenever I managed to forget it myself.

Sometimes I would peer into Mark's eyes and look for a "You don't belong here" there. As the heady haze of our first weeks together began to clear up, I would often find myself wondering what place I had in his life. For a while it seemed to depend on his mood, which in its turn depended on other unrelated-to-me factors. His best mood came after a gym session or jogging. He would walk in whistling a tune from an Italian opera, plop on the couch, and yell out in a happy and even playful voice, "Tea, please, a nice big mug of tea, a sandwich, and a remote control." He liked me to sit next to him while he watched TV, and he liked to squeeze my shoulders or pat my arm, happy to remind himself that I was there. Mark's worst mood followed the dentist and the shrink visits. On the nights after his therapy sessions his head seemed stuffed with little tampons, just like his mouth was after his visits to the dentist—half-frozen, slowly getting off anesthesia, starting to hurt. He would slump on the couch and stay there with a closed book in his hands, looking pensive and irritated. I felt that my presence at those moments annoyed and even oppressed him. He would look away when I entered the room, and he would wince if I asked him something. "Can't you see that I'm reading," he'd say. His face seemed to change in those moments. His nose grew longer, harsher, barely recognizable. I'd go to the kitchen and sit there studying the tiny cracks in the brick wall or the sluggish movements of the minute hand on the clock, waiting for Mark to start wanting me again, terrified that it would never happen. What if he fell for me by mistake? I thought every time. What if I'm not the woman for him after all, and he is just slowly realizing it, after these dentist and shrink visits? Eventually Mark would emerge from the bedroom, call for me, and seem happy to see me, but the strain of waiting through his bad moods made it difficult for me to enjoy his presence afterward.

I felt the most comfortable on Tuesdays, the day Mark spent at Bard College, and I stayed alone. With Mark out, I wasn't a bothersome houseguest anymore. I felt that I really lived in this apartment, that everything belonged to me and I could do whatever I wanted. Happy energy would fill me as soon as I heard the low drone of the elevator taking Mark down and away. I'd hum a cheerful tune, dart back and forth through the kitchen and living room, unable to choose from a medley of opportunities Mark's absence afforded me.

Usually I would start with spying on our neighbors. I'd go onto the terrace and stop by the low fence dividing the neighbors' part of the terrace from ours. The door to their apartment was often open, so I could catch a whiff of the strangers' lives while peeking over the railing. In the mornings I'd smell coffee and fresh oranges and hear some radio chatter. Later in the day, some jazz or scraps of a foreign dialogue from the VCR, soft laughter and an aroma of basil.

When I asked Mark what his neighbors did, he said that they were both teaching either philosophy or psychology, and were old, boring, and not very friendly. I didn't find them boring. The woman, when she appeared on the terrace at last, was wearing a big man's sweater and stretched-out leggings. She had a dark, wrinkly face and gray hair gathered on top of her head in a small, messy pile. She was crouching by the railing tending to her herbs and talking on the phone in a shrill, loud voice. She spoke of somebody called "Dear Charlotte" and she ended the conversation with the words "Fuck the idiots then!" I named the woman "Dear Charlotte" and decided that I liked her.

Her husband never swore, but I liked him even more. He was tall, gawky, and almost entirely bald, if not for the feathery wisps that seemed forgotten behind his ears. I named him Gosha, because he resembled Gosha, the baby ostrich from a Russian children's show. Whenever I saw Gosha on the terrace, he was sitting in the wooden armchair with a book, wrapped in a plaid blanket as if it were cold. His face was so animated that it seemed to me that I could read along in his book simply by watching him. I could tell the emotional passages from the intellectual ones by the way he moved his brows. I could tell when he disagreed with the author: he'd run his forefinger up and down his forehead and scrunch his mouth. And when he read something funny, he'd throw his head back and laugh out loud. I fell in love with the way he laughed. From time to time he would put the book down, throw his head back, and shake with his mouth wide open. Sometimes he laughed so hard that he had to wipe the tears from his eyes with the backs of both hands. He had the true, genuine laugh of a happy man, happy not because he was naïve and thought that everybody around him was good, but because he was so kind that he forgave people their follies and loved them anyway. The kindness seemed to drip from him, like moisture from a certain type of cake. Sometimes I wished that he were a cake and I could sink my teeth in and become just as happy, peaceful, and kind as he.

If the neighbors weren't home, I'd go inside, plop into Mark's favorite chair, press the power button on the remote, and flip through the channels in search of my favorite thing—commercial breaks. With Mark in, I could never watch them, because he always cruised the channels to avoid the commercials. Commercials to me were never boring. They were all about magic in ordinary life. People performed the most ordinary actions and achieved the most miraculous results. A tiny diaper would absorb buckets of mysterious blue liquid. A car would drive through a mountain range or even ascend to the sky. A woman would lather a dab of shampoo into her drab hair, and seconds later would toss a thick, glossy mane of different color, length, and texture. Another woman would unwrap a piece of chocolate, bring it to her mouth, close her unfairly white teeth on it, and a second later achieve an orgasm. I caught myself developing fleeting desires for whatever product was touted on screen. I wanted to fly above the mountains in a brand-new, clean car. Then I wanted to smash that brand-new car to pieces, pop a stick of spearmint chewing gum into my mouth, and feel perfectly cool about it. I wanted to run across the woods and deserts in new snow-white sneakers. I wanted my hair to turn glossy, blond, and long with a single dab of shampoo. I wanted cereal, chocolate, beer, pasta sauce, muffins spread with melting I Can't Believe It's Not Butter! spread and I desperately craved those wonderful, juicy cubes of dog food. The latter reminded me how hungry I was—the particularity and confidence of Mark's relationship with food usually made me too intimidated to eat in his presence.

Mark's kitchen was a rich place to explore. He would often visit the gourmet department of a food store and be seduced by some foreign-looking jar, which ended up gathering dust in one of his kitchen cabinets or sweating in the back of the fridge. I would climb up on a chair and perform an act of liberation, pulling these jars out into the light, tearing off the protective tape, unscrewing the lids. I would scoop tiny bits of food from the jars and say, "Exquisite!" mimicking the orgasmic beauties from the TV food ads. "Ooh . . . such a sensual delight!" "Umm . . . so good!" "More . . . give me more."

My next step was to taste from the careful array of opened bottles in the bar. I'd never seen Mark drinking, yet there were at least twenty different bottles in his apartment. Most often I would take a sip right from the bottle, stir it in my mouth, raise one brow, and pronounce the verdict: "Full-bodied . . . maybe just a little bit too full-bodied." "Bold and rich!" I'd have no idea what it was I'd just said and I'd giggle at the sheer senselessness of my words. Sometimes sips of those rich, passionate, and full-bodied drinks made me bold enough to make a little party for myself. I would spread some stuff from the jars onto some stale crackers or pieces of flat bread, heap them together on a plate, pour myself a little drink (not too much, so as not to provoke questions from Mark), put one of Mark's hats or scarves on, tune the radio to the jazz station, and go out onto the terrace, pretending to be both a poised and glamorous hostess and her poised and glamorous guest. "Here," I'd say to myself. "Try this. Just a drop of our divine Amaretto Disaronno will make your dreams come true." And I'd graciously accept the drink, and then just as graciously accept a bite of "our exquisite melt-in-your-mouth" cracker spread with some brown, oily, sharp-smelling paste. One drink was always more than enough to make me giddy.

Central Park, observed with a drink in my hand, looked like an enchanted forest surrounded by fairy-tale castles. The few streets that made up the grid around the big park-adjacent buildings I took to calling the castle grounds. The supermarket, the coffee shops, the stores, the movie theater belonged to the castle grounds, and all the people who worked there as chefs, waiters, movie ushers, book-sellers, or doormen, like Bruno, were there to serve the castles' inhabitants.

And I . . . where was my place in that fairy-tale hierarchy? A few reassuring swigs of my drink would give me the answer.

I was the princess from another land living with the great man, the prince, in the upper tower of the castle! I was different from other castle inhabitants, but not because I was inferior. Indeed, I was superior to all the people I saw in Mark's building and on the streets surrounding it. I was a princess from another land, a big love of the prince, and they were just castle people. Yes, that was it. That felt right.

I longed for Mark to come home to give further reinforcement to my claims to greatness.

"You look very nice today," he would say, having finished his dinner and extinguished the TV screen.

"Simple, elegant, very authentic. You know what, switch off that lamp and dim that other one to your left. No, don't switch it off, just dim it. Yes, like that. Now take your skirt off. Always the skirt first. Take a few steps away. No, no, not too far away from me. Yes, like that. And could you turn on that little lamp and move it to your right, please? Wonderful, now you're in a pool of light. No, panty hose first, then the blouse. Yes. Now you can unbutton it. A little slower, please. Oh, yes, just like that. Fantastic. You're great. You look great. Oh . . . now come to me . . . No, not there, up here. Yes, just like that. Yes. You see? You're doing great. Much better than before."

He is wonderful, I'd think each time, overwhelmed with relief and gratitude. Mark must have guessed how inept I was, and he didn't express any annoyance or disappointment but instead instructed me thoroughly and kindly, like a teacher, or rather like a movie director. I didn't have to try and guess how all those things were done and which way he liked them. I didn't have to be afraid to fail. The pressure was lifted, and I just did as told, patiently attuning my body to his needs and partialities, savoring Mark's praise, glowing in my success. "Look at him, look at him stare at me! I must be really good. I must be wonderful. Look at him rush to me. Listen to him pant. He must feel great. I must be great!"

I failed at just one small aspect of the whole deal. And that was my own pleasure. I didn't know where it had wandered, but it was never present in Mark's bedroom. Or possibly all my energy went into doing my best to carry out his commands, making sure that I'd do it exactly the way he wanted.

"One thing American men are really good at is oral sex," Dena claimed. "They know that they must do it, they know how to do it, they are not lazy, and the most important thing of all—they seem to enjoy it themselves."

But Mark didn't seem to enjoy it. The one time he did it to me, I felt his reluctance and was tortured by it so much that the faint pleasure I had felt in the beginning made me feel very guilty and then disappeared altogether. "Do you usually enjoy it?" Mark asked. "Not really," I lied. He left me alone, and once again I was grateful for his tact and understanding. He must have thought that I wasn't ready yet. He would teach me how to believe in myself as a wonderful lover first, and then, just as patiently and thoroughly as he had taught me how to make sex enjoyable for him, he would teach me how to enjoy it.

Chapter Nine

"Our journey with F.M. is quite amusing," Polina wrote on September 5, a day after their arrival in Baden-Baden. "He told me that he has hopes. I didn't answer to that, but knew that it won't happen."

When they entered their boardinghouse at night, the German maid (requisite high cheekbones, a light brown mole on a firm chin, white apron, and yellow kerchief) asked them where they wanted their tea. They had booked two separate rooms, and Dostoevsky threw a nervous look at Polina, afraid that she would refuse to have tea with him.

"We'll have the tea in my room," Polina said.

He had been so thoughtful and caring throughout their journey. He peered into her face, checking for signs of sadness. He offered to buy her drinks and ices and sweets, as if they would dispel her sadness! He asked if she was cold or tired all the time. He cited poetry to her. He told her jokes and even engaged in silly pranks, all the while hunting her smile. He trembled whenever their sleeves touched. And she brushed against his sleeve quite often, just to see him tremble. It felt good, very good to be showered with all that attention, to have a man at her feet, to feel such power. And to think about it, all she'd had to do was to dump him, to fall in love with another man! It was precisely this thought that was getting Polina increasingly angry. He obviously knew how to treat her right, and he was capable of doing that—why then couldn't he have been this way before? He said he hadn't realized how bad their relationship used to be for her. But hadn't he? Didn't she tell him, didn't she complain many times back in St. Petersburg? Wasn't he treating her badly then simply because she was his and he knew that he could?

"We had our tea around ten p.m. Having finished the tea, I, tired from the busy day, lay down and asked F.M. to sit next to me. I felt good. I took his hand and kept it in mine for a long time. He said that he felt very good like that."

In some ways this Baden-Baden room is different from the one Polina had in Paris, in other ways it is very much alike. The warm glow of candles illuminates a modest bed under white covers, a dresser, a window crisscrossed with the shadows of dark branches. A sliver of moon hiding between the black leaves. There is a round table with the remains of the tea. A teapot. Fine porcelain cups. Some crumbs on the plates. Dostoevsky sips his tea and munches on the last piece of cake, cookie, biscuit? All of that without ceasing to talk. Heady from Polina's presence, heady from the agonizing hope, he continues telling her jokes and stories as he did all day. But now she yawns, covering her mouth with a cupped hand, pushes her chair away from the table, stands up, and walks slowly to the bed. He stops talking, the unfinished sentence crushed in his teeth along with the last bite of the biscuit.

The dark shadow on the wall follows Polina's movements, making her figure appear fuller, more feminine, more enticing. She— aware of his stare—sits down on the edge of the bed and begins undoing her shoes. Could those be the same shoes that tramped the streets of the Latin Quarter in a desperate search for Salvador?

She undoes the buttons, slowly, tugs off her shoes, until at last, from the stuffy leathery depths, emerge her feet. Those famous feet—narrow, long, with straight, slender toes—capable of leaving "maddening" imprints. They seem even more narrow now, all pulled together by the tight stockings, which are a little damp and darkened on the soles. She pulls on the material on her heel to unstick it from skin, she smooths the creases around her ankles, she wiggles her toes. Then she stretches out on the bed, on her side, facing Dostoevsky, her feet innocently peeking from under her skirt.

He sits there, pretending to be deeply engrossed in the ornament the crumbs make on the table, his shoulders slouchy, his bald patch gleaming in the candlelight. He reminds her of a dog who is unsure what to expect from his master, sweet words of praise or a kick in the ribs.

"I asked F.M. to sit down next to me."

She wrote that sentence as if to drive Dostoevsky's biographers crazy. Cruel, cold, calculating! To ask a man all crazed and shaking with desire to sit down by the bed where the object of desire is voluptuously stretched, with no intention of satisfying that desire!

An evil woman!

"Come, Fedor Mikhailovich, sit by me."

He rushes to her call, like a dog suddenly promised a treat, all but wagging its tail. He sits on a chair facing the bed. His knees are just a foot away from her chest, which stirs slightly with each breath under the thick cloth of her travel dress. He wants to say something, but the words are trapped in his stiff, aching body. He is trying to focus on her face, but his vision betrays him and, bouncing off her dry half-open lips, it goes down her pale neck toward the tiny, dark hollow between her collarbones, farther down, where it loses itself in the rich folds of dress until it reaches her feet, her toes forming two delicate triangles, so helpless and so alive. He could catch them and squeeze them in his hands, and then lean over and press his mouth hard to her toes, and rub his face against the cold and slightly damp surface of her soles, smelling of smothered leather. He checks himself just in time and brings his eyes back to her face, terrified that she will sense what he is thinking, get angry, and shoo him away.

But he, too involved in his struggle, doesn't notice how her body relaxes under his stare, softens up, liquefies, aching in the process just as his body does. She doesn't toy with him anymore.

"I took his hand and held it in mine for a long time." She smiles, stroking his hard, lumpy hand. It feels good, and it's getting better, although she doesn't quite understand why.

"I feel very good sitting like this with you." The words slip off his lips, and he is terrified again. Because what he means is that he feels too good, he can barely hold himself back now. But she thinks that he means that he feels very good just like that. Basking in a mild, slow-burning desire. It's a sensual peace, not a sensual war. She knows that he wants more, she guesses that she wants more too, but it is in wanting more, as she sees now, that lies the greatest pleasure, not in getting it. She thinks that he feels the same way.

"He understands me."

And suddenly she is awash with tenderness for him. He might have been wrong in the past, but he was so good to her in Paris, so kind and unselfish. Always there when she needed him, never trying to take advantage. Warm, tangy tears come up into her eyes and her throat. "Fedor Mikhailovich, I . . . I was so cruel to you in Paris. . . . Yes, don't interrupt. I was very bad, very selfish, unkind. But, believe me, please believe me, I know that you're my friend, and I'm your friend too. I won't hurt you again, I promise."

He doesn't understand what she is talking about. The sound of her voice, low but softened by tears, reaches him in painful waves of desire. Her body is moving toward him, expanding, getting warmer.

There are her feet, so close he can almost catch the pungent smell. His head will explode if he doesn't kiss her feet this instant!

He rushes forward, knocking over the chair, but just as he makes that final step dividing him from her body, he trips on her shoes. He grasps the footboard to restore his balance. The moment is lost.

"What was that?" she asks.

"You don't know what just happened to me," he says in great agitation. "I was going to kiss your foot."

But she knows exactly what happened. Or she thinks that she knows. Never, never was he her friend. Never compassionate and understanding, but simply willing to play the game by her rules for a while, wait for the right moment, for the moment when she would yield to him. A few more minutes of her weakness and he would be on top of her, inside her, pushing and fidgeting until he had reached his release. And then he would sigh with contentment. The familiar satiated expression would spread all over his face. He would be free. But she would be full of his filth, dripping filth, branded with filth. And she would have lost. The game would go back to his rules again, her life back to the confinement of being a mistress. "You know what, Polya. I think I saw Turgenev on the esplanade the other day. We should be extra careful that he doesn't catch sight of you," he would soon be saying to her. Or "No, Polya, I don't think I will be able to see you next week, my sister-in-law is coming to town and the deadline for the new issue is approaching." Or "Come to me, Polya. Let me help to undo your coat. We have to hurry. We only have an hour and a half today."

She was lucky to put her guard up in time. She would be careful to hold on to her own game now. She would continue to insist on the "brother and sister" condition, pretending to be embarrassed and even insulted if he took a step to go too far. She would let him sit on her bed while turning her face away. She would let him kiss her, but she'd remove his hands from her body. She would shoo him out of her room, but forget to lock the door. She would do whatever she could to ensure that he stayed by her side and on his knees.

This is not a good game, Polina. What might seem rewarding in the beginning will eventually exhaust you, sadden you, make you despise Dostoevsky, make him hate you. I want to say, Don't go there, but you won't be able to hear me anyway.

A few months into my new life I yielded to the countless demands and reproaches and invited my uncle, Maya, and Dena to see Mark's place. We did it in his absence.

Mark had never expressed any wish to meet my family, and frankly I felt relieved at this, because whenever I fantasized about bringing them together, it made me break out in a cold sweat. In my first scenario, we took my uncle and Maya out for dinner in one of the restaurants in Mark's neighborhood. The whole affair was a quiet failure of forced American friendliness faced with Russian embarrassment and incomprehension. My second scenario, in which Mark and I went to my uncle's house, enfolded as a full-blown disaster, with me acquiring a sudden X-ray sensitivity and seeing my relatives through Mark's eyes and him through theirs. They would all stand by the front door to greet us, sweaty and overdressed, my uncle wearing somebody else's clothes, Maya sporting one of the three bright angora sweaters she'd recently bought on sale, Dena trying to impress Mark with a short skirt and the large VERSACE logo on her blouse stretched out by her breasts. Hopefully, she wouldn't bring Danik. Mark had mentioned that he was never especially fond of children; he definitely wouldn't be fond of the obnoxious Danik. The food and wine would be horrible, even though my uncle would have spent half of his monthly food stamps on them for our sake. A nice bottle of French wine that Mark would bring would be lost among peach, cherry, and grape Manischewitz. Imperfect gems of my aunt's cooking would vie for Mark's attention with smoked salmon, red caviar, chopped liver, boiled tongue, and the fifty-piece sushi tray that Dena, with any luck, wouldn't bring. Out of politeness Mark would agree to taste a bit of this and that, but my uncle and Maya would want to show their hospitality and force more on him. I hoped Mark wouldn't gag. And that he would compliment the food with some easy-to-comprehend gesture. It might have been more or less tolerable if we could just consume the meal in silence and say goodbye—but no, there would be an obligatory dinner conversation. "Hav var you?" my uncle would say, beaming, expecting to be showered with compliments for his fluency in English. Hopefully, Mark wouldn't say, "Excuse me?" Hopefully, my uncle wouldn't have mastered anything else to say. Hopefully, Danik, who hopefully wouldn't be there at all, wouldn't suddenly yell from under the table, "Suck my dick!" (He did that once, during Dena's birthday party.) Afterward, in the quiet of Mark's place, Mark would try to shake off his disgust and would look relieved that he was back in his world, while I would hate myself for sharing his disgust and betraying my relatives, who had meant well and tried hard, and most frightening of all, I would have to hate Mark for making me betray them.

"Mark is not fond of entertaining or going out," I lied to my uncle and Dena, and invited them to come when he wouldn't be home. On two consecutive Tuesdays, I offered two separate tours of Mark's apartment for my uncle and Maya, and for Dena.

My uncle and Maya took off their shoes as they entered and then tiptoed around the apartment slowly and respectfully, as if they were tourists in a museum. "What's that?" my uncle asked Maya in an intimidated whisper about one or another object, and she shushed him, because she had no idea what it was but didn't want to admit it. They didn't pose any questions to me, treating me with respectful restraint, as if I had become one of the objects in the apartment. Sometimes I would volunteer some information, feigning an owner's poise, blending myself with Mark: "Look, this is the terrace door, it's nice and breezy on the terrace. We like to have our coffee there." And my uncle would nudge Maya and say, "Uh-huh, uh-huh, you see how they live?" When they were leaving, Maya said, "What can I tell you, Tanya? You've done very well for yourself."

Dena started her visit by marching to the center of the living room and taking a quick look around. Then she said, "Just what I thought. Now, watch me. With my eyes closed, I will tell you what he's got. There is Prozac in the bathroom cabinet, vitamins and soy milk in the fridge, Plato on the upper bookshelf, Derrida on eye level, and an unfinished mystery novel by the toilet." She was right on all counts, except one. There wasn't any mystery novel by the toilet, but instead a colorful brochure from the recently opened health-food store.

I couldn't say what it was that was so annoying about the accuracy of her guesses, but they upset me more than anything Dena had said before. Sometimes, I too wondered why Mark cared about his physical and mental health so much. A great writer was supposed to be self-destructive, wasn't he? I could hardly imagine Dostoevsky jogging, gulping down protein smoothies, or summoning the shrink to relieve him of his sadness or agitation. Sadness and agitation made Dostoevsky grab his quill and write! Madness was the core of his writing! What would he have written if relieved of them? Gambling manuals? Engineering tracts?

I could hardly bear Dena's large, agile figure moving about Mark's apartment, filling it with the sharp, sticky smell of her perfume, flapping with the folds of her glossy leather coat, parading her wisdom. I could hardly make myself offer her a drink. I had to force myself to offer her coffee, praying that she'd refuse. She didn't.

"So, tell me, is he seeing his doctor a lot? And his shrink?" Dena continued as I moved into Mark's tiny kitchen to prepare the coffee. She sat with her butt firmly planted on Mark's couch, her thick knees gleaming under the hem of her straight gray skirt.

"No, not a lot," I said. "When he needs to."

"Right. When he needs to. That they do. That they do. They won't miss their hour at the gym, or their testicular exam. They go out of their way to prolong their sorry lives, at the same time fucking them up so badly that those lives become hardly worthy of prolonging."

Her eyes chased me around the kitchen as she spoke, as did the piercing sound of her voice. "They, they, they . . ." I'd never noticed it before, but with her beaky nose and her hair cut very short, Dena looked amazingly like our grandmother.

"They will go and cry at their shrinks then. Not because they need help, no. They know perfectly well that nobody will help them. They just want the attention, the pampering. And where do I go? Where? I can't afford a fucking shrink. I can't afford to cry. I'm expected to pamper, not to be pampered . . . while *they,* yes, *they* cry at their shrinks, cry as much as they want, fuck up their lives and the lives of others, and then take their time crying about it."

I was too upset to ponder Dena's words, too anxious to think about her at all. I just wanted her to stop talking. "Here is the coffee," I said, assembling the shaking, clinking coffee cups on a tray. Shut up and drink it! I had the urge to add.

"What can I tell you, Tanya?" Dena said before leaving. "Hold on to your horse."

I spent the following days trying to interpret that sentence, and failing that, trying to tell myself that Dena was stupid. Or else she was jealous. She might have fallen off her horse, but that didn't mean I would. Mark and I were good together. I didn't have to hold on to that stupid horse, whatever that meant, because I was perfect for Mark.

Or was I?

One morning, a couple of months after moving in with Mark, I decided to ask him a question that had been bothering me for a long time. Why did Bruno the doorman hate me?

Mark had just returned from his jogging, had taken a shower, and was enjoying his second daily cup of coffee—the situation, as I'd learned, that made him most disposed to talking. I told him how Bruno used to stop me in the lobby before, and what expression he had now when I passed him to go to the elevator.

Mark laughed so hard that he had to put his cup down so as not to splash the coffee. "You do a wonderful impression of Bruno," he said, reaching for a slice of peeled mango on a plate. He liked his second coffee with slices of fruit. "When you say 'misss' it's just great."

"Why does he hate me? He's supposed to hate you, not me."

"Why would he hate me?"

"Well, it's obvious," I said, summoning the scattered bits of hated Marxist theory that had been pushed at me at school, and which I suddenly didn't find so stupid. "Look at you and look at him. You're two men, almost the same age. You live here, in the penthouse. He has to commute from Queens. You pass through the door. He has to open the door for you. You call him by the wrong name. He has to smile at you. You give him his Christmas bonus, and he has to be all flattering and grateful, even though he knows that the amount you just gave him you could easily spend on one dry-cleaning bill. He probably does hate you, Mark. He is just afraid of you, so he takes it all out on me."

"You couldn't be more wrong," Mark said after laughing some more. "Not only doesn't Bruno hate me, but he is in love with me, he adores me, in a kind of old-fashioned lackey/master love. The two other doormen, Roberto and Mike, they are doing it for the money, but Bruno, Bruno has his heart in it. He was born to be a lackey. And since the situation of having many masters instead of one is confusing for him, he has picked a few tenants who in his opinion are worthy of being his masters."

"So you're one of those, the worthy tenants?"

"Correct."

"But how does that explain why he hates me?"

"Easy. He doesn't see you as a woman for me. For a lackey, the only source of his pride is in the achievements of his master. He wants nothing better than to feel proud of me. And you are, you are just not the stereotypical prize woman he would want for me."

Why? Why? Why? I longed to ask Mark, but he had already finished his coffee, picked up a magazine, and was heading in the direction of the toilet. The question remained unanswered. What was it about me that made me unworthy of Mark in Bruno's eyes? My slight figure, my unimpressive face, my foreign accent, my wrong clothes, my awareness of all the above?

Being around Mark's friends made me feel especially intimidated. The first thing that struck me about the parties was their uprightness. We'd enter lean, high-ceilinged rooms filled with lean, elegant furniture and tall, slender people either standing with tall long-stemmed glasses in their hands or sitting in the tall chairs keeping their backs very straight. Men—older, sparkling, with elegant, judgmental intelligence and clean, white teeth. Women—just as intelligent-looking as the men, with the added advantage of beauty and simple, yet faultless clothes. They were people of the same perfect race as the ones I used to admire on the streets. But locked in the same room with them, I felt exposed, with no place to hide and nothing at hand to help me mask my inferiority. I spent hours before each party armed with Dena's discarded cosmetics and old fashion magazines, trying to make myself look just a little bit more like them, trying to conceal my inferiority under a lovelier facade. In the dark, warped space of Mark's bathroom, I would become possessed with an idea that some tiny trick, some dab of lipstick or mascara, could make all the difference, just like it did in TV commercials. At times I thought that I was close to succeeding, that my face was almost there, in the realm of right, beautiful faces, that my charcoaled eyes had just the right amount of mysteriousness, that my contoured lips had just enough sexual appeal. I felt both proud and subdued, and I was afraid to move, as if I carried on my face an expensive and extremely breakable collection of, say, rare porcelain. Yet I could see that I needed something else, a final stroke to complete the magical transformation. The problem was that I never could find that last stroke. Did I need one more touch of dusty orange blush? A dab of peach lipstick? A hint of olive eye shadow? But when I made my choice and applied that last touch at last, I saw that instead of adding the lacking fragment of beauty, it had instead destroyed the blissful "almost" state I'd spent hours achieving.

"Oh, will you stop it," Mark would say as he passed the site of my battle for beauty. "Simplicity is your asset . . . the only thing you might need is some whitening toothpaste. Remind me to get some for you." I had an urge to grab a lipstick and cross out my reflection in the mirror with two fat brown lines. I scrubbed all of the makeup off instead, scrubbed it hard, washing off the pathetic pleas to be good enough written all over my face in charcoal and peach.

My face would still be burning from intense scrubbing as I silently moved through the long rooms hovering at Mark's side, trying to remember to keep my back straight, trying to be alert so that I understood the English, in case somebody wished to speak to me. Usually nobody wished to speak to me, and if they did, it took me too long to decipher the question and gather my thoughts for the answer. I saw just how dumb and dull I must have seemed to those people.

I was pretty sure Mark's friends shared Bruno's opinion. Some of them had known Mark for many years, had seen him with beautiful and sophisticated women, the women from the photographs in his leather bags. They must have wondered what it was that Mark saw in me. I noticed men assessing my sexual potential, and women watching them do that. What if Mark saw their reaction as clearly as I did? What if he wondered what it was that he had seen in me too? What if he became embarrassed with me? And what if later, when we were alone and Mark was in one of his dark moods, he would finally agree that I wasn't the woman for him after all? I longed to slump on the couch and find comfort in eating, as I would at my uncle's or Dena's parties, but the food, trimmed and toothpicked, just as upright as everything else, strove to be inconspicuous. It was either served in elegant, unfriendly arrangements with the accompaniment of confusing silverware, or it resided on little serving dishes hidden from view by people's backs, or it circled the room elusively on trays protected by waiters. I spent most of the time skulking next to massive bookcases, feigning interest in the books, watching in disbelief at how perfectly Mark blended in with the party guests. He moved around the room, partaking of conversation, laughter, smiles, contributing his own, never shy or out of place, swimming smoothly among them, swimming away from me. "I loved your book, I loooved your book," a woman with enormous nipples pushing against her simple brown T-shirt was bleating to Mark. Her nipples looked as if they'd been removed from a baby bottle and pasted to her body, and maybe they had been, but Mark seemed excited to talk to her! He was flushing a wide, content, perfectly genuine smile.

"Hey, haven't seen you in a long time, pal," he was saying to a balding long-haired man in a green corduroy jacket, having slapped him on his ugly green back. This man had just asked me a question about the severity of the Moscow climate and walked away before waiting for an answer. I hated him! But Mark didn't. "Your last book was pretty good," Mark was saying to him. "Hey, yours wasn't bad either. That scene, you know, where the mother chases the father into the basement . . . Strong stuff." And Mark laughed happily at the green man's words, laughed so hard that his eyes narrowed into wet, quivering slits. Mark was turning into one of them, a perfect stranger to me. I couldn't share his excitement, his smiles, his poise. At those moments, I wondered if I knew him at all, if the deep knowledge of him I believed I possessed wasn't just an illusion.

But once we got home after a party he'd turn into my familiar Mark again. "God, I'm tired" or "The food was awful, wasn't it?" he would say, and ask me to make some decaf for us and sit next to him on the couch.

"Remember the man I was talking to in the corner?" Mark would start. "Green jacket? You won't believe how crazy he is! He actually thinks that he is a good writer based on a couple of reasonably good reviews and the sales figures for his book, that for some unexplainable reason have been going up. I haven't met anybody with so little talent. Our Bruno would make a better writer if he chose to write a novel in between opening the door."

Or: "Did you notice Barry Steele, the tall, hawkish man, bald and ugly? What? You don't find him ugly? He's a brilliant record producer, but so crazy! He has a wife—oh, what a bitch—and two mistresses, but he says that he doesn't enjoy sex with any of them. For sex he only uses prostitutes."

"Why does he need mistresses then?"

"To talk!"

"And why two?"

"Oh, that's because Martha, the first one, doesn't appreciate music."

I laughed, finding comfort in the thought that we were together in this, two castaways washed up on an island surrounded by a sea of craziness and bitchiness. I cuddled up to Mark and breathed in his homey, familiar smell, trying to separate it from the strange odors of the party—somebody's strong perfume, tobacco, wine. I kissed him on the mouth, which was sweet and warm from the coffee. I unbuttoned his clothes as if unpeeling all the ugly influences of the strangers layer by layer. I pressed myself to him tighter and tighter, trying to shield our intimacy from the hostile winds that threatened us from the outside. We were good together, very good, I thought. I didn't have to hold on to that stupid Dena's horse. Mark wanted me. Mark loved me. There was only one thing that could bring me closer to him, make our relationship stronger. I had to learn how to read English, so I could understand his work.

My approach was straightforward and stubborn. Every Tuesday, as soon as Mark left (I decided it would be embarrassing and even rude to struggle over a book in its author's presence), I took a copy of his latest novel and my big English-to-Russian dictionary and carried them out on the terrace. There, I sat down in one of the folding chairs, put the dictionary in my lap, put the book on top of the dictionary, and looked up the definition for every single word I didn't understand. Usually I would give up within an hour or so. Mark's sentences were long, endless freight trains carrying heavy loads of unknown words. My knees started to hurt under the weight of the dictionary before I was through with the first sentence. There were too many words that I didn't understand, the definition entries had too many different meanings, and most of them were explained by still other words I didn't understand. A little math exercise that I did right in the margins of the dictionary showed me that since an average Mark sentence had about five or six words I didn't know in it, and each dictionary entry gave me an average of two definitions, I would have to try some sixty-four combinations before I found the one that worked! All that to decode a single sentence! Yet I was determined to succeed.

Once, as I struggled with Mark's book, Dear Charlotte's head appeared over the railing that divided their side of the terrace from ours.

"What are you reading?" she asked me. It was the first time she'd ever spoken to me. I rose in my seat and showed the book to her, terrified that I would mispronounce the title in some horrible way. Dear Charlotte leaned over the dividing wall and squinted at the cover. She was wearing her usual stretched-out sweater covered with fresh dirt. Her hands were dirty too; she must have been doing something with her plants. "Oh, that," she said with a faint trace of disappointment in her voice. "So, how do you find it?"

I shook my head. "I'm not really reading it. I'm just trying to learn how to read in English. So far it's been very hard." She caught sight of my mammoth dictionary then. "Oh, don't tell me you look up every word! That's the worst method ever."

The next Tuesday when she saw me reading, she said, "You know what, come to my place tomorrow, I'll give you better books."

When I rang her doorbell, the "better" books were waiting for me in two crumpled Lord and Taylor bags. All paperbacks, with bright gleaming covers, titles in golden embossed letters—*Sweet*

Enchantment and *A Heart to Come Home To.* I read off the top two and looked up at Dear Charlotte.

"Oh, no, no," she said. "Don't get me wrong. I didn't mean to insult you or the author you were reading. But these are the best for somebody who is just starting to read. The vocabulary is limited and consistent. You will have no choice but to memorize the words and expressions once you see them for the hundredth time. Predictability of plot is another advantage. You will know the line that is about to be said before you see it on the page. They are perfect, believe me."

Gosha waved at me from depth of their living room. "You can trust my wife here. Nobody's read as many romances as she does. Teaching *Beowulf* by day, reading drugstore romances by night. One of those dear, annoying peculiarities I fail to understand about her."

Mark was watching TV when I walked in with the two Lord and Taylor bags. I put the books on the shelf behind the coats in the closet, to read them when Mark wasn't home. I couldn't possibly open a drugstore romance in his presence.

The next Tuesday, I read the whole first chapter of *Sweet Enchantment* in less than an hour, and understood most of it. I couldn't wait for Dear Charlotte to come out on the terrace so that I could tell her.

"Great, wonderful," she said when she appeared on her side of the fence at last, wearing a stained apron over her usual dark pants. "Once you're comfortable enough reading those books, you'll effortlessly graduate to more serious writing." She wiped her hands on the apron and invited me to come over for tea.

They liked their tea dark and strong, and they served it in broad, very thin white cups with tiny sugar cubes in a chipped dark-blue bowl. Plop-plop . . . plop-plop-plop. The sugar cubes made cheerful little sounds as they fell into the tea.

"We buy sugar cubes just to hear this sound," Gosha explained. He had exceptionally bad teeth that looked like tiny, crowded, crooked pine nuts, the worst teeth I'd ever seen in an American mouth. That made me like him even more.

I put two sugar cubes into my cup, pausing to savor each plop.

They asked me questions about Moscow and about my former studies, making them sound like the most fascinating subject. "Isn't it amazing?" Gosha said when I told them how nineteenth-century Russian merchants liked to put a sugar cube between their teeth and suck their tea through it. I knew that my English was muddled and awkward, but it was such a joy to talk in it, or possibly to talk at all, that I embarked on more stories of nineteenth-century Russian habits.

"What were you doing up there, charity work? Entertaining the elderly?" Mark asked me when I came back from their place.

"They're helping me with my English."

"Always a good thing," he commented. There was irritation in his voice, but not too much of it. I felt a hint of guilty pleasure at having enjoyed something that didn't involve him.

Dear Charlotte and Gosha never mentioned him. Whenever I dropped by, they behaved as if Mark didn't exist, as if I lived in the apartment next door all by myself. It felt exciting and not altogether real, as if I were engaged in a make-believe game, and was playing the titillating part of a single immigrant girl who was getting to know this country, this city, and this different life all on her own.

Soon Dear Charlotte and Gosha started inviting me to tea every two or three weeks. They loved to talk about the city, about their favorite paths in the park, their favorite streets and neighborhoods, their favorite buildings and cafés. Dear Charlotte also enjoyed talking about people who lived in our building. I listened to her, marveling how the people of her stories emerged one by one as interesting, complex individuals breaking away from the hostile crowd of strangers created by my perception of them. Once I asked Dear Charlotte about "the woman in the hat" who looked at me in the elevator.

"Oh, Vera! Her name is Vera," Dear Charlotte said. "We don't know much about her, but what we do know is very sad. I heard that decades ago Vera started out as a promising young artist, but some traumatic event made her stop. She even wound up in a hospital."

Dear Charlotte turned to Gosha. "Was it something mental or physical?"

Gosha shrugged. "I don't pry into strangers' lives."

"Oh, and I do? Well, we don't know what happened. It was before we moved in here. All we know is that Vera's been in and out of hospitals and eventually had to move in with her aunt, who took care of her. And now that the aunt is dead, poor Vera has been living like a hermit, slowly fading away. She has a sister who visits once in a while, and the housekeeper drops in to help a couple of times a week. Other than that, I don't think Vera sees anybody at all."

"How old is she?" I asked.

"Fifty? Sixty? Why?"

"And she's never had a man in her life?"

"A lover, you mean? No, not that we know of. Anyway, if she had, my guess is it would've been a woman, not a man."

I couldn't stop thinking about Vera as I lay in bed that night. Old, sick, and alone. Horrible, horrible fate. Like my grandmother. Like my mother, now that I was gone. I was so lucky to have a man in my life. To lie in bed next to somebody warm, breathing, responsive. A man. And a wonderful man at that. A writer. I will be reading Mark's books in no time, I thought before falling asleep. And wouldn't it be wonderful if he started working on his new book just as I learned to understand his writing?

Chapter Ten

Mark didn't start writing until two months after our one-year anniversary. That night, he came home from his therapist and announced that he was ready to write and would start as of the next day. By then I thought it would never happen.

"Wonderful!" I said to him in a squeaky, nasal voice and reached for another Kleenex. I'd been plagued by common colds and other petty illness for the whole year. "You don't take vitamins, and you exercise appallingly little," Mark complained whenever my coughing or nose-blowing erupted in the middle of the night, during one of his favorite TV shows, or at some other inappropriate moment. "You don't eat right," my uncle and aunt commented when I visited them on their birthdays, and on the morning after mine.

But I secretly attributed my constant ailments to boredom.

Our routine never varied. Bard Tuesdays were followed by stay-at-home Wednesdays. Breakfasts of granola by avocado sandwiches for lunch. Mark wasn't fond of air travel, and when we traveled by car it was only to the summer houses of his friends—the same people we saw at the Friday and Saturday parties. The woods, the shores, or the meadows where the houses were located seemed to me coated by the protective film of those people's presence, which made the landscapes look cold and fake—impossible to enjoy.

Even our sex schedule became as predictable as everything else.

"Now come here," Mark would say once or twice a week, often after one or another party, never after the gym or the dentist. "Tell me what a bad little girl you were."

At first, Mark asked me to say anything at all. For the sake of my accent, I guessed. Then, when the novelty of my accent had faded, he demanded more complicated narratives. And if I couldn't come up with the right narrative at once, he would guide me and prod me, as if tuning a radio in search of a suitable station.

"Did your schoolteachers want to fuck you?"

"Um . . . well, one did."

"Did he fuck you?"

"No."

"You can lie!"

"Yes, he fucked me."

"Where?"

"On a camping trip."

A moan.

"Was it your first time?"

"Um . . ."

"It must have been your first time!"

"Yes, it was my first time."

A big moan.

"Details!"

"We did it in complete darkness, behind the tents, by the fallen pine tree, on the warm (warm? why would it be warm?) mushy ground covered with pine needles."

"Great! Great! Did you love it?" Mark moaned with his eyes

closed and his teeth grinding. He had the most stupid expression like that.

"Did . . . you . . . love . . . it?" Mark moaned again. "What is it? Where are you going?"

"I'm sorry, I have to blow my nose."

"Vitamins! How many times do I have to tell you that!"

And then I had to make out as though Vovik had fucked me every Wednesday after school.

"Details! Details! Be evocative!"

"We did it right in his classroom, by the little cabinet filled with framed portraits of Marx, Engels, and Lenin. As we fucked, Vovik would bang his head on the cabinet door, and the door would open, and the portrait of Lenin wearing his famous hat would fall out, and the fallen Lenin would watch us."

"What about now?" Mark would moan. "Do you think Lenin is watching you now?"

The image of Lenin risen from his grave and traveling to New York specially to watch Mark's pale butt writhing between my thighs made me burst out laughing. I turned my face to the side and bit the pillow in vain attempts to stifle the laughter, so as not to spoil it for Mark. It had been a long time since I'd given up on my own pleasure. I knew that I could have more or less enjoyable sex only on Bard Tuesdays, on Mark's couch, alone. In the beginning, I fantasized about the first times with Mark. The first time I felt Mark's beard tickling my neck, the first time I felt his rough hand under my blouse, the first time he came. Those images evoked in the slow silence of the empty apartment worked much better than the same actions performed by Mark. With time, however, my favorite images faded, worn out by frequent use, and I had to resort to my imagination rather than memory. New fantasies would be born, at times involving the men I saw at Mark's parties, at other times my old

Moscow boyfriends, made much smarter, sexier, and more mature. Then, after the last shiver had left my body, I lay there just as lonely as I had been at fourteen. Sometimes the irony of the situation would strike me. I used to dream of the old bearded writer coming to my bed, and now that I could have that writer, real and alive, I preferred to exclude him even from my fantasies. This thought frightened and depressed me, as did my urge to laugh while I was making love to Mark. I tried very hard if not to participate in his enjoyment then at least to focus on it. Here, I forced myself to think, is a truly intimate moment. Mark and I are one, with his most intimate part moving inside me. But lately I'd found myself increasingly uncomfortable. What intimacy could possibly be between us if Mark didn't know or didn't care how I felt?

"Intimacy!" Dena laughed when I complained to her in a crowded lunch place. By the middle of my first year with Mark, I had stopped avoiding Dena's company. I accepted her invitations to have a quick cup of coffee or lunch in a downtown Au Bon Pain, close to the gray bulk of the Chase bank building where she worked. We'd buy some soup in bread bowls, or cups of papery-tasting coffee, and settle down in shiny metallic chairs that mercilessly screeched against the marble floor whenever we moved them. After a few spoonfuls, Dena usually asked me how I was and plunged into her stormy "they" tirade, often without waiting for my answer.

"Intimacy is the last thing they need. The lack of intimacy is what they strive for. You're a foreigner for him, you're exotic, you're different. Don't fool yourself with that 'intimacy' shit. You're different, and that's exactly why he wants you. Some of them believe that we're these wildly erotic creatures, but that's only because out of stupidity we let them do to us what no other woman in her right mind would let them. Or else they think that we're those complacent little fools ready to take their shit at any time."

Dena was breaking off pieces of crust from the edge and using them to sop up the remaining soup at the bottom. She talked of the erotic creatures with her mouth full of wet bread. I would've had an urge to laugh if not for the pain that her words were causing me.

"Some women know how to work it to their advantage. They give the bastards their coveted freedom from intimacy and then just milk them to their bones. Not me. Couldn't do it. No. One day, I just told him to go fuck himself and left."

But Mark wasn't like that, was he? Mark strove for intimacy. Didn't he share his childhood memories with me? What could possibly be more intimate than that? Although, there at the table across from fuming Dena, I saw Mark's reminiscences in a different light. They were smooth, well-rehearsed performances rather than intimate confessions. He hadn't tried to become closer to me; he just wanted me to listen, to admire, to be fascinated. And the more I lived with Mark, the less I actually understood him. On one hand, I knew everything there was to know: the names of the places where he'd vacationed as a child, the names of his cousins and uncles with whom he never spoke, the kinds of herbs he preferred in his salads, and what subjects were appropriate conversation during sex. I could count his scars from memory and draw a map of the birthmarks on his body. Yet the accumulation of all those bits of information failed to bring me closer to him, failed to provide me with some larger knowledge of Mark. I didn't know his plans for future novels. I didn't know whether he was satisfied with his work. I didn't even know what his favorite books were. He said that he loved Dostoevsky, but I'd never seen him reading any of Dostoevsky's works. Nor did he talk about him, except for that first time, when he asked me three Dostoevsky questions.

Mark's feelings for me also remained a constant, annoying puzzle. "What is it, a year? Have you been with him more than a year?"

Dena asked. "Watch out. His interest is about to wane, and then you'll see how he starts to find more ways to be annoyed with you."

But Mark's interest wasn't waning. On the contrary.

"Isn't it amazing?" he once asked in the middle of one of my "bad girl" narratives.

"What?"

"How it doesn't get boring?"

Somewhere in the beginning of Polina's diary there was a draft of her letter to Dostoevsky, the letter that she wrote during their Petersburg period and where she tried to explain what she hated about their relationship the most. "You behaved," she wrote, "like a serious, busy man who pays due attention to his work, but at the same time doesn't forget to enjoy himself. On the contrary. He considers enjoying himself a duty too, the way one great medicine man or a philosopher claimed that it is necessary to get drunk once a month."

Was Mark like that too? "You don't know what sex is for me," he said to me once, after one time that was particularly good (for him). "Sex is like . . . um. It both charges and discharges me. I don't drink, like some people. I don't do drugs. I don't play sports. I don't even smoke. Sex for me is the only way to get off." And then he kind of patted my neck . . . so I would take his words as a compliment? So I would take as a compliment that I was his tool to get off, like a whiskey on the rocks for some people, or a soccer ball, or a few grains of cocaine?

In other ways too, Mark was getting increasingly comfortable around me. He didn't mind my presence anymore, even when he was in his worst mood. "It's astonishing how little your presence bugs me," he would say. He was testing me in the beginning, trying me on. Now he'd become certain that I fit. I should've been happy, and relieved, but instead his ease around me, his contentment, made me feel alarmed. Something was very wrong with our relationship, and I couldn't quite put my finger on it. One thing that bothered me immensely was how little Mark seemed to want to know me. He either assumed that he had a very good idea of me already, or he didn't care to know me at all as long as I suited him. He never asked how I liked my coffee or whether I preferred a tuna or chicken sandwich. He never expressed any wish to know about my childhood, my life in Russia, my former studies, or my friends. He never asked about my relatives. "If you plan to be calling your parents in Russia, I'll have to switch to a better long-distance plan," he said once. My parents! I thought, taken aback. I had told Mark that my mother lived alone. I had told him that my father was dead! It was one of very few things that I'd told him about myself. I remembered exactly how it had happened. We were sitting on his bed (it was in the beginning of our relationship, before we'd even slept together). Mark was telling me another story about his parents, and in the middle of it he asked what my father did. I said that he had died almost twenty years ago. I said that in a very calm voice, which made it even more awkward when a minute later I suddenly started to sob, shivering and hiccuping, trying to hide my face in Mark's bed linens. Mark pulled me close and stroked my tangled hair and my shaking back, wiping the tears off my face with a corner of his soft light-blue sheet. I sat very quietly, soaking up the warmth of his touch, and then as he was about to pull away, I buried my face in his chest and whispered through the damp darkened cotton of the sheet that I loved him.

How, how could he have forgotten about that?

"Tanya, are you there? Tanya?" my mother yelled from the strange, unreal universe on the other side of the telephone line.

"What do you mean you haven't found a good school *yet*?

Tanya, it's been two years! And you quit your job too? What were you thinking?"

Where exactly was my mother's voice? It seemed to sputter off the warm surface of the receiver right into my ear. She was in Russia, thousands of miles away, moving about in our little apartment, untangling the telephone cord as she spoke, her feet clad in scuffed slippers over woolen socks, her wispy hair touching the receiver, but her voice was right here, ringing and sputtering in Mark's penthouse above Central Park. Her shrill, loud, annoying, impossible, enormous voice.

"Tanya, tell me, I don't understand. What do you do?"

"I'm working on my English, Mom. So I can enter a better school."

"But what do you do for money?"

I lived with Mark and inspired him. And since I didn't do anything else, was that what I did for money? And since he hadn't been writing, what exactly did I inspire him for?

"Mom, you see, this man, my boyfriend, he has enough for both of us, and we decided that—"

"You're dependent on him? He keeps you?"

"Mom, just get off the Soviet propaganda, okay? Nobody thinks like that anymore."

"What do you mean?"

"Mom, it's as if we were married. A lot of married women here don't work. It doesn't make any difference, that Mark and I are not married."

"You're right, it doesn't. You would still be dependent on him if you were married!"

"God, what is so wrong about it?"

"God, everything!"

I slammed the receiver down at that point—as I did at the end of most of our conversations. I wanted my mother's voice to leave Mark's apartment, fly back into a tiny Moscow kitchen and die there in my mother's throat. But it wouldn't. Like a stubborn mosquito, my mother's voice seemed to hover around, invisible and malicious. I wished that the voice were a real mosquito and I could just smash it against the wall.

Even without my mother's assaults, the question of money popped into my mind more and more often lately. I couldn't believe that there was a time, and not so long ago, when I'd admired the elegance and grace of the people who lived in Mark's neighborhood. I had a firm conviction now that neither their sophistication nor their elegance was inborn. It was all simply bought with money. Expensive education, expensive European travel, expensive opera tickets, and living in expensive areas among people who were exposed to the same made them sophisticated. Having no money made you live in a subsidized apartment and hunt for rotten tomatoes, like my uncle did. A little money bought you a programmer's class in a community college, a house like Dena's in an ugly New Jersey suburb, Ikea furniture, too-tight, outdated clothes from end-of-the-season sales, and discounted tickets for the not-so-popular Broadway shows. Big money bought you Harvard and Yale, country houses, Manhattan apartments, one-of-a-kind furniture, simple clothes that suited you without your trying too much, season tickets to the opera, understanding of opera music, good taste, elegance, beauty, confidence, contentment, peace. I admitted that it was possible to have money and no culture—I'd seen all too many examples of that—but not vice versa. Of all people I got to know here, Dear Charlotte and Gosha had the easiest, the most natural, the most unpretentious relationship with culture. It seemed to come from within and come effortlessly. But would it be possible, I thought, if not for the money they had, and their parents had, and their parents before them? The very unpretentiousness had its price, and a very steep price at that. I caught myself wanting the money, hating myself for wanting the money, hating people who had it, and hating myself for unfairly hating them.

Sometimes I wondered if my muse ideas were simply convenient. Maybe I was just scared of the hardships of immigrant life and had snatched a rich older man who would take care of me, and had come up with all that muse stuff afterward to make me feel better about myself. What if it were only here, after I'd met Mark, that I'd put Dostoevsky, Polina, Anna Grigorievna, my grandmother, and Vovik together, and simply talked myself into believing that being a muse had been my destiny from the very beginning? I felt disgusted with myself and suspected that other people should be just as disgusted. Our new cleaning lady, for example. The old, invisible cleaning lady had quit, and the new one was coming on Tuesdays. "I trust her completely," Mark had said to me. "But since you don't have to be anyplace anyway, better stay in the apartment while she cleans. She's new, you know."

She was a sullen woman in her late forties, with dingy reddish-brown hair and sallow skin. "Good morning," she said without smiling, in an accent similar to mine, and proceeded to clean quickly and silently. Her thin gold earrings swayed gently as she moved. My mother had the same earrings, and I imagined that, in her country, the cleaning lady used to be a math teacher too. Just a few years before, she was knocking with crumbly pieces of chalk against a blackboard to produce long white equations, and now she was kneeling by a bathtub to fish wet slimy hair out of a drain in the apartment of an untidy rich man whose lazy bitch of a girlfriend was lurking around watching her, lest she steal something from him. Her presence made me feel such intense shame that regardless of the weather I spent all the time on the terrace while she cleaned. But while on the terrace, I thought about Gosha and Dear Charlotte and wondered if they disapproved of me as well. "Tanya, the head of the history department at City College is a good friend of mine. Why don't you go and talk to him?" Or "What about social work, Tanya? Do you think it might be something to consider?" they kept saying to me whenever I stopped by for tea. Did they mean to suggest that my present way of life was wrong, unacceptable? I imagined that disgust crept into their conversations with me, seeped like a poison into the tea we drank. I stopped going to their place. I started dodging them on the street, and if I was inside the elevator and saw them approaching, I rushed to flatten my thumb against the Door Close button. The only person I longed to see was Vera. Her stare was kind, attentive, nonjudgmental, and I fantasized that it could cleanse and redeem any person at which it was directed. But Vera must have rarely left her apartment, because I almost never saw her in the elevator.

I spent more and more time on the couch with drugstore romances. Every time my head swelled up with another cold, I felt happy, because it gave me a good justification for doing that. Contrary to Dear Charlotte's prediction, I didn't graduate to reading serious books. I couldn't appreciate the humor, the insights, or the beauty of the language, so most of the serious books I attempted to read seemed poorly written, annoying, and boring. The thought of the great intellectual effort the serious books would have demanded sickened and depressed me. I didn't want to make an effort; I needed to be distracted.

"What is it you're reading?" Mark asked when he announced his decision to start writing again. "*Death at Sunset*? Sounds nice, sounds fascinating." He studied his flushed face in the hallway mirror and flicked off a few raindrops stuck in his hair. "Now close it quick. We're going to celebrate!"

We went to a dim, homey Italian café that looked a lot like the one where Mark had kissed me for the first time. This place was just as tiny, and our knees bumped against each other from time to time. Mark squeezed some roasted garlic over his bread, took a bite, and moaned. "Oomh, just the way I like it! Apparently, I had some unresolved issues with writing, but now that's over. My shrink said that's completely behind me. Nothing is holding me back. Do you understand this?" Then he laughed and said, "The bread is simply amazing here, right?" I nodded and laughed too, rushing to wipe a smudge of garlic off his beard.

He is wonderful. Our life is going to be wonderful, I thought all the way through tricolor salad, the bottle of Montepulciano, the gnocchi, tiramisù, and cappuccino, and then all the way through the quick, silent lovemaking, and a couple of hours after that, which I spent unable to fall asleep. I longed for the sharp morning light to break through the one missing slat in the blinds, signaling the beginning of our new life: the writing life, an exciting, meaningful life. This would be the true beginning that would dispel all the doubts, and redeem everything that had gone wrong. The lack of intimacy wouldn't be a flaw but a requisite attribute of living with a writer. A writer could be truly intimate only with his work. If he wasted his innermost thoughts on his partner, what would be left for his novels? Mark's egoism wouldn't be a flaw either. A writer had to be so perfectly receptive to his own feelings that he couldn't possibly understand the feelings of others.

Around two a.m. I remembered that I hadn't taken my cold medicine that night, and realized that I didn't need it. My nose was still dripping, but my head didn't hurt anymore and my chest felt free of congestion. I felt sprightly and vigorous, like a hunting dog about to enter the woods for the first time after a long stay inside the house. My uncle once said that good hunting dogs get sick if their owners don't let them run in the woods. Possibly, muses were just like that, sickly and depressed while their partners were taking a break from art, alive and full of energy during the working period.

When the morning came at last, I dug out my long-forgotten diary from a drawer with my clothes, blew some dust off the cover in a symbolic gesture, and wrote, "March 7. Mark is starting to write."

Mark didn't physically write anything for a couple of weeks, but he was visibly in the process of creation.

"Mark spent the whole day looking through his old drafts. 'What a piece of crap,' he said most of the time, or 'I can't believe I was serious' or 'Was I drunk when I wrote this?' But once or twice he looked pleased with what he read. 'Now, this is a fine piece of writing. I can't imagine why I ever abandoned it.'

"Sometimes Mark drops the manuscript page he is reading and lies very still, thinking. At other times he announces that he has to go for a walk, obviously with the same purpose, to think."

And finally the long-awaited moment came:

"Today I woke up to the sound of the typewriter's keys!" I wrote this in handwriting so firm that it was possible to decipher the imprint of the words on the following pages. "I wanted to get up and watch what Mark was doing, but I didn't want to disturb him, so I just lay there and listened to the clanking. Today's sound was entirely different from the usual one, when Mark typed his letters and papers for school, lighter and more energetic, even urgent, as if Mark were hurrying to catch his thought and bring it safely to paper."

I paused to savor the vividness and precision of my entry. I planned to beat Anna Grigorievna by being not only the perfect companion to a great writer, but also an excellent biographer. Unlike her, I wouldn't devote my diary to the description of minor purchases or petty domestic battles, but instead I would document the writing process, something almost entirely missing from Anna Grigorievna's notes. Dostoevsky wrote his greatest works while married to her—*The Brothers Karamazov, The Idiot,* and *The Possessed,* among others—and she didn't seem to have noticed! Not me. I would register and preserve every detail about Mark's writing, and do it in a clever and engaging way. It would be a wonderful gift from me to generations to come.

"Today Mark sent me to get some hard green pears, which he needed for inspiration. Chewing on something hard must have sent some helpful vibrations up to his brain.

"Mark's mouth is a little agape when he writes, which makes him look like a schoolboy laboring over his homework.

"He sometimes sits, perched on a chair, with one leg bent and serving as a prop for his elbow, and the other folded under his butt."

Gradually, however, the entries in my diary were getting shorter, scarcer, boasting more and more abbreviations and neglected misspellings.

"Today Mark typed for three hours.

"Has sat at the typewriter for the whole night. Possibly watched TV some of the time.

"M. finished ch. 6.

"Typed for an h-r and a half."

I began getting bored with my new job. Mark's work didn't look like a thrilling dramatic process anymore, but rather like another daily activity effortlessly incorporated into his schedule. Two hours squeezed between jogging and lunch. One more hour before the evening news. Sometimes Mark read aloud to me. "So what do you

think, Tanya?" he would ask after reading two sentences or two passages to me. "The second one? Right? Yes, it's probably the
strongest. But the first has more dialogue in it, and more humor.
Most readers won't have patience for a philosophical thought; they
need to be entertained. The first is very funny, don't you think?" I
didn't think anything—my still imperfect English allowed me to
understand the content, but made me blind to the philosophical
depth of the second passage as well as the humor of the first. I didn't
even have to feign understanding though. "The first, yes, definitely
the first," Mark would say and go back to his typewriter, never waiting for my answer. The content of his work wasn't that exciting
either. The novel-in-progress was supposed to become the last in a
trilogy about a gifted but troubled Jewish boy growing up in a very
ordinary, reasonably happy, moderately well-off New Jersey family.
The main character's name was Mark. Mark (the real one) said that
he was planning to end the narrative by the time the boy turned
fourteen. "Sixteen, tops." Which meant that there would be no
place in his novel for the "maddening imprint" of my foot. I would
rather Mark wrote about a gifted, troubled Jewish boy who grows
up to be a gifted, troubled man, chases cold and empty beautiful
women, and suffers a lot, until he meets a woman from Eastern
Europe, unimpressive at first glance, but endowed with so much
more than simply brains and beauty, who changes his whole life
and . . . well, the rest was up to him. But it wasn't the content of
Mark's work that disappointed me. I consented to the notion that a
muse didn't necessarily have to be a model to influence the writer.
But how exactly did I influence Mark? He seemed pleased that I was
documenting his writing in my diary. "So, how's our hardworking
chronicler doing today? I wish I could read Russian," he said from
time to time. He liked me to watch him write. "Your presence is
soothing," he said. My presence was soothing, that was good, if only

I hadn't spent my whole life hoping to be inspiring rather than soothing.

I continued to write in my diary, but keeping it began to remind me of my sixth-grade biology assignment. We had to pick an animal, watch it for two weeks, and jot down whatever it was doing. My animal was a hamster borrowed from my mother's friends. Watching him was exciting for the first couple of days. He ate! He slept! He tore a newspaper page into tiny bits! He ate some more! He slept again! But soon the excitement faded. He ate. He slept. He ate. He slept. He tore the newspaper page. What in hell was the point?

Even the sounds of Mark's typing, which I used to love, started to irritate me. Dull and consistent, they resembled the drumming of an incessant summer rain against the roof. And Mark himself, Mark too, seemed perfectly dull as he sat slumped over his typewriter, opening his mouth very wide to take a good bite out of a pear. From time to time he paused in his typing, yawned, and rubbed his eyes. I had to plead with my memory to tell me what it was that used to excite me about Mark. Sometimes I would come up to him and hug him from behind or ruffle his hair a little, all the while chanting in my head, He is wonderful he is so wonderful I love him I love him so much I'm crazy in love with him. Mark would usually smile or pat my hand, but the forced exultation of my unsaid words left me frightened and uncomfortable. In search of distraction, I tried to go back to romance books, but discovered that I couldn't read them anymore. Their emptiness and stupidity and false optimism, which I used to find funny and even endearing, now irritated the hell out of me. The only books that gave me some kind of comfort were Mark's countless writers' biographies. I didn't care to read them, but I liked to look at the pictures wedged in the middle of the book. My favorite were group portraits of the writer as a child, surrounded by his siblings. Here they were little boys and girls, all staring at the camera with the same strained smiles coaxed out of them with threats and promises. Wearing britches or pinafores, in wrinkled stockings and scuffed little shoes, with sharply cut bangs hanging above their eyes, or tight braids fixed with ribbons. Some held a doll by its arm, others squeezed a string leading to a toy horse or a tugboat. One of the group, only one would become a genius writer, but there was no way to tell which one.

One evening I stumbled upon a book about Dostoevsky. There were no pictures, but the title at once captivated and enraged me. *The Three Loves of Dostoevsky.* Three loves? Dostoevsky had only one love—Polina. His first wife, Maria, didn't count. She never loved Dostoevsky, and I firmly believed that he didn't love her either. Mad crush quickly faded into pity and guilt, never quite touching on love. And Anna Grigorievna was just . . . well, Anna Grigorievna. He couldn't possibly have been in love with her. Yet, the author of *Three Loves* picked her as the most important one. "Anna: The Happy Marriage" the section about Anna Grigorievna was called. That part of the book was also favored by Mark. The pages inside "Anna: The Happy Marriage" were the shabbiest in the book, motley with yellow highlights, pricked by little notes.

I started reading, expecting the author to paint a phony romanticized portrait, but to my surprise he had a pretty realistic take on Anna Grigorievna and her relationship with Dostoevsky. A very similar take to my own. "He trusted Anna; he felt that she was near to him and kind, but he was not in love with her," I read in the first of the highlighted passages. Of course, Dostoevsky wasn't in love with her! I snorted with approval and was about to turn the page when I saw something that made me short of breath.

In the margin, next to that passage, were penciled scribbles in Mark's hand. Four letters and an exclamation mark: "tan'a!"

Just like that: a lowercase *t,* and an apostrophe instead of a *y.* My name. I started leafing further, hoping that the next one would disprove my discovery somehow, that "tan'a" would turn out to be just a mistake, or somebody else's name. Mark couldn't possibly have meant me!

It wasn't long before I saw another "Tan'a."

"In general he was touched because she was so simple and unpretentious," the author wrote in that passage. Simple and unpretentious. Simple and unpretentious. Mark commented on that, Mark praised me for that. He meant me. It was me.

I read on, hunting for the highlights, swallowing angry tears. "She was a rather young, none-too-well-developed average girl, not remarkable in any way, yet possessed of a lively mind and an unerring intuition wherever Dostoevsky was concerned." This was about me? This? Badly developed average girl was me? Mark's answer was yes. "Tania." "Tan." "Tan'a!!!" All over the chapter. "After the hysterics of Maria and the imperial posturing of Apollinaria, Fyodor welcomed Anna's neutrality with profound relief." "Anna's youth, her inexperience and burgher ideals had a soothing effect on him."

And finally the gem of gems came: "He could do with her what he willed, he could train her as a companion in his erotic fantasies. . . . According to her own expression she 'permitted' him a very great deal, and not only because she liked his 'tricks,' but because in her great love for him she was ready to endure everything, to bear anything submissively." This was me. I couldn't argue with that.

I looked closer at the book and saw the traces of other female names next to the highlighted sentences. So that was who the women in the photographs were. Failed Anna Grigorievnas. Too beautiful, too smart, too difficult for the role. Mark must have been auditioning women for a long time. Now he'd picked one. The perfect one. The most obedient, the most devoted, the most ordinary of them all. The "authentic" Anna Grigorievna. Tan'a!

I looked at Mark in the living room, stretched in his favorite chair in front of the TV, perfectly comfortable, sipping the coffee that I had brewed for him. He must have felt my stare, because he turned around and smiled at me. So that was how he saw me.

Not mysterious, poetic, erotic, inspiring.

But ordinary, naïve, obedient in bed.

Mark had never been in love with me.

Mark had chosen me for purely practical reasons.

How could I have been so blind? So deluded? I couldn't even blame Mark. Didn't I behave like that from the very beginning, rushing to bring him food, crying with gratitude when he came inside me, pretending to be somebody I was not? But maybe I didn't have to pretend. Maybe that was precisely what I was? That was probably why I'd always hated Anna Grigorievna so much—I saw myself in her, and I wouldn't admit it.

"Tanya," Mark called for me from the couch. "I need a refill, please." There was a thin, grayish trickle of milk on his beard, and I thought that as Anna Grigorievna, I should rush and wipe it. Swiftly and tenderly, with a happy smile. I would have done it effortlessly before; now the mere thought of acting like her made me shiver. The mug, still warm, still smelling of coffee and cinnamon, felt heavy in my hand. I imagined lifting it above Mark's head and smashing it hard against his crown. The image didn't last more than a second, but a faint satisfying sensation lingered as I washed and refilled the mug.

A scene from the abandoned but never forgotten Anna Grigorievna's diary flashed in my mind:

"Whom do you think I should marry, Anechka, a smart woman

or a kind woman?" Dostoevsky asked her after one of their stenography sessions.

"A smart woman, Fedor Mikhailovich. Of course, a smart woman. Why, you're such a great writer!"

"No, Anechka, I better marry a kind one."

Soon after that, he proposed to her, and Anna Grigorievna was so overcome with happiness that she didn't get the insult.

Dostoevsky was looking for dumb and kind. So was Mark. Only Mark had made a mistake. I might have been dumb, but I wasn't kind.

Not to him, not anymore.

"Rome. September 29, 1863. Yesterday F.M. badgered me again."

I don't know when and how it ended, but by the time Polina and Dostoevsky arrived in Rome, three weeks after Baden-Baden, their "brother and sister" game was over. Sex was now out in the open.

This time I don't feel like imagining their hotel room. I don't care if it was lighted by the soft moonlight or by the glow of candles, if there was any food left on the table or if there was a table at all. This scene is all about the bed. I picture a dark, empty room with a single bed in the center. An eyesore of a bed. Tall, plump, with an ugly brass railing and a sand-colored coverlet. An arena of deadly battle, just like the Colosseum looming in the dark not too far away from their hotel, a place for gladiators.

I see them walking around the bed in circles. Watching each other, glowering, mouths shut tight.

He takes a few firm steps around the bed toward her side. She takes a few steps too, keeping the distance the same.

"Why, Polina, why?"

She shrugs.

He takes some more steps. She does too.

"Why are you being so serious about this?"

She shrugs again.

"We used to do it before, remember?"

Oh, yes, she remembers.

"You used to love it."

She just stares at him.

"You used to want it. You keep wanting it. You want it just as badly as I. I saw some signs of it."

He takes a few very big steps in her direction. She takes a few very big steps away.

"Why do you give such importance to this entirely common act, anyway? These are simple bodily needs, one has to satisfy them. Back in Petersburg, I used to go to the 'houses of fun' on a regular basis."

She winces.

"What is it? You've suddenly become prudish? Prudishness doesn't suit you."

A step.

A step away.

"I am not prudish."

"What then?"

She glares at him.

"Are you enjoying torturing me?"

She shakes her head. She isn't enjoying torturing him anymore.

"Are you trying to tease me? You can't refuse a man for a long time, you know. He might stop insisting at the end."

She smiles. She has evidence to the contrary.

"I might have to force you, Polina, because we Russian soldiers never retreat."

A step in her direction.

A step away.

"Oh, I know. I know why. You are hoping. You still cherish hopes that your charming Southern prince will come back?"

She shudders.

"That's it then! You are hoping. Can't you see what you were for him? Nothing more than a convenient mistress!"

Wasn't I just that for you too, she thinks, closing her eyes. Her eyelashes are wet.

He looks at her and stops talking. Slumps on the bed. Hides his face in his hands.

"Polya, please forgive me," he says. "I don't know what possessed me to say all this to you."

She sits down on the bed next to him. They are both silent for some time, and then he says, "I'm tired, Polya. I'm unwell. I'm doing sightseeing here as if somebody were forcing me to, as if I were learning a school lesson. I'm walking around in a haze. I cannot go on like this."

She takes his hand in hers. He looks up at her and shakes his head.

They both know that it is time for them to part.

Chapter Eleven

Vera died in the middle of October, about a week before my twenty-sixth birthday. The housekeeper found her lying on the living room floor.

I heard her telling the story to Dear Charlotte through the open door: "She was all white, your palest grayish white. And very still, still like a doll."

Of course Vera was still. Why wouldn't she be? She was dead.

Vera's sister, a sharp, skinny woman in tweed slacks, came to pack her belongings after the funeral. The faceless boxes criss-crossed with packing tape crowded the elevator that day, a gloomy reminder of the senselessness of Vera's life.

"Vera died," I said to Mark.

"Who's Vera?"

He sat at his desk, nibbling on a pear and leafing through his manuscript; his novel was almost finished.

"A woman who lived downstairs. She wore knitted hats and big coats, and she had this strange, anxious, but kind expression . . ."

"Uh-huh."

He didn't lift his eyes from the manuscript.

His beard, caught in the pool of light from the small overhead lamp, cast a weird shadow on the pages. It looked like a small, mangy rodent, a gerbil or a tailless squirrel, clutching onto a human face.

Ever since I'd found out that I was labeled as Anna Grigorievna, I'd been discovering more and more things that disgusted me about Mark. I would wake up in the morning and add another detail to the collection. I hated the long, satisfied yawns he made in the morning, the dazzled expression on his face when he read a restaurant menu, the sight of pear juice on his beard, his snoring, his sighs, his upper front teeth, his left shoulder, his big toes, the puffs of his breath coming out of his mouth on a cold day. I developed a physical revulsion to his habit of drying his toothbrush with a towel after using it. "It's a good toothbrush," he said when he once caught my stare. Even Mark's childhood photographs that I used to love nauseated me now. I would peer at the charming, innocent face of the boy in the pictures and see some tiny feature of the adult Mark in it, which was enough to make the boy seem revolting.

One day, I decided that I hated Mark's smell. He smelled exactly like overripe plums left rotting in the company of onions. I hadn't minded his smell before, so I hadn't bothered to define it, but now I saw it clearly. Plums and onions, sweating and leaking through a string bag forgotten in an aluminum shed in the hot August days, and no added scent of lavender shower gel, lime deodorant, or mint toothpaste could conceal the truth.

But nothing repulsed me more than Mark's smugness and especially his conviction that people were happy to serve him. If he happened to catch our cleaning lady, he would always stop her and chat. "So, Adila"—he had made sure to ask her name and he remembered it correctly most of the time—"did you find a boyfriend yet?" From what I could gather from her brief and hushed phone conversations in a language similar to Russian, Adila had a husband and at least two children. But she always said yes to Mark's question. "Yes, yes, Mr. Schneider. I find. Can I go now?" Mark liked to joke with supermarket cashiers, waiters, and doctors' receptionists, sure that they all glowed in his attention. "Patience, Bruno, patience," he said to my favorite doorman, if he inquired about Mark's new book. When Bruno asked him that about a week before, Mark had said:

"As a matter of fact, Bruno, yes, I finished it."

"Oh, wow, sir. Oh, that's great. I'll send my wife to Barnes and Noble to get it."

"It's not out yet, Bruno. But you know what. As soon as it comes out, you're getting a signed copy."

And he was the same way with me. "Bring me another cup of decaf, sweetie . . . Yes, skim milk, please. Thank you, my darling." He must have thought I was happy to serve him coffee, and he probably felt very good about giving me little rewards in the form of all those "sweeties" and "darlings" and other benignly patronizing compliments: "Look how good you've become at brewing coffee; we are talking real talent here" or "Stripping is art, Tanya, and you've mastered it perfectly." Every time he offered me praise or a compliment now, I had the urge to either laugh or slap him across the face.

I thought that I should leave Mark, but what was the point? Leaving him equaled summing up my whole life with a fat red stamp that read FAILURE! I was twenty-six. I had never had a real boyfriend, I had never had good sex. I had failed at my studies. I couldn't even learn English to read well. What guarantee did I have that I would ever succeed? At anything at all? At least now I had hope that I would make an impression on Mark's writing, or ensure with my being there that he wrote under favorable conditions.

Meanwhile, I discovered that I couldn't bear to be in Mark's presence, or simply stay in one place for a long time. I developed

bouts of geographical restlessness that sent me on various purpose-
less, chaotic expeditions.

I would tell myself that I urgently needed new shoes, a particular blouse, or a pair of socks, and I would head to the Macy's on
Thirty-fourth, and walk and walk while there, dragging my feet
across the vast space of the store, going up and down on slow, torturous escalators, running my hand over blouses, shoes, and socks,
changing my wish as soon as I found the ones I had thought that I
wanted. One day, I decided that a tense tea conversation with Dear
Charlotte and Gosha would still be better than staying with Mark.
But as I was standing at their door about to knock, I suddenly
changed my mind, rushed to the elevator, rode downstairs, exited
the building, and started walking downtown, hoping to think of
some urgent errand I had to make. Somewhere in the vicinity of
Battery Park, I saw that I was hoping in vain and took the subway
back. Another day, I thought that visiting my uncle would be a nice,
and even noble, idea, so I headed out to Brooklyn, having taken a
bag with Mark's dusty gourmet items with me. I sat in my uncle's
kitchen watching how he shuffled about in search of a can opener,
then cheerfully spread the contents of Mark's tins on thick slices of
Russian rye bread. "What is that? Chopped liver, right? And this?
Smells like fish . . . tastes like . . . no, no, wait, Tanya, don't tell me,
let me guess . . ." He talked with his mouth full, greedy for the audience and food alike. By the time his sandwiches were almost finished, he embarked on a long story about some Isakov, who'd tried
to squeeze him out of the committee of the Society for Former
Doctors from the Former Soviet Union, when my uncle had a very
good chance to become the vice president, and maybe even the president in time. I sat and listened until it dawned on me that even my
uncle's life with his Isakov struggles had so much more purpose and

energy than mine, that I suddenly felt nauseated and tired, and anxious to leave. But nothing was as bad as Dena's place, where I ventured one morning in the beginning of January, lured by the prospect of the long ride—by subway, then train, and then bus. I walked the succession of sidewalks leading to their place, marveling at the flatness of the suburban landscape and the gloominess of the identical houses, which looked bleak in the harsh sunlight of cold, leafless streets. I was counting on the comforting sense of boredom and misery that I always associated with Dena's home, but once inside, I was overwhelmed with the cozy smell of coffee and burned bread and the bright picture of a family morning. A three-pound Price Club box of Cheerios and a half-gallon container of orange juice dominated the table. Yawning, shaggy-haired Dena sat half hidden behind the box, cradling a steaming mug of coffee. Igor, dressed in a bathrobe over striped boxers, flipped pieces of French toast at the stove. Danik, taller and more mature than I'd remembered him, carefully took a mug with milk out of the microwave and carried it to the table. "Tanya, want to see a trick?" he asked me after we had all settled down for breakfast. "Look, this bowl is filled with cereal, right? To the top, right? Now look. I'm pouring the milk in, lots of milk, and it doesn't overflow. Want to know why?" And Dena smiled proudly at Igor, patted Danik on the back, and then laughed when the milk finally spilled over the bowl. Danik might have been a little monster at other times, and Dena might have been angry and tense, and her husband apathetic, but they didn't seem so at the breakfast table that morning. They were simply a family. A family, where I didn't belong.

The image of Danik's skinny hand squeezing the mug handle haunted me the entire endless ride back to Manhattan. I suddenly longed to have a child, but not Mark's child. The idea of having

Mark's child, a little Mark, was revolting. Then I thought of my mother, how she called me less and less frequently lately, and always seemed to be short of words. Our conversations now consisted of sad, solid pauses sullied here and there by weather comparisons.

"Is it already warm in New York?"

"No, not yet. Is it getting warmer in Moscow?"

"No. There is still snow in some places."

The subway car was almost empty, and as the train was approaching my stop, I had the urge to curl in my scratched corner seat and stay there, like a sick, homeless dog.

The finale of Mark's working period came quickly, quietly, and almost unexpectedly, probably because I had been too depressed to ponder what our life would be like once the novel was finished. One morning, he gave me a neat stack of pages and asked me to make a copy of it and mail it to his publisher. Later, we had a quiet dinner in the same restaurant where we'd celebrated his decision to start writing again. And the next morning, after jogging, instead of going to his desk, Mark happily stretched out on the couch with a hefty Henry James biography and a mug of coffee. I had heard that writers go into postpartum depression once they've finish their work, but Mark simply went back to his usual routine. I didn't detect any signs of sadness or anything unusual about his behavior until the following Sunday.

"Tanya, bring me the paper, will you?" Mark said as soon as I appeared from the bedroom that morning. He was sitting at his desk with his back to the typewriter, right hand resting on the copy of his manuscript in his lap, left hand combing through his beard, glazed stare glued to the wall.

When I got back with the paper, Mark shoved his hand in the middle and dug out the *Book Review,* letting the disheveled rest drop to the floor. "Is the review of your book already out?" I asked in disbelief. "No," Mark said slumping onto the couch to read. "I need to know what they say about the others."

He proceeded to read the reviews, either making frequent grunts and long sighs, kneading his forehead with an open palm, or pulling on his beard and saying, "Unbelievable!" Sometimes he would nod in cheerful contentment, scratch his beard, and say, "Exactly!" There was a system to his responses, as I found out, having peeked into the discarded pages. He said "unbelievable" about a rave, and "exactly" about a bad review. For the first time in a long time I watched him with interest.

Later that afternoon, Mark tore a contents page from the *Book Review,* marked some titles with red marker, and told me to go to Barnes and Noble and get them.

"I don't want to be seen buying this talentless crap," he explained to me.

When I returned with the needed books, Mark picked the one that had had the most enthusiastic review and slumped back on the couch. He lay on his back, his head supported by three little pillows. He was very still, except for his eyes moving quickly over the pages, left to right, left to right. He didn't pause until he'd finished the entire book. Then he dropped it to the floor with a sigh of relief and said, "Whew, I thought he really did it this time. Okay, Tanya, time to eat."

The next Sunday, Mark followed exactly the same scenario. And the Sunday after that didn't promise anything different. Mark read the reviews and circled the titles for me. I brought the books home, and Mark slumped on the couch with the book about which the reviewer had written, "it soars." "We soar, do we?" Mark said, chuckling. "Well, let's just see how high." He proceeded to read the book just as swiftly and silently as he always did, the only difference being that he sucked sharp intakes of air from time to time, as if he had stomach cramps. When he finished reading, he dropped the book to the floor, stood up, and went out on the terrace, mumbling, "Soars! What the fuck does that mean? Is it a fucking airplane or is it just a book, after all?"

On the terrace, he roamed slowly and sadly among the folding chairs and empty pots. His head hung so low that his beard touched the collar of his T-shirt. The book must have been very good, and Mark was suffering. I knew that I should go to him and say something comforting, or simply touch him in a warm, affectionate way. I tried to come up with some gesture of kindness, but I couldn't. I couldn't move or take my eyes off him, so I just stood and watched him suffer. There he was, usually so cool and confident, exposed to the pains of envy.

That night, Mark's hands felt cold against my body and his mouth felt flabby and dry. His movements were fidgety and strangely angry. He kept pushing me, tugging and squeezing me, all in complete silence. He used to be like that at times. When he returned from his shrink in an especially bad mood, or after he'd talked to somebody at one of those parties. Silent, fidgety, faintly hostile. I didn't understand what was happening then, but now I knew. This was his dialogue with the author of the "soaring" book. By pushing and tugging and squeezing *me,* he was trying to prove his strength and his power to *him. I* didn't matter at all, and my body was just a vessel for his frustration. I felt a wave of repulsion so strong that I thought I was going to be sick right there in Mark's bed. I was about to push him away when his body, as if aware of this, suddenly went slack. "What is wrong with you today?" he mumbled with irritation before turning away from me.

The next morning he told me to get rid of the book. "I don't care how!" he said. "No, don't return it. I don't want them talking at the store. Just get rid of it! Put it in the garbage! Give it to your Russian relatives!" (Which apparently was the same thing for him.)

I carried the book to Central Park, where I sat down on one of the benches, took the book out of the bag, and opened it in my lap with the pleasant shiver of doing something illicit. It took me about an hour to get through the first couple of pages. The style was significantly more difficult than in other English books I had read, and the thoughts were more complex too—I often had to go back and read certain passages again to make sure I'd understood them. By the middle of the second chapter, though, the most difficult expressions and the author's way of thinking became more or less familiar, and I was able to gain a good, steady pace. By the third chapter, I understood almost everything, and even smiled in some funny places. Just as it used to happen when I read Russian books, the words effortlessly formed sentences, the sentences produced images, and from those images emerged a whole world filled with characters so real that they seemed to sit right there on the bench next to me, as well as existing on the pages of the book. I couldn't tell if the book really "soared," but it was clever and funny, and certainly entertaining. I kept reading until my neck became stiff. I put the book on the bench and leaned back with a tired and contented sigh. It was the first real book I'd managed to read (and to enjoy!) in English. It was the book that Mark hated. I felt as if I'd just cheated on him.

The weather was mild. I liked how the sun warmed my face, but the breeze immediately cooled it off. I unbuttoned my coat. There were many people in the park, and everybody seemed to be in movement. Joggers passed me by, and mothers with strollers, kids on their cute little tricycles, squirrels chasing one another, dogs, bikers, pigeons chasing after crumbs of bread. It had been a long time since I was aware of the busy, complicated life of the park. One jogger, a tall, muscular man in his thirties, stopped on the path across from my bench and bent to retie his shoe. He had beautiful calves—thick, hairy, drenched with sweat. I thought about the appeal of men's calves, or about their appeal to me, until I realized that I was thinking about a man. I made another happy sigh and continued with the book.

And so it went on like this. Most Sunday mornings, Mark would spend with the *Book Review,* most Sunday afternoons he would read the touted books, and the next week I would spend reading the one that had hurt him the most. I can't say that I liked all of them. Some books were too foggy for me, others seemed downright absurd. But even with the most boring of them, the fact that I was reading and understanding them never failed to make me feel victorious, energetic, and strangely aroused. Images of sex now haunted me everywhere, regardless of what I was doing—whether I was reading, watching TV, doing the dishes, shopping for food, or simply walking the streets.

Soon I became conscious of a game I'd been playing in my mind. Wherever I encountered a number of reasonably attractive men—at the supermarket, at Starbucks, in a post office line, in a subway car—I would start arranging and rearranging them in order of preference as bedmates. In the process, I had vivid images of our potential lovemaking. I could see the changing expressions on their faces as they were getting closer to climax; their moans rang in my ears, their hands seemed to leave fingerprints on my skin. And I was having an acute physical reaction to those images—I had to remind myself to keep my knees closed. I enjoyed coming home after my walks and talking to Mark about some casual stuff, as if I'd already cheated on him and was just acting normal to pretend that nothing had happened.

Meanwhile the weather grew warmer, and Mark's friends started inviting us to the country. "Barry wants us to come to his new place in the Berkshires," Mark said in the middle of March. "He says it's still cool up there, but pleasantly so." I feigned the onset of a cold, but urged Mark to go without me because he needed some rest and some fresh air. I didn't have any secret intentions. I thought that I just wanted to enjoy a weekend in the apartment alone. But on the Saturday morning, as soon as Mark was out the door, I found myself going out too, and spending a couple of hours walking in the park, and then stopping in the crowded Starbucks on the corner of Columbus and Sixty-seventh Street. I bought a large regular coffee and sat down to engage in my game.

After some deliberation, I counted six attractive individuals.

Number One was a wiry, dark-haired man in his thirties with a soft, sexy mouth and a deep baritone that floated across the room to caress my ears, even though he wasn't talking to me but to his appallingly beautiful girlfriend.

Number Two was a stout, slightly stooped guy with a powerful jaw and wisps of dark hair visible through the opening of his shirt. I imagined how good his hairy torso would look when arched above mine.

Number Three looked a lot like Number One except that his nose was of a strange slanting shape that I found sexy or weird, depending on the turn of his head.

And it went on, down to Number Six, a waiflike blond girl. I fantasized how her breasts, seemingly absent when clothed, would come into view as she undressed, and wondered if they would be just as light and pale as I imagined. The fantasy was so vivid that the girl went up in the line to Number Two or even One, at which point I got nervous and reshuffled her back to sixth place.

Eventually, I slept with Number Four.

Number Four had the shaky feverish expression of somebody

who was not having enough sex, was thinking about sex all the time, was conscious of thinking about it all the time, and was terrified that this was noticeable. He had a pear-shaped face with large, dark, downturned eyes. Number Four looked both safe and most likely to accept my proposition. I didn't come up with any graceful seduction plan, but simply complained to him that I couldn't find milk and sugar, even though I'd been sipping my coffee for quite a while. "Right behind you!" Number Four showed me where, and then said that I had a lovely accent. "Are you from Russia?" Yes, I was. The conversation slowly traveled from Moscow by way of Amherst, where Number Four was working on his thesis, to the New York apartment of Number Four's grandfather, where he was staying for the weekend. A nice, spacious, empty apartment on the Upper East Side, where we eventually ended up.

Now what? I thought as we sat at opposite ends of his grandfather's soft leather couch, both of us squeezing the increasingly warm glasses of "a drink" (Will you come to my grandfather's place for a drink?) and getting slightly uncomfortable. We had talked up a storm since we met, covering a vast range of subjects from the topography of Moscow and New York to the funny peculiarities of our college professors. It was very easy to talk to Number Four, he listened with attention, he joked a lot, he laughed generously at my jokes—he made me feel how starved I was for a conversation with a person my age. His warmth and friendliness, his soft childlike smile, the kind, receptive expression in his eyes, made me forget about the main purpose for our being together, and whenever I remembered, it seemed impossible. In theory, he was sexy: His mouth was large and firm, his thighs strained the faded material of his jeans, his hands made swift, promising movements as he talked, yet I couldn't imagine him engaged in the sexual act. There was no way that our friendly chitchat could turn into something that involved sharp actions, sweat, penetration, sexual craze. And then I thought that maybe we should be great friends rather than lovers.

I was proved wrong on both counts. The lovers part was accomplished surprisingly easily. I put my glass on the table and leaned closer to Number Four, prepared to make a "let's be friends" offer, when he, mistaking my intention, pulled me close and kissed me with unexpected confidence and force. The last time I'd had an encounter with a man other than Mark was shortly before leaving for the United States, in the freezing, drafty, creaking dacha of my last Moscow lover. Then there were the three years of the unwelcome warmth of Mark's bed. I'd managed to forget how strong, how completely overpowering the sensation of a man's touch could be! It didn't take us long to get to Number Four's bedroom and get undressed. I felt as thrilled, overwhelmed, and out of control as if I were rushing down a long, slippery, and very steep slide. And as if I were on a slide, I felt like squealing with pleasure rather than moaning or gasping, which would have been more appropriate. The only thing that I found annoying was Number Four's dogged thoughtfulness. He would stop what he was doing, look into my eyes, and ask, "A little slower?" "Like that?" "Right here?" I had no idea which way I liked it best. I had been a muse, I had been used to serving, not to being served. One day it might be fun to find out, but not at that moment. I didn't want to stop and think. I just wanted everything, and lots of it, and quick.

"Are you hungry?" Number Four asked afterward. "I am." He brought two bottles of spring water, a sliced orange, and a plate of chocolate chip cookies, and got back into bed with the plate in his lap. "You know, as a child I used to stay with my grandfather a lot, and he always kept cookies in the cupboard. He still does." There was some strained earnestness in his voice, as if he believed that since we'd just had sex we should automatically move onto a higher level of intimacy. Or maybe he was just starved for conversation and thought this was the appropriate subject now: childhood memories. He then switched to talking about his dog, a Labrador named Tsarina, who had been dying of cancer and had to be put out of her misery. "My dad took her to the vet, but I read in her eyes that she didn't want to die, that she'd rather live even through the suffering. I should've stopped him, but I didn't." He looked sincerely sad, but he was talking about it naked, with his large pink penis folded cozily between his legs, on the bed smelling of oranges and chocolate. "I'll never forget Tsarina's eyes, as my father put her on the car seat on the way to the vet. It's the biggest shame of my life," Number Four said. There was a long, expectant pause. Did he want me to talk now, to be a good friend and share my biggest shame?

His was such a lovely shame. I could have told him that the biggest shame of my life was not being kind enough to my dying grandmother, bullying her, laughing at the sight of her shorn head. It would be true in a way, but I knew I had other, uglier things to be ashamed of. I lived with a man who thought that I was "average" and "not too well developed," who treated me like a grateful servant. I hated that man, I hated myself, yet I had no intention of leaving. Was Tsarina really Number Four's biggest shame? If so, we existed on different planets. I felt increasingly uncomfortable and tired of listening to him. I wanted him to shut up, and I couldn't think of a better way than to remove the plate of cookies from his hands, climb on top of him, and cover his mouth with mine. This way, we would be doing something good, something completely sincere.

I got home on Sunday, around ten in the morning. I fixed myself a bowl of cereal, ate it up, and plopped on the bed, facedown, in my clothes. There were two messages from Mark on the answering machine. "Tanya, are you there? Pick up, please," said the first. "Tanya, I think I'll be home around eight or nine at night," said the second. "Good." I smiled. "Still the whole day without Mark." I thought I'd fall asleep right away, but instead I felt giggly, vigorous, and fully alert. A bath suddenly seemed like a good idea. I made it extra hot and bubbly, with a generous amount of Mark's bath salts. I got in, wincing as the water touched the sore spots. Being sore is a whole pleasure in itself, I thought, stretching as far as the bathtub allowed, ready for the show to begin, sure that my mind wouldn't hesitate to produce some delicious images of the recent lovemaking. The lovely Number Four, I said to myself, urging my mind to start working, but images of Mark and myself swarmed in my head instead. I was alarmed, I didn't want this encounter to be about Mark, this was something that I did purely for myself, but then my fantasies turned out to be even better than everything that had taken place in Number Four's grandfather's place, and I let them loose.

I would be on the couch when Mark opened the door.

Hi, Mark, I would say. How was your day? I just slept with somebody.

Or this: Hi, Mark. I cheated on you today.

Mark, I have something to tell . . .

Mark I have a terrible, terrible confession to make.

The little sentences zigzagged in my mind, fighting for the prize of being said aloud and actually heard by Mark. It even crossed my mind that the main purpose of my little dalliance was to hurt Mark. If he was so jealous about his writing, he must know sexual jealousy as well. I would hurt him, oh, yes, I would hurt him so much. He mentioned that his beautiful women of the past used to drive him crazy. I wondered how. Did they cheat? Did it hurt? What I'd done must hurt more. He thought that I was his Anna Grigorievna, his eternally devoted cow, the one woman in his life who was safe, who would never betray him. He had chosen me precisely for that reason. I thought about another passage from the book *The Three Loves of Dostoevsky*. The author noted how jealous Dostoevsky was of Anna Grigorievna, in spite of the fact that she didn't give him any reason to be. "Anna had to belong to him indivisibly," the author wrote and Mark highlighted, "body and soul, like the things on his desk that nobody dared to move about or even touch." Here, Mark, take it from Anna Grigorievna! He would suffer. He would suffer so much. He would go on the terrace and roam there slowly and sadly among the folding chairs and the empty pots, just as he had after reading a really good book by a rival writer. His head would hang low as he made small, unsteady steps. He would sigh. He might even moan. Yes, let him moan. I had never enjoyed a bath that much!

And then my mind produced another idea. The pain I caused would finally make me his muse. The real one. It was not Polina's love but her betrayal that made her Dostoevsky's muse. It wasn't the sexual satisfaction of their Petersburg days, but the agony and frustration of their Italian journey that had made him write about her. How, how had I not thought of this before! Mark, too, would write his greatest work now. Fuck the troubled, gifted boy from New Jersey! Mark would write about a grown man who had a habit of falling in love with beautiful, difficult women, who in their turn had a habit of torturing him and driving him crazy. He became disappointed in love and lived alone for many years, afraid to get too close to a woman. And then he met a woman who was perfectly unique, unlike any other he'd ever met. Not as beautiful, not as sophisticated, but so kind and loving, so awed with him, so fascinated by everything he said or did, ready to do anything to please him, grateful for the smallest attention he would pay to her. He allowed that woman to love him, he allowed himself to love her back. For the first time in his life he felt happy and safe, only to be viciously betrayed by her.

Now I had to see how my ideas would fit into Mark's novel. With all the reading practice of the recent weeks, I was pretty sure I would be able to understand his writing. I climbed out of the tub, threw a bathrobe on, and rushed into the living room, leaving a fast-melting track of soapsuds behind. Mark's manuscript was on the floor next to the typewriter. A fat, white heap of paper blackened with letters like dirty snow, luminescent in the semi-darkness of the room. I carried the manuscript to the couch, put it carefully in my lap, and read the first sentence.

"Mark is the name my parents gave me, a simple name, a common name, yet a bothersome one, full of forced elegance and dignity, which I never desired to achieve or maintain myself."

I had heard this sentence before, read aloud by Mark to me and to his friends on the phone, but it was the first time I had truly seen it, and I saw how much I disliked it. I read on. Mark's command of English was excellent and he did know how to weave a long, intricate sentence, but that somehow failed to bring his characters or descriptions to life. Dead dummies wandered around in a dead landscape that looked more like a stage set, exchanging words that were supposed to be clever but were in fact empty and boring. I kept reading, pleading to discover some magical reversal that would redeem or explain the stillness of the rest. I didn't lose hope until the very last sentence. This was a bad book. Completely, hopelessly bad. I never claimed to be an expert in literature, and even among Russian books there were plenty that I'd simply failed to understand, but this one . . . this one . . . was simply dead. I took Mark's first and second books off the shelf, with the faint hope of finding some life there. The first one was a little more inspired than the rest, but the glimpses of life there were stifled with Mark's desire to impress. Every sentence seemed to cry out for attention: "Look at me, look! Look how clever, how elegant I am!" There was something pathetic, something sickening about those pleas.

I wrapped myself tighter in the robe and walked out onto the terrace, where I sank into the folding chair, welcoming the numbing sensation as the backs of my legs touched the cold surface. I wondered if Mark was aware of how bad his books were. He must have suspected it, but he probably comforted himself with the thought that all writers doubted themselves, even the best ones. His obsession with writers' biographies must have sprung from that. He was looking for proof that they were just like him, and he came to the reassuring but mistaken conclusion that he was just like them. I went through the same delusion when reading about Polina. Mark and I were very much alike, if you thought about it. Two people with immense aspirations, and limited abilities, except for our one great gift—the belief that we were what we wanted to be and the stubborn insistence on that belief.

I went back into the living room and pressed the Replay button on our answering machine. "Tanya, are you there? Pick up, please." Tanya . . . Tanya . . . Tanya . . . Pick up . . . Pick up. I couldn't hear a trace of smugness in Mark's voice. He needed me. He needed my kindness. I remembered another highlighted passage from *The Three Loves* that I'd chosen to ignore before. "He gasped with horror before the realization of his own nothingness and his fear of death. Very few people were aware how great his need was at such moments for a kind word, for the warm pressure of a woman's hand."

My hatred for Mark was gone, and the space that it used to inhabit was now hollow and uncertain. I wondered if we had had a chance at love, if back then, when we met, we had seen each other for what we were, and if Mark hadn't reduced me to Anna

Grigorievna, and I hadn't elevated him to Dostoevsky. I wondered if he would have been able to see with time that I needed his kindness, the warm pressure of his hand too.

Mark came home around nine.

"I'm beat," he said, lowering his bag to the floor.

"Want something to eat?"

"No, I'll go straight to bed. The trip was a disaster. Apparently the furnace broke down, and it was freezing in the house. I mean it. Freezing. I kept going outside to warm myself up. Shit! I think I got my feet wet."

I took his damp socks away and gave him warm ones from the drawer.

"You know what, Tanya," he said. "I don't think I thought once about you while I was upstate, but now I see that I missed you."

He fell asleep very quickly, and I stretched out next to him on the bed, listening to his sharp little snorts.

A few weeks before, Mark had said, "You know what, I might want to marry you." We had just returned from another dinner party and Mark had taken off his shoes and socks and was curling and uncurling his toes. I felt a surge of repulsion so strong that I had the urge to crush his ugly toes with the heel of my boot. Now, I felt that if he did ask me to marry him, I would probably agree.

I fell asleep feeling that the emptiness, absurdly heavy, was pressing down on my chest just like the marble slab that was pressing on my grandmother's grave.

Chapter Twelve

The final piece of correspondence between Polina and Dostoevsky is dated April 23, 1867. The last letter—at least the one that survived the caprices of time and people and reached the biographers, the books, and me. It has always made me cringe in pain.

So, you must know nothing about me, my darling, or at least you knew nothing, when you mailed your letter. I got married in February of the present year. . . . My stenographer, Anna Grigorievna Snitkina, was a young, nice-looking girl, twenty years of age, from a good family, graduated from Gymnasium with honors, with a remarkably kind and sunny disposition. Our work together went very well. "The Gambler" was finished in 24 days. By the end of the novel I noticed that my stenographer sincerely loved me, even though she never said a word about it. I too became better and better disposed to her. Since my brother's death my life was very empty and difficult. I offered her my hand in marriage. She accepted. The difference in years is terrible (20 and 44), but I'm getting more and more sure that she will be happy. She has a heart

and she knows how to love. . . . Your letter left me feeling
sad. You write that you're very sad. I don't know your life
during this past year, but judging by what I do know about
you, it will be very difficult for you to be happy . . .

Goodbye, my eternal friend.

Yours F. Dostoevsky.

Did he still love her when he was writing this letter? I'm sure
that he did. He is apparently protective of Polina—so careful to
spare her the description of his feelings for his new bride. He writes
only about Anna Grigorievna's love for him. But at the same time
aren't there some gloating notes? Isn't he hinting that after his and
Polina's messy battle of love, it was he who emerged as the winner?
Polina is alone and sad. He is joined with a young, nice-looking,
sunny, sincere, adoring woman. "She knows how to love." Did he
mean to suggest that Polina didn't?

Dostoevsky's first wife died in April of 1864, and even though
his relationship with Polina was hardly intimate at the time, he
rushed to propose to her. I wasn't surprised in the least to know that
she refused. Resolutely, vehemently refused. There was no difference
for her in the confinement of being a mistress or being a wife to
somebody like Dostoevsky. Polina then embarked on a series of ill-
fated attempts to make something out of her life, suffering through
the humiliation of yet another failed project, yet another disappoint-
ing love affair. Fairly or not, she blamed Dostoevsky for the latter.

"People talk to me about F.M. I just hate him," she wrote in her
diary. "He made me suffer so much when it was possible to avoid
suffering. Now I feel and see clearly that I am unable to love, unable
to find happiness in the joy of love, because the caresses of men will
remind me of the pain and humiliation. D. was the first to kill my
faith."

The last of Polina's humiliations was a disastrous marriage to a young (almost twenty years younger than she) scholar, ironically a Dostoevsky scholar. Dostoevsky once told Polina that if she married she would start hating her husband on the third day and leave him. His prediction proved to be correct: Polina left her husband fairly quickly and she continued to hate him for the rest of her life. She died alone.

She lost. Except for one thing. She left that "torturous imprint of her foot" on the pages of some of the greatest novels of all time. Whether she wanted it or not, the fact remains: She became a muse. Yes, immortality doesn't do you any good. But how many people don't wish for it?

Many years later, I'm sitting on the small patio of a two-story New Jersey house, alone, with a cup of rapidly cooling coffee, a random section of the *Times,* and my old diary. The breeze ripples through the leaves of a young maple tree in the backyard, tickles the newspaper pages. The time is 1:15. I've finished my work for today and I still have two long, wonderful hours before I have to pick up my daughter at the school bus stop. I turn my face to the sun and squint at the maple tree, trying to imagine that I'm on a beautiful country estate somewhere in eighteenth-century England, trying to block from my vision the neighbors' barbecue that stands not five feet away from our patio, my daughter's all-American pink bike resting in the pile of last year's maple leaves in the backyard.

I didn't marry Mark. By the time his novel came out, it was perfectly obvious that to continue living with him would be pointless and impossible. What feelings I'd had for him were exhausted by my excessive and unfair admiration at the beginning of our relationship and scorched by my excessive and just as unfair hatred at the end.

And while Mark might have been aloof, he was not stupid or completely insensitive. I'm sure he'd finally developed some doubts about my real attitude toward him and his writing. When I told him that I was leaving him, he seemed upset but not very surprised. I tend to think (or I want to think) that he did love me in his own selfish way, but it was certainly easier and less painful for him to lose me than to lose his delusions about himself.

The second my daughter steps off the bus, the whole street will seem to shake its faceless suburban quiet and start vibrating with noise and movement, the electrifying energy of a five-year-old. She will be running ahead of me, one of her ponytails bouncing happily above her ear, the other all messy and loose with a bright scrunchie hanging close to the tips of her hair. Or if it has been a bad day, she will trudge by my side, holding my hand, sniffling loudly, complaining that Katie M. didn't want to be her friend anymore or that the teacher didn't praise her drawing as much as she apparently should have. "She gave me one smiley face, one. Nicholas got three of them." Then we will have three busy hours filled with the smell of apple juice, the chatter of TV cartoons, and homework struggles. Up until my husband comes home from work. "Daddy!" my daughter will shriek and dash downstairs to our little hallway. She will climb up on him, clutch onto his neck with her hands and onto his waist with her feet, and stay hanging off him like a baby koala. I will watch how a happy smile breaks through my husband's tired face, and I will become overwhelmed with an absurd, shameful envy. I will still feel a faint residue of that envy as we put our daughter to bed and tuck her in along with her two Winnie the Poohs and one plush lobster bought in a souvenir store in Bar Harbor. The rest of the evening will belong to my husband and me. We will either spend it peacefully—dozing off in front of *Seinfeld* reruns. "Wake up, George is about to say your favorite line," we will say to each other from time to time. Or not so peacefully—engaged in another of our so-called "surprise" fights. Something that starts as an innocent argument about politics or art and within moments grows into a full-blown battle, where we shout accusations in heated whispers so as not to wake our daughter.

Am I happily married? I often wonder, probably more often than necessary. "Happily" really depends on your definition of the term. My most satisfying definition to date is this: If I look forward to my husband coming home from work, and he feels the same about me, and we engage in energetic fights when we can't stand each other, rather than plunge into stale, bored silences, then, yes, the marriage can be considered happy. I don't tell my husband, but I secretly enjoy our fights very much. That's one thing that had been completely missing from my life with Mark. Sometimes I wonder if Mark might have been a factor in my choice of a husband, if it wasn't accidental that I married a man so drastically different from him. My husband is a very tall, slightly stooped man who speaks English with an accent, knows nothing about clothes, doesn't believe in therapy, and needs serious coaxing to go to a dentist. He feels uncomfortable when he is being served, to the point where he apologizes to a waiter when he drops a fork or rushes to grab the heaviest piece of luggage when he gets out of a cab. He likes to read but doesn't have any artistic aspirations.

My husband is a microbiologist, and I often catch myself admiring the specific, tangible nature of his work. He can actually see what he is doing, if only through a microscope. The subject of my work can be resurrected only through hundred-year-old documents, pictures, and, shamefully for a historian, my imagination, which is always on hand to fill in the missing pieces.

With Dear Charlotte's help, I was able to attend graduate school, where eventually I learned how to focus and choose a narrow topic for my research. My thesis was called "Domestic Life in Late Nineteenth-Century Russia." I was amazed that many details of Polina's life as I had imagined them turned out to be wrong, but still more amazed that so many turned out to be right. "Domestic life" on the page doesn't quite make a living, so I had to succumb to teaching, and surprised myself by how much I actually enjoyed being around teenagers. Sometimes my job has its other little perks. About three years ago, I was picked as a historical consultant for yet another movie version of *Anna Karenina,* this one called *Anna— A Study in Passion.* It probably sounds very small, but I was excited that millions of viewers would be watching Anna and Vronsky eat a meal where I was in charge of the menu! My husband was even more excited; he insisted on renting a DVD of the movie and showing it to our daughter: "You see that piece of bread in Anna's hand? That was Mommy's idea."

Another person who repeatedly watches *Anna—A Study* is my uncle. He brings it with him to all the dinner parties, even at Dena's house, with the same proud line: "My niece done that." I'm not sure which part of the movie creation is ascribed to me. And I'm glad that Dena has never tried to clarify that. My mother, on the other hand, isn't so impressed with Anna's breakfasts, but she firmly believes that the day will come when I will make some groundbreaking historical discovery. Well, I am a mother too, now; I guess I can understand her. My mother comes to visit us every year, and to my great surprise she and my husband tolerate each other pretty well.

I should be perfectly content with my life, and most of the time I am. Yet it is these lonely moments, with the undrinkable remains of coffee in my cup, with the neighbors' dog yapping its brains out, with the mean shore wind ravaging the *Times* pages, that I enjoy the most. This is my own time, when whatever I feel or think belongs solely to me. I'm not accountable for any thoughts I might have and I'm free to dream any dreams I like.

Right after I left Mark, Gosha and Dear Charlotte found me a job in the college library and a place to live. Three of Gosha's students used to share a tiny apartment on Twenty-third Street; one of them was moving out, and I took her room. That room, with its chipped door and windowsills, its darkened wallpaper, and only a smidgen of sky visible through the grid of the window, became the first place in America where I liked to be, where I felt at home. I draped my bed with some bright blue-and-orange cloth I'd found at a flea market, took my photographs out of the suitcase and placed them on all the available surfaces.

When I had free time from my job, I spent it making tours of the neighborhood. My routes were random and unwise, based on whatever fleeting interests I developed, attracted by a funny store window, an unusual stoop on a building, or a seductive smell from one or another café. I was learning to savor the city anew, learning to enter the shops, galleries, and cafés, learning to see the crowd as a group of distinct individuals rather than a hostile mass, learning how to feel a part of the crowd myself.

One morning, I stopped by a tiny art gallery called Bridges. The door made a loud screech as if breaking the space between the bustle of the New York weekday morning and the quiet of the gallery. The two rooms were empty except for an elderly woman in the back and a middle-aged man chatting with a happy, chunky receptionist.

The black-and-white photograph pinned to the front wall pictured the artist, a young woman with a wild frizzball of hair and serious, slightly protruding eyes. I passed by the long description of the show and went straight for the paintings. The gallery was very cold, with dry, chilly air drifting somewhere above my feet, yet the paintings were strangely warm. A half-open closet door, the hem of a dark old dress visible through the slit. A massive, also dark armchair with its back to us, with somebody's sprawled elbow barely visible against the upholstery. The years on most of the works ranged from 1965 to 1969. The frizzy-haired woman must've been some famous artist from the past. I wasn't too excited by the paintings, but I was pleasantly touched. They were beautiful, as far as I could understand them. Sad, restrained, and at the same time alive. As if each forgotten sock, or old dress, or drab elbow was redeemed by the comfort of light.

An elderly woman smiled understandingly as she moved past me to the front room. She liked the paintings too. I took up her place in the back, darker room and walked to the largest, six-by-eight canvas. It took a while for my eyes to adjust to the change in light, so the painting seemed to emerge slowly from darkness, getting more and more definite the longer I looked at it. In a few moments I was able to see that the two shaky light-blue lines in the center of the painting were in fact the legs of a woman, half-hidden by the flaps of a heavy coat, clad in some wide, ugly boots. The rest of the body was drawn as a fuzzy, misshapen cone with just a smudge of blue paint in place of a head. The lower part of the coat was depicted very clearly, so clearly that I could see flaps with the herringbone pattern and stray threads coming off the shabby hem. A strange anxiety came over me.

They couldn't be . . .

They were my legs!

Yes, they were my legs; there could be no mistake about it. And my Russian boots that were a size too big for me. My old coat with the herringbone pattern and loose threads; there couldn't be another coat like that in New York. My first reaction was for some reason embarrassment; I was terrified that somebody would recognize me in the picture. Even though I knew that this was impossible—I wasn't wearing the coat or the boots anymore, and at first glance there was hardly anything else in the painting that spoke distinctly of me. Then I felt sorry that nobody would recognize me. I wanted to yell, to call for somebody, for the elderly woman, for the chunky receptionist. I needed some support, some recognition, some proof that it was me, that I wasn't suddenly going crazy.

I peered closer to read the title of the painting. "A girl in the elevator." The elevator! Of course. Now I recognized the lines indicating the corner and the floor, the pattern of the elevator wall in Mark's building. It was me, standing in the corner of the elevator in Mark's building, slumped against the wall, just as I'd always stood there.

I rushed back to the front room to read the description of the artist. It was then I saw her name: Vera Mielich. Vera! And it was she in the picture, only decades younger. Those were Vera's eyes. I read the short bio: a promising young artist, a tragic illness, decades of silence, a sudden and powerful comeback shortly before her death, starting with a series of paintings called *A Girl in the Elevator.* A series! I darted back.

There were three more, smaller, paintings with the elevator's interior and my legs in the center. They were painted differently in each piece, seen from another point of view, basking in stronger or weaker light, but they all were very thin, thinner than physically possible, and they all were done in shaky, seemingly unsteady lines. I wished I understood more about art and were able to describe the paintings better, but all I saw while standing in front of them was the shame, the heavy, smothering shame of those days, mixed equally with the hope that managed to sustain me. Vera was able to catch and transfer all that into a painting. This wasn't even me, just my legs and my coat, yet it was me, the whole of me, and beyond it was more than me and more than Vera.

Between the last and next-to-last pages of my diary there used to be a piece of paper folded in two. A reproduction of *A Girl in the Elevator.* I had torn it out of the exhibition's catalogue. I used to save it for last whenever I looked through my diary. It got lost in the violent mess of moving into this house. All I have left now is the fading image in my mind of the thin-legged girl in the funny Russian coat slouched against the elevator wall.

It's time to pick up my daughter now. Just one last tiny peek at the diary before I shut the book and snap out of my selfish bliss to return to family life.

ABOUT THE AUTHOR

Lara Vapnyar's book of short stories, *There Are Jews in My House,* was nominated for a Los Angeles Times Book Prize and the New York Public Library Young Lions Fiction Award, and was the winner of the National Foundation for Jewish Culture's 2004 Prize for Jewish Fiction by Emerging Writers. Vapnyar, whose work has appeared in *Open City, The New York Times,* and *The New Yorker,* emigrated from Russia in 1994. She lives on Staten Island with her husband and two children.

A NOTE ON THE TYPE

The text of this book was set in Simoncini Garamond, a modern version by Francesco Simoncini of the type attributed to the famous Parisian type cutter Claude Garamond (ca. 1480–1561). Garamond was a pupil of Geoffroy Tory and is believed to have based his letters on the Venetian models, although he introduced a number of important differences, and it is to him we owe the letter that we know as old style. He gave to his letters a certain elegance and a feeling of movement that won for their creator an immediate reputation and the patronage of Francis I of France.

Composed by Creative Graphics,
Allentown, Pennsylvania
Printed and bound by R. R. Donnelley & Sons,
Harrisonburg, Virginia
Designed by Robert C. Olsson